The Ocean Inside

JANNA McMAHAN

KENSINGTON BOOKS
http://www.kensingtonbooks.com

ISBN-13: 978-0-7582-5393-4
ISBN-10: 0-7582-5393-1

First Kensington Books Trade Paperback Printing: April 2009
First Kensington Books Mass-Market Paperback Printing: July 2010

10 9 8 7 6 5 4 3 2 1

Printed in the United States of America

*This novel is dedicated to my beloved mothers-in-law,
Ruth Ann Cotterill and Anne McConnell Cotterill.
Both librarians, these two women happily clipped and
collected for me.
They were greatly loved and are most sincerely missed.*

Acknowledgments

Special thanks to fellow cancer survivor Elizabeth Grimball, a brave young woman who freely shared her thoughts and feelings about battling this disease in childhood.

I'd also like to thank Dr. Laura Basile and Dr. John Cahill for their medical advice, John Bolin for his theology guidance, Monica Francis for her insurance knowledge, Gerald Lonon for insight into real estate development, and First Sergeant Angus MacBride of the South Carolina Department of Natural Resources for beautiful descriptions of shrimping. Thank you to all the helpful reference librarians at Richland County Public Library, Debra Bloom in particular. Also, thank you to the South Carolina Law Enforcement Division for information on drug smuggling.

My gratitude goes to my supportive friends and family who read my work, catch my mistakes, share great ideas, and in various ways contribute to my success as a writer. Thank you to Amy Barnes, Robin Riebold, Doreen Sullivan, Mary Jane Reynolds, Deirdre Mardon, Jeffrey Day, Brian Ray, Kate Spurling, Jill Todd, Shelby Miller Jones, Lisa McMahan, and my mother, Edith McMahan.

A big ole thanks to my brother, Robb McMahan, for the catalyst of my first laptop and the missive "Now you have no excuse. Write that novel." You're the best brother in the world.

Thank you to my bighearted friend Carolyn Mitchell

for sharing her Pawleys Island beach house with my family. I can never repay your generosity. Also, thank you to Bunni Crawford for an invitation to a swanky party at her island home. The crab cakes were divine and the gossip even better.

My appreciation always to Katherine Fausset, my insightful and encouraging agent at Curtis Brown. I'm so pleased we found each other.

Thank you to John Scognamiglio, Editor in Chief of Kensington, for lovely covers, editorial guidance, marketing support, and creative freedom.

Thanks to my family, Mark Cotterill, and our daughter, Madison, for being ever patient and supportive. I'm glad you're both artists who understand that creativity takes time.

The Silver Gardens

Come to the silver gardens of the South,
Where whisper hath her monarchy, and winds,
Deftly devise live tapestries of shade,
In glades of stillness patterned,
And where the red-bird like a sanguine stain,
Brings Tragedy to Beauty.

—Archer M. Huntington

CHAPTER 1

Night Swimming

Not halfway there and yet her shoulders tingled with fatigue. Going out was always a fight, the incoming Atlantic shoving her back, impeding her progress. Sloan swam slowly, methodically, one stroke following the next in perfect rhythm with a head turn and measured breath in between. Pier lights appeared from behind a jetty and she stopped, treading water, triangulating herself against the faint illumination of home.

An occasional figure moved on the beach, dark against the lights rising behind dunes. Tonight she hadn't worried that her mother might see her drop her clothes to the sand. Her parents were at a charity benefit in support of a cure for some disease or another. They were always attending these events even though her father grumbled. But her mother was poised for the next illness or disaster, always extending her checkbook to those less fortunate. Sloan had come to question her mother's commitment to these causes. Somehow, her actions appeared desperate at times rather than altruistic.

Her parents looked like old money when they left,

Sloan's father in his worn tuxedo and her mother in a rose-colored dress, understated as always. A string of inherited pearls encircled her delicate neck. But her parents seemed somehow out of kilter in their evening attire with the summer sun bright on their shoulders. It was the gentleness of his hand against her back as he helped her into the car when only moments before they had argued. This particular argument was the same as always—money, work, the pressure of social obligations.

They seemed at a truce when they left. Sloan stood on the screened-in porch watching them pull away, the oyster-shell drive popping under the car's tires. Ocean breeze fingered her hair while a lump of dread formed in her stomach. Sloan had come to anticipate this emptiness, the sensation of a roller coaster hung at the bottom sweep of a drop, pressing down, never leveling out.

She was nearly ill with this sinking feeling at times, but she could never pinpoint why. Sometimes it didn't have anything to do with her parents or her SAT scores or even her total lack of social life. When that vacant sensation crawled in her stomach she gravitated to the beach. It was an odd impulse that had made her wade into the dark water the first time.

She hadn't meant to go so far. She knew better, but she walked forward into the waves until she was gently lifted, her tenuous connection with solid earth dissolved. She had floated there, her arms moving listlessly, barely enough to keep her head above soft swells, knowing an undertow could carry her to sea.

But she had sensed the tide was coming in and she had been correct on that all-important account. The current caught her up and swept her along parallel to the beach. At the northern tip of the island she was pushed inland where the water squeezed into the creek behind their home. There she was deposited on the steps of their dock as if the hand of a god had laid her there.

She crawled into their barnacle-encrusted wooden boat. Like most everything else of value in their lives, the watercraft was inherited from her great-grandfather, a once regal thing grown shabby under her father's watch.

Stars had been distinct that moonless night as she tiptoed down the dry planks of the slender walk from the dock. Palmetto fronds clacked and marsh grass shushed as she sneaked toward her back door. Inside, her parents dozed on the sofa, a movie playing soft blue against their faces.

She had remained careful since then, checking the weathered tide chart on the storage shed door to make sure of the water's movement before she ventured into the surf—a calculated risk. She was a strong swimmer. Her mother had made sure of that, hauling Sloan and her little sister to lessons at the YMCA for years, until Sloan had flatly refused to go another chlorine-stinging lap.

Her mother would have a meltdown if she knew Sloan was out at night, swimming into the distance, leaving her younger sister alone in the house. She'd be grounded for a month if discovered, perhaps for the rest of the school year. Still, Sloan craved the heart-pounding adrenaline from this secret endeavor, a feeling far preferable to the palpitations of anxiety and dread that came upon her so naturally. She felt wild and independent knowing she could slowly drift to the black below or be attacked by a rogue shark. Everyone would wonder what had happened to her. Was she kidnapped? A runaway? There would be headlines in the *Pawleys Island Gazette*— "Local teen disappears, worst feared."

Gauging her level of exhaustion as moderate, Sloan started toward shore. She'd make it. She always did. Today was not her day to die. She struggled on. The journey back was always easier, as if the world were behind her pushing her home.

Twenty minutes later her feet found sandy purchase and she stumbled onto the beach so limp it was impossible for her to feel any emotion, except perhaps relief that she had survived once again.

Soreness would grip her muscles the next few days, a constant reminder of her triumph over the abyss, over exhaustion, over herself. Her mother would comment that her moody nature had ebbed. Her grades would improve. She would be at peace for a time.

It was not the death-defying act that buoyed her but the clandestine nature of it that was her companion. *I have a secret*, she would think to herself over the next few weeks when she quarreled with her mother or struggled with calculus. *I'm strong. I'm a survivor.*

CHAPTER 2

Island Life

Emmett Sullivan pressed open the hatch to the widow's walk atop his house. His golf shirt billowed in the rush of salty air as he climbed the last few ladder rungs and stepped into a 360-degree view. The Atlantic tumbled in on the east side of the island. To the west, the creek was placid, the marsh grass still and straight. Only a cat's-paw ripple in the channel betrayed the current below where the incoming tide married the creek. Here at the northern tip, a wide sandbar tightly packed with cordgrass squeezed the channel more narrow each year. It was healthy compared to the southern end, where the clockwise motion of the Atlantic chewed away the island's sandy fringe and depleted the creek.

Emmett scanned the beach for his daughters' bright bathing suits. They were in their usual spot, away from the grip of undertow between islands but close enough to be seen from the widow's walk.

He clicked the walkie-talkie. "Sloan, it's Dad."

One of the tiny people on the sand below moved. A

moment later, he heard his older daughter's bored tone crackle to life in his hand.

"Yeah, I'm here."

"Your mother says it's time to come in."

Sloan motioned to Ainslie and began cramming things into a bag. Ainslie, true to form, ignored her sister, enthralled with something in a tidepool, probably crab holes or a starfish. Emmett knew how things would transpire. Ainslie would ignore her sister. Sloan would practically drag her to the house. Later, Sloan would let her mother know, in that universal sardonic teenager tone, how much she hated having to baby-sit, AGAIN.

The girls trudged back, lugging buckets and bags. Sloan wore her straw hat and Jackie-O glasses. She was no doubt slathered from head to toe in sunscreen in her battle to stave the freckles that sprinkled her mother's skin. Then there was Ainslie, his sun-drop baby, all nut brown skin, dark eyes and hair just like Emmett's before the gray invaded. Emmett could relate to his nine-year-old's desire to stay out all day. His own childhood had been spent in similar pursuits on this island, he and his brothers wading tidal creeks and crawling sand dunes from first light to dark.

The girls left the hard-packed beach for the loose sand of a path that snaked between dunes. The sand pulled at their steps, their flip-flops kicking up sprays of granules behind them. They worked their way through gnarled cedars, a stand of only a dozen or so trees. When he was a boy, this island had been thick with cedars, low-slung and hardy from weathering storms. Emmett and his brothers hacked through them, cleared secret rooms in their dense branches.

Their mother banished them from the house each day until supper, so Emmett followed Rick and Judd around the island. They rode bikes the three miles down to the public beach at the island's southern end where new, pale girls in bikinis appeared each week. They hung out with locals who leaned over the creek bridge, fishing poles tailing line into rippled waters, buckets and coolers smelly with flounder and spot. At low tide, the boys dug oysters and clams. They came home with split fingers and a sack of jagged bivalves.

They shed their cut-off high-tops in a muddy heap outside, hung their stinky shirts and shorts on the clothesline and showered in the changing area under the house. The shower stung their skin with sweet prickles of pain and washed rank pluff in a gurgle down the drain. They ran up the back stairs in the buff, their mother snapping a tea towel at their bare bottoms as they streaked through the kitchen. A few days later their clothes would appear, fragrant and folded, in their chests of drawers.

Emmett often lamented that his girls would never know the luxury of being kicked out and free to roam. Lauren kept a close eye on them—they were never unaccounted for, never left to their own meanderings, particularly Ainslie, who was still a baby in so many ways. But Ainslie was tough, athletic, and energetic. Emmett wished Lauren would let her join the other kids who explored the island on bikes and slender scooters. Often Emmett thought Ainslie should have been born a boy; perhaps then her mother might have cut her some slack. But to Lauren, girls were supposed to be pink bows, tea parties, and piano recitals.

Poor Lauren had struck out with both girls in that respect. Where Ainslie was rambunctious, Sloan was introverted and somewhat dark of nature. She had inherited his family's artistic talents but also a more brooding, sensitive side that was puzzling. Sometimes when Sloan would give him a certain look Emmett could see contempt, so bald and honest it seared his soul. She apparently found him incompetent, but then the girl would roll her eyes and he would convince himself it was only puberty talking.

He could feel the girls rattle into the house, but up this high, wind smothered most of their noise. He sensed water running in their bathroom beneath him. He reclined against the bench and scanned the horizon of startling orange burn pooling over the mainland, its reflection quivering in the creek. Out to sea, the sky was licked with lavender like the heavens of a Renaissance painting.

"Want some company?" Lauren appeared at the hatch. Wind whipped her blonde bob in a frenzied dance. She held a glass in both hands. "I come bearing gifts."

"Please join me."

He took the gin and tonics from her outstretched hands. She climbed up and slid onto the bench opposite him.

"I assume Ainslie's in the bath." He sipped his drink, and the distinct taste of juniper and lime tingled his nose.

"Sloan's supposed to be helping her wash up, but I heard the TV on. I think they're watching *Titanic* for the forty-fifth time," she said and sighed dramatically. "It's pretty up here tonight."

"We always have the best sunsets in the fall."

"Have you heard when they're going to start dredging the creek?"

"Spring, I hope. The channel has to be opened up again or we won't be able to get the boat out."

"Mom?" Sloan's frustrated voice floated up to them.

"What now?" Lauren leaned over the opening and yelled, "I'll be down in a minute." Then to Emmett she said, "Well, I guess I need to go stir the soup anyway."

"What are we having?"

"She crab."

"My favorite."

Lauren backed down the ladder, grasping the rungs with one hand while she balanced her drink in the other.

Emmett sucked down the rest of his cocktail and tossed the ice cubes onto the sharply pitched roof. He watched as they rolled down and bounced off where the curlicued façade poked above the gabled roofline of his funny house, the only Victorian on Pawleys. When his grandfather built it in the 1920s, locals had hated the giant burgundy, blue, and green house. Now it was considered a landmark, a house locals advised tourists not to miss.

Emmett Layton Sullivan Sr. bought this northern part of the island as a family get-away and erected an exact replica of his house on Cape May. Shortly thereafter, Victorians started popping up in nearby Georgetown, but there was never another frosted cake house on the island. The houses served as the logo for his grandfather's company, Painted Lady Greeting Cards. His brother Judd lived in the New Jersey house now and was CEO of the company. Rick was their lawyer and CFO. But Emmett Layton Sullivan III had stayed behind, married a Low-country girl, become a landscape architect. Along with his brothers, Emmett had inherited this house. His end of the deal was upkeep and taxes, both of which escalated each year. Lauren had been so enamored of the house that Emmett continued to tease her that she'd married him for real estate. They had both envisioned the many rooms overflowing with a large family. But now their home was a money pit, a hulking house of deterioration that would have served a larger family well, but which seemed empty with only their two children padding the halls.

Emmett backed down the ladder and pulled the hatch closed with a final swish of air. Before he could get it latched Ainslie was calling for him, drawing her words out long and pleading. "Daaaadeeee. Daaaadeeee."

He pressed his palm against a bumper sticker on her bedroom door that read, *Lights out! Turtles dig the dark.*

"Watch out. Here I come," he said in a low growl. He pushed the door ajar and stomped into her room. Ainslie squealed and jerked away from Sloan, who was struggling to pull pajamas over her sister's wet legs. Posters of frogs, snakes, and butterflies were stuck at odd angles along the walls. An entire bookcase was given over to prized seashells, contorted driftwood, and smelly bits of coral. Ocean musk came from the bank of aquariums housing the luckless creatures Ainslie plucked from the beach.

"You do this, Dad. I can't get her to sit still," Sloan said. "She's old enough to put on her own p.j.s anyway. Y'all just baby her."

"Go on. I'll take care of her." Emmett raised his arms over his head and swayed into the room like Frankenstein. "Get those pajamas on. I'm the daddy monster who gobbles up little girls who don't have on pajamas. Aarrgghhh!"

"Oh, no. Oh, no." Ainslie jerked on the damp pajama bottoms. "I'm done! I'm good! You can't eat me!"

"No?" He stopped and turned his head as if thinking. "But I'm still hungry. Maybe I'll just GOBBLE YOU UP ANYWAY!" He stomped to the bed, grabbed her ankles, and dragged her toward him.

"No, Daddy! Don't eat me." She gasped around gulps of laughter. "Don't!"

He buried his face in her soft tummy. "Yum. Yum. Yum."

"I'm not sweet! I'm not!"

"Yum. Yum. Yum."

Emmett stopped. Ainslie was still slick from her bath and Emmett's fingers moved smoothly over her abdomen. He could discern a distinct mass below her ribcage.

"Ainslie, does this hurt?"

"Get me, Daddy!"

"No. Stop a minute. This spot right here. Does it hurt?"

She calmed and laid back. "No."

"How long has this been here?"

"I don't know. Get me, Daddy."

"Stay right there." He walked to the top landing of the stairs and yelled down for Lauren.

"What?" she called up.

"I need you to look at something on Ainslie."

She came to the bottom of the stairs, a tea towel in her hands. "What is it?"

"Did you know she has a lump in her stomach?"

"No." Lauren's forehead wrinkled. She draped the towel over the banister and took the stairs two at a time. Ainslie lay still, her arms above her head, her top bunched up against her neck. Her innocent eyes moved from her mother's face to her father's and back as they poked her stomach.

"Right here," he said, moving his fingers over the firm lump.

Lauren touched her gingerly. Her eyes focused on the spot. "Ainslie, how long has this been here?"

"I don't know."

"Does it hurt?"

"No."

Lauren pulled the pajama top down slowly and said in a forced, cheerful voice, "You hungry, baby?"

"Yes! Yes!" Ainslie said. "I'm starving."

"Good. Go tell your sister it's time to eat."

Ainslie bounced off the bed and ran into her sister's room.

"What is it?" Emmett whispered.

"I don't know. You get on the Internet and see what you can find. I'll call the doctor's office and leave a message. I'm taking her in first thing in the morning."

CHAPTER 3

Taking a Ride

Since she was twelve, LaShonda had known how to maneuver the school boat around the snaking river bends from the mainland to the Sandy Island dock. Older children were instructed each year how to guide the boat, cut the chugging diesel engine, throw a life preserver ring. All this was a safety precaution in case the captain, Mr. Heriott, ever fell overboard or had a heart attack.

When she was younger, LaShonda frequently envisioned Mr. Heriott falling off the boat so she could jump to the wheel, cut the engine, and fling the orange donut into the Waccamaw's gator-infested waters. But the old boat captain was as dependable as sunset and LaShonda had never seen him lose control of the watercraft or the children. When Mr. Heriott spoke, the children listened. They said, "Yes, sir" and "No, sir." LaShonda had always admired Mr. Heriott as having the same sort of self-control as her father. Both men were sweet-natured, but they saw the world in terms of the right choice and the wrong choice. Both men tended to say things like, "Now, just take a look at the choice you're making and decide if that's what you really want to do."

Low-lying trees trailed tangles of moss in the Waccamaw River. Sunlight scattered flashing patterns on the surface of the water downstream as the white, steel-hulled school boat made way toward Sandy Island. The boat slid smoothly parallel to the dock and a young man tied off the aft while Mr. Heriott stepped off the boat and tied down the fore. The children knew the rules, and they all stayed seated on the wooden benches that lined the hull inside the cabin.

When all was secure, kids began to spill out of the boat, lugging heavy backpacks festooned with superheroes and filled with assignments for the weekend. LaShonda watched the children drift into the woods, disappearing into the underbrush as if they had only been spirits. She threw her backpack on the floorboard of the school Jeep. Mr. Heriott always drove her the last mile to the center of the island, down a sandy, lumpy track where turkey oaks and long-leaf pines scrubbed the sides of the vehicle. The primitive road ended at LaShonda's house, a place her father had inherited from his great-great-grandfather Philip Washington, a slave who had purchased the land from his former owner and established the Sandy Island community with thirty-two former slaves. Today, their numbers hovered around twelve dozen, depending on births and deaths.

LaShonda saw her father's legs sticking out from underneath his truck. Some days, if shrimping was bad, her father would be home when she got there, tinkering with his truck or fixing some old lamp or iron for a neighbor. He wriggled out from under the truck and wiped his hands on a cloth. LaShonda stopped for her father to kiss her forehead.

"Welcome home, sweetheart," he said.

LaShonda went inside to see what she could cook for supper. Her father walked out to the Jeep to speak to Mr. Heriott. They often conferred on island events. While Mr. Heriott held control of the school-boat children, LaShonda had seen her father calm drunks, break up fights, and shame wife-beaters to tears. It was her father, Abraham Washington, the police came to when they had a problem with a Sandy Island resident. Plenty of times that problem had been her first cousin, Ronald, a drifter who always returned to his home community when money ran out, worming his way into an invitation to eat, waiting around afterward for a chance to sleep on couches and porch swings. Abraham Washington felt a responsibility to take in his sister's son, lecturing him on life choices in return for a bite of food and a place to sack out.

While LaShonda felt no such obligation to her slacker cousin, she was proud of her father, the unofficial leader of Sandy Island. There were no elections, but ask anyone and they would tell you Abraham Washington was their mayor. People came to him to settle disputes, whether over property or over love. He was the man the island turned to back in the 1990s when a development company planned a bridge so they could log Sandy Island. Her father had known it wasn't just the lumber those people were after. He knew once the bridge was built and the timber cleared that it wouldn't be too hard to justify throwing up a development. And sure enough, plans had been leaked for an "exclusive and elite" community with marina, golf course, riding stable, and hundreds of houses and condos.

Sandy Island residents knew development companies had been eyeing their land, and they feared it would go the way of other islands where property values and taxes were driven up by unchecked development and poorer residents were quickly priced out of their own homes. LaShonda's father worked with conservation people and their lawyers to fight the bridge. LaShonda clipped the newspaper articles describing her father's presentation to legislators in Columbia at the statehouse. One of the tree-huggers on their team claimed Sandy Island was a pristine ecosystem, and that the island is "culturally, biologically, and geographically unique." Eventually Sandy Island was declared a wildlife preserve under the jurisdiction of the state of South Carolina, the centerpiece of eighty thousand acres of the Waccamaw National Wildlife Refuge. The citizens of Sandy Island were protected just like the red-cockaded woodpeckers and American alligators at least for a while, was what her father said.

The screen door slapped shut behind LaShonda. Her cousin Ronald turned his gaze from the television to her. His budding Afro smashed flat in the back where his head rested against the couch.

"Hey, Ronald," she said deadpan.

"Hey," he replied. "What's for supper?"

LaShonda ignored him as she took stock of the refrigerator's contents. Cars crashed and gunshots rang from the living room. She was pulling frozen peas from the icebox when Ronald stepped into the kitchen.

"We need more beer," he said. "I'll be glad when you're old enough to buy beer."

"Buy it yourself," LaShonda snapped. "And while you're at the store, feel free to buy some food, too."

"Whoa, who peed in your cornflakes?" Ronald grinned.

"You're lucky I don't pee in your food. What're you doing here?"

Ronald continued to grin as he leaned against the door facing. "Nothing much."

"How's your job with the state?" Ronald had lucked into a well-paying flagman job for road construction.

"Too hot," he said. "That job's for suckers."

"God, Ronald. All you have to do is stand in place and turn a sign around. Why don't you go out there and help Dad with the truck? Do something useful."

Ronald snorted. "He don't need no help from me. Ain't nothing wrong with that truck. He just likes to think he's doing something, even when he's not."

LaShonda propped her hand on her hip and said in an exasperated tone, "You got that right. The poor man can't sit down for a minute. Always got to be doing something. He wears me out. Go out and crank up the grill. You can cook the hot dogs."

"Why, yes, ma'am," he said, bending low. "I's be happy to do that fo you, ma'am."

"Shut up! And pick out that nappy head of hair you got," she yelled at him as he pushed through the screen door into the yard.

"I wouldn't be talking like that, Miss Freckle Face," he said. Although LaShonda didn't exactly love her coppery, speckled complexion, her cousin's nickname for her always brought a slight smile to her lips. Ronald had a way of charming people. He was never mean. He was just one of those people who self-sabotaged—always making the wrong decision, bringing other people down with him.

"No stick-with-it," was what her father said. Growing up, LaShonda had watched Ronald drop out of school, pass on job opportunities, and blow off jobs he did get. The bosses were always too bossy, the work beneath him in some way. He was a get-rich-quick sort of fellow, always with the big idea.

One summer during high school, her father had forced Ronald to take a job on the shrimp boat. Ronald spent one afternoon picking overcatch out of netting and tossing the undesirable sea animals back into the ocean. By afternoon, Ronald claimed he was seasick.

When that got no sympathy from the crew, he said he was afraid since he didn't know how to swim. The river, he said, was smooth water and the banks were close enough that he could make it out if he fell in, but open water was more than he could take, and wearing a life jacket was little comfort.

This had been just another of Ronald's excuses to get out of work, but there was some validity to his argument. While many Sandy Island natives made their living from fishing and shrimping, very few of them could swim. It was simply a skill not mastered nor passed down within the community. No family on the island had been spared the loss of a loved one to drowning. Every couple of years a child would wander into the water or someone would fall from a boat. Residents feared the gators that lurked the murky waters, but while dogs and chickens disappeared on a regular basis, people did not appear to be of great interest.

LaShonda couldn't swim. There had never been an opportunity, no public or school pool where she could learn. The ocean was definitely not the place to practice swimming, so on the rare occasions when she accompanied her father shrimping, he cinched her into a life vest so tightly she could barely draw breath. Even the mighty Abraham Washington was a marginal swimmer, a burden to him to know he would not be able to save anybody who fell over the side of his vessel.

The tang of the ignited grill wafted into the kitchen. The door banged open and Ronald stepped inside.

"Gas's going. Give me the dogs."

LaShonda handed him a plate with five wieners rolling back and forth. Ronald stood mesmerized, staring down at the raw tubes of meat.

"What?" LaShonda finally asked.

"I was thinking a hot dog stand at Myrtle Beach might

make some good money. Uncle Abe might invest in a hot dog stand with me."

"Only if you can make hot dogs out of shrimp."

"Shrimp dogs. That's just wrong."

"I tell you what's wrong. You always trying to squeeze money out of my father."

Ronald stared at the hot dogs.

"Hell, I'll give you some money myself if you'll just go away," she added.

The microwave beeper went off.

"Why do you hate me?"

LaShonda reached in and extracted a bowl of peas. "I don't hate you, Ronald, it's just you wear everybody out. When you come around it's like you take all the oxygen; you need so much there isn't any left for anybody else. You've always got some agenda. What's your deal this time? Is it just money or are you in trouble? After everything he's done for you, I'd think you'd be ashamed to ask for anything else. Why don't you just take your unskilled labor ass out of here and leave us alone."

"I got skills," he said, halfheartedly.

"Skills at bullshit. If you spent half as much energy working as you spend trying to get out of working you'd be a millionaire. You looking for a place to sack out tonight?"

"You couldn't pay me to stay here. I know when I'm not wanted."

"Then why'd you show up in the first place?"

He moved as if to walk out, but stopped. "I swear your old man'll think a hot dog stand's a great idea. After all, it's perfect for unskilled labor."

She was glad her back was to him when a smile pulled at the corners of her mouth.

"I bet you," he continued, "he'd be glad not to haul stinky shrimp all day. He'd get to hang out at the beach, watch girls in bikinis, and get away from your holier-than-thou bitchy little ass."

"Oh, I know you ain't talking to me that way!" she snapped, but he was already gone, the door raining its racket over her words.

CHAPTER 4

Preexisting Condition

Emmett had hit his stride, his legs in perfect pace with his heart. The morning sand was hard packed and more responsive than it would be later in the day, after the sun sucked out moisture, and granules crumbled under his steps. He watched his path carefully, always alert to holes where sandcastles were mined. The wind was gentle, and even though he was finishing the seven-mile round-trip from the south end of the island, he had barely broken a sweat. He liked to run on Saturday mornings. He passed friends casting into the ocean. These neighbors usually drove sections of PVC pipe into the beach to hold their rods and reels while they swigged from thermal cups and threw driftwood to their Labs. Occasionally Emmett stopped to check out their coolers of sea bass or pet their dogs, but this morning the beach was empty.

The top of his house came into view ahead. He cut through the dunes on a spongy boardwalk buckled with age and hit the gravel road that ended at home. He ducked under the boom security gate, rounded the crepe myrtles fronting his drive, and sprinted up the two dozen steps to his porch, where he stood panting in front of his wife who was curled up in one of the white rocking chairs sorting mail.

"Hey," Lauren said without looking up from her task. "Good run?"

He nodded, still catching his breath from his last burst of energy up the stairs. He walked the length of the porch and back, his right knee talking to him. His hands on his hips, he felt his muscles ripple with each exhalation. He had dropped weight the last couple of weeks, as had Lauren. She was looking more like the woman he had married nineteen years ago, her cheekbones becoming more pronounced, her hair growing longer, roots showing through blonde.

Lauren picked through the mail in her lap. She ripped open envelopes, dropping advertisements and solicitations into a sloppy pile at her feet or carefully folding bills into their return envelopes and laying them neatly on the side table. When he had shaken the tension from his legs, Emmett lowered himself into a rocking chair beside her.

She held a slender envelope from Common Good Insurance. Lauren slid the letter opener under the flap, pulled out the contents, and read. Her brow wrinkled and she bit her lower lip.

"Emmett," she said, handing him the paper. "What does this mean?"

Emmett read.

Dear Mr. Sullivan,

After completing our evaluation of your recent claim number 343345, we regret to inform you there are no benefits payable at the present time for the following reason(s):

Your sickness policy does not provide benefits for pre-

existing conditions during the first 12 months after the policy's effective date. Preexisting conditions are diseases or illnesses for which the insured received treatment, advice, or medication within twelve months before the effective date of your policy.

According to our information, your policy was effective 1/15/2008, and your dependent, Ainslie Sullivan, received treatment from Dr. Richard Jessup on 9/9/2007 for stomachache and kidney problems.

We review every claim in a thorough and timely manner because we want our policyholders to receive all the benefits their coverage can provide. You are a valued customer, and we want to ensure you understand your coverage and its benefits.

We hope this letter explains our evaluation of your claim. However, if you believe our understanding of the facts is incorrect, or if you have additional information concerning your claim, please submit information in writing to our office.

The letter was signed *The Department of Claims and Customer Affairs,* with no particular person taking responsibility for the correspondence.

Emmett read it a second time. He could feel Lauren's expectant eyes upon him.

"Well?" she said when he had lowered the paper.

"They're denying the claim."

"Why?" Lauren said.

Emmett shifted uncomfortably in the rocker. "I think they're saying the problem is the office had just switched to Common Good Insurance and we knew Ainslie had cancer before we took the policy so they don't have to pay. I think it's called a preexisting condition. We'd had another insurance carrier for five years before that and we could have kept that active policy had we known."

"Why'd you switch?"

"Cost. I thought we needed to switch carriers. Get something more affordable. We'd had Common Good for two months when Ainslie got sick."

"Is there a waiting period you didn't know about?"

"According to the insurance broker we used, the minute we wrote the first check and put it in his hand we were covered."

"But obviously within parameters. Parameters that are no doubt in the fine print of the contract."

"I guess."

"Oh, so we knew she had cancer, but we waited two months before we got her treatment so we could rip them off?"

"I suppose that's how they're approaching it."

"That logic works against itself. If we were that smart, we would have found a policy without an exception for her illness."

"All we've paid are, well now, five months of premiums, and they're going to have to pay tens of thousands of dollars or maybe even more. They view it as a huge loss."

"A loss?" Lauren was suddenly animated. "What do they know about loss? What about losing a child? There's no bigger loss than that!" Bills blew off the table and scattered around the porch, but she didn't notice.

Emmett chased the blowing papers and gathered them up. "Look, it's all going to be okay. I'll take care of it. They have to pay for her treatment. We paid the premiums. It's all going to work out."

"What does the policy say about cancer coverage?" she asked.

"I'm not sure."

"Why don't you know? You bought the policy."

"Look, I trusted the agent."

"You didn't even read the policy, did you?"

Emmett didn't answer. He studied his feet, a wad of

errant mail clutched in his fist, trying to formulate an answer that didn't make him sound like an idiot.

"You're scaring me. You didn't, did you?" she asked solemnly.

"No," he mumbled weakly.

"Why'd you buy this policy?"

"Look, Lauren. My company was being eaten alive with insurance premiums. Shit, how was I supposed to know this was going to happen? I'm no insurance expert. The policies are so long and complicated."

"Have you read it yet? It's been three months since this all started. Have you even read the policy yet?"

"No. Have you?"

"You know you're the one supposed to take care of this. Is her surgery covered? Is chemotherapy covered?"

"Nobody ever reads all of those contracts. Look, when you're in business you make decisions every day based on hunches. This was a reputable company. I bought a name brand with lots of years in business. They don't stay in business by having their policyholders die on them, so what was I supposed to expect?"

Lauren's gaze burned a hole in his heart. "I'll tell you what I expect. I expect you'll look out for our well-being. This is Ainslie's life we're talking about here. I expect . . ."

"Stop it." Emmett held up his hand to her. "I may have made a mistake, but blaming me isn't going to solve this problem."

Tears simmered in her eyes. "Okay," she said. "How do you intend to fix this?"

"Larry. I'll talk to Larry. He'll know what we should do."

Eric Clapton was singing about Layla when Larry came into The Pub. Like most of The Pub's patrons, Larry was a fixture. Emmett and Larry had their usual spot at the bar where they'd been hanging since they became drinking age. Larry was older by a few years and had been friends with Judd and Rick when they were all young. But after his brothers left the island for places north, Larry and Emmett had continued the routines of island males—fishing and crabbing and cracking oysters with pocketknives. They washed the salty critters down with cans of cheap beer fished from filthy coolers. There were a few years when Larry was gone pursuing a law degree, but he came right back home and slid up onto his bar stool without missing a beat.

But things had changed some. Larry had a little more heft after law school and he had continued to gain weight, Emmett suspected, mostly from drinking. His backside spilled over the bar stool and his jowls drooped over the starched collars of his button downs. He'd been married briefly in law school, but this short marriage was something Larry rarely spoke of. Other than a heavier body and a heavier heart, he seemed like the same old Larry—dependable, sarcastic, sharp as a tack.

Larry glanced at the golf game on the wide-screen above the pool table, then he checked their usual spots at the end of the bar only to find their stools empty. Emmett raised his hand to his friend from a booth in the back. Larry squeezed onto the bench opposite Emmett, his belly grazing the edge of the table.

"Hey," Emmett said.

"Hey, yourself," Larry said.

"You been lawyering all day?"

"Nah, been sitting at home listening to that damn police scanner. You wouldn't believe the crazy fool stuff people do."

"You still have that thing?"

"Free entertainment. Old habits die hard. Still have it from my defense days when I was always looking for my next customer."

Emmett snorted and slid the insurance letter across the rough tabletop.

"Here, looks like I'm your next customer."

Larry fiddled with the salt shaker and tapped a smidge into his beer while he read. Vonda walked a second round of beers over and set them down beside the first without her usual banter, respecting the apparently serious nature of the men's discussion.

"Shit," Larry said when Vonda walked away. "Looks like it's time to start appealing."

"What's that entail?" Emmett asked.

"They have a process you go through. You have to write a letter appealing their decision, substantiate why the claim should be paid, it goes to a review committee that will stick by the company's initial decision. Bunch of crap most people give up on. It's just one more roadblock a certain percentage of people won't make it past."

"How can they stay in business if they treat people this way?"

"Insurance companies stay in business by collecting premiums from people who don't get sick and by denying claims from people who do," Larry said. "They deny, deny, deny until they wear you down. They make the policies so complicated and boring most people won't read them. When you call to find out what's covered you're almost always told you don't have coverage for your particular illness. They exclude things. They make you get everything preapproved. You have to use certain providers. They bounce bills back hoping you'll pay and not question. You have to stay on top of every single bill. It's a game. A big-dollar game."

Emmett considered his friend, the lawyer, master game player. "This isn't a game. This is my daughter's life. What do I have to do?"

"We have to go through the proper channels first."

"And what happens to Ainslie while we're going through channels? What if she dies while we're going through channels?"

"It's not dire, is it? She's pretty stable, isn't she?"

"Right now she is. She recovered amazingly fast when they removed her kidney, but the radiation is really harsh. I don't want to even think about how sick she's going to be if she has to do chemo."

"What's the chances?"

"I don't know. They haven't told us anything solid yet. I can hardly keep up with all the medicines and procedures and shit. Lauren's the one who deals with all that. So, what if she does need chemo or something else? We're talking tens of thousands of dollars, aren't we?"

"Maybe hundreds of thousands. How have you paid for everything so far?"

"Most of the bills are outstanding. Everybody's been cool about waiting on claims approval, but now that everything is denied, all the doctors and the hospital will be getting antsy."

"Don't pay for anything yourself yet. We'll write all your healthcare providers that we're appealing the denial. We'll guarantee they'll be paid, one way or another. It'll buy us some more time. What kind of money do you have if this takes a while?"

"Savings. Kids' college funds. I can sell my boat." Emmett suddenly slammed his fist down on the tabletop. "It's not right."

"Lack of medical coverage is one of the main reasons people go bankrupt. Even people who have coverage, if they miss enough work they lose their jobs, then they lose their insurance. You're not the only family this is hitting hard."

"My father always said most people were only one major illness away from the poorhouse. I should have been more careful. I should have taken insurance more seriously, but I just always viewed it as another annoying expense."

"Everybody loves insurance that pays, but when it doesn't, well, now you know. Look, don't go down the damn pity path and blame yourself. You can't let this be about emotion. We've got to beat them at their game now."

"You're right."

"Don't think of me as your friend anymore. I'm your lawyer now. It's my job to be logical. This is business."

"Okay."

"This company doesn't want to get a bad rap for a child's death, so we can play that card if we have to. Insurance companies hate bad press."

"How long will it take to get a response to our appeal?"

"It should say in the handbook."

"The handbook. More shit I don't understand."

"Bring it to me. I'll read it for you."

"What do you charge for all this?"

"Don't worry about my bill right now. I'll get on the appeal letter first thing Monday morning. But if I were you, I'd look into St. Jude Children's Hospital. Just in case. You know that hospital in Tennessee? They treat kids who don't have insurance."

Emmett watched Larry neatly fold the denial letter into a pocket.

"What do people do who don't have a friend like you?" he asked.

Larry shrugged his massive shoulders and finally took a sip of beer.

"You don't want to know."

CHAPTER 5

Focus

Lauren's cart was wobbly and creaked along as she racked her brain for the item she had thought of in the car but neglected to scribble on the shopping list. She was unable to retain such minor things anymore, although she did have a hunch it was on the pickle and salad dressing aisle. Perhaps if she found that aisle something would jog her memory. Lauren whisked past the end displays, but the signage was poor. She was having trouble focusing in this unfamiliar store.

Lauren had driven inland a mile to a grocery she knew was far less expensive than the ones along the coastal highway where she normally shopped. She'd decided she should cut corners wherever possible, but now she was struggling to find what she needed. She headed down an aisle and stopped cold when the familiar powdery smell of baby products hit her nose. She reached for an amber shampoo bottle and flipped open the top. The aroma of bubbles and giggles flooded over her and she snapped the top down quickly. She picked up a package of diapers and squeezed them until their sweet chalky scent filled her with longing. A baby's cry brought her back to reality, and she shoved the diapers onto the shelf. Tears rimmed her eyes as she tried to maneuver out of the cascade of baby products, but another cart, one with tiny arms flailing from an infant seat, blocked her passage.

She lost control then. Frustration, rage, fear, and baby envy rushed her, and she shoved past the startled mother and fought tears until she was safely in the produce section. She ached to turn back time. She wanted her girls to be the baby in her arms and her sweet nine-year-old again. If she had that chance she would figure out what went wrong. Her research had told her that Ainslie's Wilms' tumor most likely developed in the womb and there was no known cause. But a mother couldn't help but question and the doctors were short on satisfactory answers. It seemed a spontaneous occurrence, but how could that be? There had to be a reason. Lauren believed there was always a reason.

She couldn't turn off the questions. Had Ainslie's illness resulted from something Lauren had done? Something she hadn't done? Had it been fast food or lack of proper sleep? Chemicals in cleaning products or the wrong laundry detergent? Was there something in the pool water or the ocean that had contaminated her daughter?

And now she was willingly allowing her daughter to be poisoned with chemotherapy. The doctors had all warned Lauren she needed to be more enthusiastic about chemo, that therapy always worked better if patients believed it would work. Ainslie certainly took emotional cues from her. She knew she should be more supportive of this therapy, but watching her daughter disintegrate, literally, hair thinning and body growing gaunt before her eyes, made it impossible for Lauren to believe in the positive effects of the drugs they streamed into her daughter's black-and-blue arms every other week.

Lauren headed to the bank of registers and checked out, blindly handing a credit card to the bored clerk. She refused help from the bag boy and smashed bread and chips as she flung the flimsy white bags on top of each other in the old Volvo's trunk. She drove back toward the island with signs swimming in her vision as she fought back sobs. By the time she pulled into their drive she had regained some control of herself. It was a Saturday, and Emmett would expect to help carry the groceries up the steps, so she called him on her mobile.

She kept her sunglasses on so he wouldn't be able to tell she had been weeping. They carried the first load up to the kitchen, where she noticed a large book open on the dining table with beautiful photographs of sailboats, powerboats, and yachts. It was a library book on how to restore wooden boats. Emmett saw her looking at the book and explained.

"I'm thinking about cleaning up Granddad's boat."

She began unloading the sacks of groceries, situating items in the proper slots in the open refrigerator door. The cool licked her arms as she stuffed frozen vegetables in the freezer.

When he saw she wasn't going to offer an opinion, he began to explain.

"I've been thinking about this for a long time. According to the Internet, there's a big demand for classic powerboats. If she cleans up good, I could get a pretty penny for her."

"You'd sell your grandfather's boat?"

Lauren was glad he couldn't see her clearly behind her sunglasses.

"Well, it's my boat now. Our boat I mean. We're talking maybe thirty grand in good shape."

"That's what we're going to do? Sell off our lives one piece at a time until there's nothing left?"

"You're being a little dramatic, don't you think?"

"Am I? You really think working on that old boat is going to be a windfall for our financial problems? I think it's just an excuse for you to spend time downstairs away from everything going on around here."

"That's blatantly unfair and you know it."

"Oh, really? You take up this new hobby, try to say it's for money, when what we really need is a good insurance policy. It just seems like screwed-up logic to me. Your time could be better spent."

He stood stunned for a moment, then he said, "I'll bring up the rest of the groceries."

Was she unfair? Lauren could see the future; he'd be working on his pet project and she would be holding back her child's hair while Ainslie rested on her knees in front of the toilet bowl. There. That's what Emmett would call bitter. But she wasn't bitter. She was exhausted, both mentally and physically.

He said she had changed—well of course she had. Her life had become doctor appointments and medicines, Internet searches and worry. Her days were filled with her daughter's struggle to home school on par with her peers, those fortunate children whose brains were not racked on chemotherapy.

Emmett would never voice his opinion of her personality in crisis, although he made sure she was aware of it in subtle ways. But Lauren believed that if she were truly bitter she would be asking why her child, why their family? She'd turned to God for answers, but none had been forthcoming. That was another place where she and Emmett parted company. While she tried to have faith, Emmett seemed to have very little. Where she wanted to believe life had purpose, he believed things were simply random.

Did she believe Ainslie was sick because God wanted to teach their family some sort of lesson? No. Of course, she'd thought about it, but she'd finally come to the conclusion that God didn't directly affect physical things here on Earth. If a child and a bowling ball were both tossed from a high building you couldn't pray for God's hand to catch the child and spare her. Both child and bowling ball would hit the ground at the same time with very different results. Lauren had decided that praying was for comfort. Hope was necessary. She didn't expect God to spare her child when other children died. That was too self-centered. She had never asked why her child, but she had asked why any child.

Emmett thought she had unexamined faith, that she believed blindly, but that was simply not the case. The people with blind faith, the ones who assured her God had a plan for Ainslie and it wasn't up to her to question His plan, made her want to scream. In Lauren's opinion, those people were simply too weak to face the fact that life can be shit sometimes. They want to think that ultimately they are not responsible for their decisions, for their lives.

Faith for her was not about turning over responsibility for her child. It was about comfort and mental health. She knew God was there, and how anyone couldn't feel this was a foreign concept to her. Her faith was basic in her bones, a truth she felt as solidly as she felt her own fingers, but it wasn't an excuse to be blind to life's darker moments.

Still, her faith hadn't translated to the rest of her family. It seemed that very little God shine, as her oldest daughter called it, had rubbed off on any of them. The girls had both been raised in a church family, but neither girl ever sought the church or any type of faith when they had problems. They never gravitated to the young Christian clubs at school nor wanted to spend a week of their summers at Bible camp.

Where Sloan and Emmett were openly disdainful of organized religion, Ainslie continued to be the only one willing to attend services with Lauren. Still, as soon as Ainslie left church, she left that train of thought behind. After lunch, when they arrived home on Sunday, Ainslie immediately went on the hunt for bugs and lizards, and all thoughts of God vaporized. Lauren tried to inject the beauty of God's creativity into her nature talks with Ainslie, but doubt always hovered behind her daughter's eyes.

So of course, Ainslie had taken a scientific approach to disease. She'd asked doctors if she could look in the microscope to see what her cancer was like. Ainslie had expected it to be moving and was surprised to find the cells were dead. She told Lauren that the slide looked like tadpole eggs or a pink-and-purple polluted river, but the pathologist had told her the color was from dye used to stain the slide.

Lauren had prepared herself for the questions Ainslie would have about God and why he allowed her to get sick. Lauren had spoken to her minister, but Reverend Michael had been vague and less helpful than she had hoped. He certainly hadn't equipped her with the solid answers she was seeking. Presbyterians were a contemplative bunch, independent of thought and questioning. Reverend Michael had simply said that times like this tested us all and that she needed to show Ainslie how strong faith can ease pain and give meaning to life's struggles.

But Ainslie hadn't asked many religious questions. Instead, she watched Animal Planet and movies. She read the wildlife books people sent her and made beaded jewelry and ragged potholders. Lauren had prayed with Ainslie, but she guessed that her daughter just saw it as another thing she was required to do. She wasn't as questioning or as angry as Lauren had expected, although Lauren could see anger building in her other daughter each day.

Some sort of faith could help Sloan deal with what was happening to them, but Sloan was deep into the independent-teenager phase. She was never without white earbuds snaking down from her head to block conversation. Sloan pulled her sunny hair into elastics and let it spew angrily from her head. She wore jeans with artfully placed holes, and unusually feminine baby doll tops. And the flip-flops, the ubiquitous things she wore most of the year, even on days when Lauren was sure her toes would freeze. No. Sloan was her own person and she had used Ainslie's illness as a source of freedom. Ainslie had felt the sting of her sister's long absences, but who could blame Sloan? It was hard to watch these terrible things happen to a person you loved. It was wearing on everyone's psyche, this daily reminder that doom lurked around the corner.

Luckily, the girls had a special connection. Last week, Lauren had been coming around behind the house with a bag of trash when she'd heard the girls talking inside the latticed carport. Ainslie asked Sloan what she thought getting an MRI would be like.

Sloan said, "Like this." And she had climbed into the old fish sink where three generations of Sullivans had cleaned their catch.

"And they'll take a picture of your insides," Sloan said.

Ainslie said, "Duh. I know that. What I mean is, will it hurt?"

"I don't think so."

"Move over." Ainslie crawled into the tub beside her sister.

Lauren stood there, waiting for them to talk more, but they didn't. They just lay beside each other, dangling their feet over the edge of the tub.

Sloan had successfully hidden this part of herself since she hit puberty, and sometimes Lauren forgot this side existed. She was such a moody little thing, Lauren feared she was on the verge of being one of the pitiful goth kids who lurked in bookstores and outside hamburger joints around their little town of Litchfield. But she hadn't gone over that edge yet. Sloan had rejected nearly everything Lauren had suggested as far as clothing, hobbies, or social graces. Still, she made good grades and kept out of trouble. She wasn't drugged out or pregnant and she hadn't run away. Now she was eighteen, so technically she couldn't run away. For all intents and purposes she was an adult—able to vote and get married, hold a job and pay taxes. She was more independent now than ever, with all of Lauren's energies focused on Ainslie. Emmett had said to let her go, that it was unnecessary to try to keep track of her anymore, and Lauren had decided he was right. She had held on longer than most parents do these days.

But it was hard to let go. Lauren had wanted her girls, had never even blinked when Sloan came along unexpectedly. She and Emmett were married, and they moved into this house, and Emmett started his company, and life was good. Along came Ainslie, and life got even better. Lauren had never really regretted dropping out of college after her sophomore year. There hadn't been any one thing she'd been passionately interested in. But once her girls came along, she finally knew who she was. She was a mother, and to Lauren, that was the perfect job. She took selfish pleasure in being able to bake cookies with the girls and give them elaborate birthday parties and take them to Brownies and church. She'd been dedicated to photographing them every year. Her favorite image was one of the girls in matching white dresses, barefoot on the beach, big white bows in their wind-tossed hair.

When the girls were small, Lauren had taken them

to ballet lessons. She loved their cute protruding toddler tummies, and little bottoms in pink tights. Their tiny feet were so sweet in dainty ballet flats. She'd collected Sloan's curls on top of her head, but in mere minutes Sloan always found a way to have her hair tumbling around her shoulders. Her little redhead had been only six when she told Lauren ballet "wasn't her thing." Yet, her grace of movement was apparent still. Of course, Sloan would never admit to the benefit of her dance background, but Lauren enjoyed the way she glided rather than walked.

Ainslie's ballet days were spent peering through the giant glass window at the butterflies lighted in the garden there. She had stayed with ballet longer than Sloan, not wanting to upset her mother. But Lauren had realized one day that her little girl was miserable. She would never be the graceful, long-limbed swan other girls seemed to be, nor did she even care. On the day Lauren asked Ainslie if she wanted to quit ballet she saw relief wash over her child's face. This second failed ballet experience made Lauren vow never to force her own agenda on her girls again. While Lauren was neither artistic nor scientific, she was supportive of her daughters' interests. She let them choose their own paths, although she was chagrined she would not be getting even one ballerina out of two girls.

Sloan hadn't liked swimming lessons either, but the pool had been Ainslie's passion, at least for a while. Her younger daughter had taken to the water and moved up through the YMCA's program from Guppy to Porpoise in no time. From the kitchen window, Lauren watched her tomboy daughter saunter to the end of their boardwalk, pocketknife and plastic critter box in hand, bug net thrown over her shoulder like Huck Finn. It comforted Lauren to know that if Ainslie fell into the creek or onto the muddy bank she wouldn't panic, she'd more likely find a clam to examine before she hauled herself out.

Occasionally, Lauren would climb to the widow's walk to check on her if she couldn't see her from the kitchen. Sometimes she would join her, this daughter in cutoffs smeared with pluff mud, a favorite snake T-shirt, fly-away baby hair escaping her ponytail. Ainslie was always eager to share her finds, and sometimes they would sit for hours on the dock examining shells and gory bits of animals her daughter found fascinating. It had never occurred to Lauren that she would find rocks and animal bones in a daughter's pockets, but she was constantly amazed by the mysterious dead things that crumbled from Ainslie's clothes.

Emmett banged into the room carrying the balance of the groceries. He deposited them on the counter, and then, before she knew it, he had disappeared. *Of course*, Lauren thought, *it would be too much to ask for help putting the groceries away.*

She heard a squeal of glee from upstairs. She left the groceries and sneaked up the steps, following the happy sound. The bathroom door was ajar and easy to nudge open. Straight brown hair pooled on the tile floor and Lauren sucked in a shocked breath. The girls had taken the matter of Ainslie's thinning hair into their own hands. Lauren knocked gently on her daughter's bedroom door expecting to see a distraught girl buried under the comforter. But her girls were perched on the bed, books strewn around them, permanent markers tossed thoughtlessly on the pale sheets. They turned to her, wide smiles across their beautiful faces.

"Mom, look what Sloan did for me!" On Ainslie's deathly pale scalp, her sister had drawn a colorful, undulating Chinese dragon.

"It's the coolest thing I've ever seen!" Ainslie said,

checking herself in the mirror. "Thank you so much!" The girls embraced and fell over on the bed, giggling.

So here it was, one of those times when hope renews. When Lauren was forced to reevaluate. It was this occasional glimmer of optimism that kept Lauren going. Just when things seemed most bleak, when thoughts of losing their home, wrecking her marriage, or Ainslie's illness were foremost in her mind, something miraculous would happen.

She heard Emmett push into the room behind her and turned in time to see him whip off his white running cap.

"So what do you think?" he said, running a hand over his own bald head.

The girls kicked their feet in the air with laughter, and Emmett climbed onto the bed next to them.

"Let me pick out one," Emmett said.

"Here," Sloan said and handed him a book of tattoos. Lauren recognized the book. She'd found it in Sloan's room a couple of years ago and had talked to her about how tattoos were tacky and not acceptable.

Perhaps that was another thing Lauren had misjudged. Emmett pointed to a tattoo of an Indian elephant and Ainslie clapped her hands. Lauren settled on the bed too. This was what she prayed for, that her girls could find some happiness each day, that her husband would come back to them, and that her family would be strong enough to live through this.

CHAPTER 6

The Black Fountain

Everybody had to have a favorite place, was what Sloan thought. Her mother's place was the bathroom, where she steamed and creamed and conditioned, a flowery funeral smell trailing her for hours afterward. The beach held a special allure for her little sister. Ainslie would hunch over tide pools for hours, her toes digging sea stars from under faint outlines. Her dad had The Pub, although he thought nobody knew how much he hung out there, but his happy, cigarette-tinged demeanor gave him away.

Sloan's place was Brookgreen Gardens, and on occasion, the remaining shell of Atalaya, the Spanish-style mansion across the road. She never knew when she drove there which way she would choose to turn. To the right lay Atalaya, the salt-crusted walls and empty stone rooms cool even in summer. The front opened to a sand path leading through a thicket of crusty cedars to a beach scattered with shell fragments.

To the left, America's oldest public sculpture gardens, as Sloan had learned early in life. An independently wealthy couple, Anna Hyatt Huntington and her husband had created the gardens, now the pride of the local community. He was a poet, and she made the garden's more dramatic sculptures. Sloan's favorite Huntington sculpture marked the highway entrance—horses as big as cars locked in writhing combat with a snarling lion, a rider clinging to one horse, tossed and feckless, another rider thrown to the ground at the feet of the massive animals.

It was February, and plants were beginning to leak buds. By March, the gardens cascading down to the Waccamaw River would blaze with azaleas like a Valentine's Day parade. Today she headed back through the gardens, past stone animals and an allee of giant live oaks to the black fountain, Ainslie's favorite place. There was something creepy and disturbing about the water oozing from the foundation of the original house, which had burned in 1901. The corner was always cooler, a breeze up from the river constant and welcoming even in February, when short-sleeve days were frequent.

On the outside of this raised pool, lusty ferns grew, and in this tiny tropical paradise anoles thrived. Sloan imagined how they must recognize Ainslie by now and run to hide from her. Her sister took some notice of the various animal statues in the gardens, but her main focus was always a huge game of catching every anole unlucky enough to be within reach. She would hang lizards from her earlobes, their fragile limbs flat to their bodies, paralyzed with the effort of biting. Ainslie always put her friends back carefully, saying they had favorite places. It seemed even tiny reptiles had spots of reprieve.

Sloan dropped down onto an ancient millstone and found her drawing pad and pencils in her satchel. She eyed the sculpture atop the black fountain, a stocky man with large feet and hands wresting an alligator backward into a U. Both man and beast were straining, but the man was on the winning end, perpetually compressing the beast in upon itself. She loved the *Alligator Bender* for its symmetry and contemporary lines.

Ainslie loved this sculpture because it reminded her of her hero, Steve Irwin. She thought of the statue as an ancient crocodile hunter. As Sloan's hands jumped across the paper, she envisioned the smile Ainslie would give her for this sketch. Sloan had drawn starfish, seashells, birds, fish, and every manner of creepy-crawly thing her sister had ever requested. It was the only thing she could think to do to help her sister now. She wasn't allowed to even breathe in Ainslie's direction if her mother was hovering around.

Both Sloan and her father found it easier to simply stay out of the way. "You know how your mother is," he had said. They were on the beach watching leggy sand-pipers skitter away from a dog's awkward advances. "She's focused on Ainslie, and that's the way it should be. It's what's best for your sister that matters right now."

He hugged her to his side, making it awkward to walk. This path of least resistance suited Sloan, and when her father slipped her the keys to the old battered Jeep, she had known without it being spoken that he was giving her the vehicle. Previously a point of contention between her parents, it was quietly dismissed, ignored really, like everything else where Sloan was concerned. She floated around, standing always on the outside of conversation, like a ghost on the periphery of her family. After she got the Jeep, she'd come to Brookgreen so frequently her father finally told her to keep the membership card.

"I don't imagine the rest of us will be going for a while," he'd said.

Sloan was crosshatching to represent the scales on the bottom of the alligator's body when she heard laughter. Usually Sloan could sketch here for hours and not be bothered, but occasionally people wandered near. She heard a giggle, and then a group of six stepped from behind a hedge into sight.

"Wow, this is cool," one of the guys said.

"I'm bored. Let's go," a girl whined.

The guys sported khakis and pop-collared Lacoste shirts. The girls each wore pink sweatshirts emblazoned with the College of Charleston and short cotton shorts with Greek letters across their butts.

He was the sort of boy she immediately disliked. Shiny bangs, polo shirt, sports legs like ropes. As he drew near, she recognized him. He was from real money, new money, Lafayette Isle money, where everyone was a perpetually tanned, logoed, CrackBerry'd drone. He'd graduated the year before, although he'd spent his younger years in private school. Calhoun Wannamaker. The list in the yearbook beside his name showed letters in golf, tennis, baseball, and track. Sloan was appalled that she remembered this information, that she could even see his photo's position on the page. But such was the curse of the artist's photographic memory. His hair was much shorter in that photo. Today his bangs hung down over one eye, and he whipped them to the side every few minutes. He moved fluidly, like an athlete. He was quickly beside her, leaning over her shoulder toward her drawing.

She hesitated, slightly irritated at the intrusion, but also flattered by the attention. She held up her work.

"Shit. That's really good."

"Thank you."

"You come here and draw a lot?"

"It's kind of my space, my time to be alone."

"Oh, hey." He threw up his hands and made a show of backing away. "If you're running me off."

"No."

"No, you're not running me off?"

"No."

"Okay. Well, like, I've seen you around school. I mean last year I did."

She simply looked at him.

The whiny girl appeared from nowhere and laid perfectly polished nails on his arm.

"Come on, *Cal.*"

"In a minute. Y'all head on back. I'll catch up."

The girl gave Sloan a hateful glance. "Whatever," she snapped. When she was some distance away her voice carried across the surface of the black fountain. "This place gives me the creeps."

"So anyway," he continued, rolling his eyes, "you're Sloan Sullivan, right?"

"Yeah."

"So if I asked you to go out sometime, what would you say?"

"Out with you."

"Sure. Dinner or something."

"Dinner or something."

"Damn, do you always repeat everything?"

"No."

"Okay, so give me your digits." He pulled a slim phone from his pocket.

She hadn't said she would go out with him. She watched him program her name and wait patiently for her number. She considered him for a moment, let him sweat just a little. He was used to having his way, and just briefly she thought of telling him no, but just as quickly she rattled off her numbers, which he punched in. Her phone rang in her pocket.

"Now, I know you have my number," he said.

"Are you always so aggressive?"

"What if I never saw you again?" He smiled a perfect smile. "I gotta run and catch up with my friends, but . . . I'll call you."

"Sure."

He started to walk away.

"Wait."

"What?"

"You never told me your name."

He seemed slightly amused by her.

"Oh, sorry. I just thought you knew me."

"Not really."

He grinned. Did he know she was lying?

"Cal Wannamaker."

"Okay, *Cal.*" She drew out his name in a mocking tone. He grinned in a crooked way.

"Yeah, okay."

Sloan watched him go, then she lowered her head to draw again but her fingers were frozen. Her pulse fluttered and her mind was blank. Unable to concentrate, she suddenly decided she needed caffeine to help her focus. It was a habit she had recently developed. Since there were so few good coffee places in their vest-pocket town, she often treated herself to a cappuccino at the garden's café. It was this habit that had introduced her to LaShonda Washington, a girl she had always gone to school with but had never really known. Once Sloan started hanging at the café at off-hours finishing sketches, she had found LaShonda amusing and easy to talk to.

"Hey," LaShonda said when her friend walked in.

"You totally won't believe what just happened."

"What?" She continued to count dollars into the cash register. The café was empty except for two people conversing excitedly in German.

"Germans always talk so loud," LaShonda mumbled.

"Do you remember Cal Wannamaker from school last year?"

LaShonda raised her eyebrows. "Sure. Rich, preppy, jock. Good-looking, though. Why?"

"I just ran into him outside and he asked me out."

"You lie."

"I swear." Sloan held up her hand as scout's honor.

"Girrrrl." LaShonda seemed unconvinced. "What'd you say?"

"I gave him my number. Maybe he just wanted to prove he could get my number."

"Be careful. Isle boys make for the quick hookup and even quicker breakup." LaShonda slammed the register's drawer shut.

"That's with summer girls. They don't try to pull that crap on locals." Sloan knew her friend had never been out with a boy from Lafayette Isle. Blacks weren't even able to own real estate there. Although it was supposed to be a secret, everybody knew the private island would never be integrated. The Lafayette Isle charter stated that two residents had to recommend a potential buyer before a sale could take place, and nobody wanted to be the leper responsible for lowering property values.

"Maybe. But you know how those rich boys think. They got entitlement issues. Like everything in the world's supposed to come easy. You want a cappuccino?"

"Sure. Are you saying I should play hard to get?"

LaShonda frothed milk. She raised her voice to be heard over the screech of the steamer. "I don't know. Seems like boyfriends always turn out to be more trouble than they're worth."

"Who said anything about a boyfriend? I'd just like to go on a real date. Somewhere nice, like Al's by the Creek. Not hooking up at the mall or parking at the beach."

LaShonda set two foamy mugs on the table and slid into a seat across from Sloan.

"He called me so I'd have his number."

"Don't you dare call him. Make him work for it."

"I wasn't drooling all over myself if that's what you're thinking. I was cool."

"I'm just saying don't make it too easy. Guys like him are used to getting what they want, when they want it."

"True."

"I can't believe you'd go out with him anyway. I thought you hated those fake people on Lafayette Isle." She sipped coffee. "You know, come to think of it, ain't his dad that developer dude, always finding some island to mow down or some swamp to drain so he can throw up mansions?"

"I don't know. You sound like my dad. Can't you be at least a little happy for me? He's hot."

"Yeah, he's hot all right. Just be careful or you'll end up burned."

CHAPTER 7

Side Effects

Adults were secretive. Her parents and the doctors and nurses whispered in the hall outside her door. While that might have worked with some kids, Ainslie's hearing was sharp, and she strained to make out their conversations. Sometimes she would lie in bed and pick certain sounds out of the hospital noise, slippers soft in the hall, the call button at the nurses' station, a cry from down the corridor. And she could smell better, too, which usually wasn't a good thing in a hospital—alcohol and urine and that too sweet hand lotion all the nurses seemed to like. Ainslie could even smell the brownish antiseptic still lingering on her skin from the surgery.

And the pain. If she lay perfectly still it was like nothing was wrong with her, but if she twisted left or right her back hurt. So she stayed still, the pain medication swimming in her mind. All the details of the humming hospital, the smells and sounds, made Ainslie wish for the calm of waves and the scent of tea olive that drifted through her bedroom window at home. But the hospital windows were shut tight, and even though she was in Charleston at the Children's Hospital at the Medical University of South Carolina, she could have been anywhere in the world. Sometimes she imagined she was in India where sleepy-eyed camels pulled carts below her window, or she imagined she was in the Arctic where polar bears prowled outside and Eskimo children slept in other hospital beds.

When she was first diagnosed, Ainslie hadn't tried to understand what was happening to her. She'd just done what was asked, submitted to whatever tests. But then they removed one of her kidneys and the things they did to her hurt more. She was tired and cranky from the meds and all she wanted to do was run away, to rip the tubes out of her arm and run out of the hospital into fresh air and sunshine. Instead, she got a parade of kids in pajamas dragging IV poles past her door. Sometimes they would look in and see Ainslie, and they would wave or smile. Other times they just stared like they didn't really see her there, and then they would just walk on down the hall.

The longer Ainslie stayed in the hospital the more things began to hurt. They took blood and started IVs, and each time a nurse stuck a needle into the top of her hand or the tender part inside her elbow, Ainslie imagined she was being burned, that a tiny flame was shooting into her arm. Of course, they put numbing cream where they stuck in the needles, but that didn't really help much. The doctors had promised her something called a port, some thing they put inside your chest, just under your skin. They said they could stick the needles in the port and it wouldn't hurt so much, but she wasn't sure that she wanted some creepy thing inside of her. This was when she started to tune in to adult conversations instead of watching cartoons.

Once she tuned in to what was being said, things

started to make sense and they started to scare her. She'd learned about chemotherapy. Everybody knew chemotherapy was medicine to kill cancer, but she found out that chemotherapy killed good cells along with bad ones and that was what caused you to be grossed out and to vomit. She'd been scared when she'd overheard the hall-lurking adults talking about the possible weird things that chemo could cause to happen to your body later. They called these side effects.

Ainslie wanted to know what these side effects were, but she didn't ask her mother. The hospital staff had made a book where they kept all her medical information. They called this the roadmap, and it had all her medicines and all the reactions she could expect, but her mother never wanted her to look at the roadmap book. She told Ainslie not to worry, that the doctors would take care of everything. Ainslie suspected that her mother never told her the whole truth. And her father wasn't an option. He didn't know much of anything about medical stuff.

When her mother wasn't looking, Sloan helped Ainslie decipher the roadmap book. Sloan brought her laptop and they got online. It didn't take long before they found a link and had document after document off the Internet about Wilms' tumor cancer. The deal was usually that a kidney got removed, the kid got radiated, sometimes they got chemo, other times not. Most kids survived and were never bothered with it again.

"Piece of cake," Sloan said. "You're tough."

She also said that they probably shouldn't read a bunch of the stories of other sick kids, that it might be too depressing. Ainslie had agreed. All the research was enough for her to think about without being sad over some other kid with worse luck.

They were in bed together, looking up her chemo

cocktail on the Internet. They had both become good at medical lingo.

"I can't find this drug anywhere. I wonder why."

"Go ask Miss Vivian. She's my favorite nurse."

At the nurses' station Sloan asked for Miss Vivian and a few minutes later the woman arrived in Ainslie's room. Vivian flipped through her own reference materials and then said, "It must be new."

"Is it experimental?" Sloan asked.

"Honey, I didn't say experimental. I said new." Vivian flipped her book closed with a frustrated sigh. "I don't have much info here on that, but I'll see what I can find out. Sure you want to know all this? It can be scary."

"It won't scare me," Ainslie said.

"We won't tell anybody you helped us," Sloan said. "Especially not our mother. She thinks she needs to shield us from all of this."

"Sure, I understand," Vivian said. "A lot of parents feel that way."

Ainslie nodded. "It's okay. I want to know."

But that hadn't been the case when Vivian brought them a printout the next day.

"You didn't get this from me," she had said. "I could get fired for this." Sloan promised to destroy the paper as soon as they were finished.

"What does it say?" Ainslie asked.

"Just a bunch of doctor stuff I can't understand. A few side effects you know about. Nausea, hair loss, blah, blah, blah."

She stopped her finger on a line. She reread the passage, then moved on quickly.

"What?"

"Nothing."

"What?"

"Nothing, I said."

"You can tell me. What does it say?"

"You really want to know?"

"Yes."

"Okay. It says this drug here can cause sterility."

"What does that mean?"

"It means . . . it means that you may not be able to have babies when you grow up. Sterility, you know, like sterile."

"Is that bad?"

"Well, it is if you want to have kids, but hey, you don't need to think about that right now. Look, that's the worst thing listed here. Your chemo won't like, make you deaf or blind or anything awful like that."

But from then on, every time Ainslie arrived at the oncology clinic for another round of chemo, she thought about that word—sterility. She had to push it down and try to focus her thoughts in a positive direction. They told her to imagine chemo moving through her body like a video game character blasting away cancer cells. One time, she had asked to see what her cancer looked like. Her pathologist had been thrilled to show her, had adjusted the microscope eyepieces until the cells were large and like gobs of purple Jell-O stuck together. It was hard to hold her head still enough to keep the focus, but she'd stared through that microscope for a really long time. The cells didn't move like she had expected because they were dead. The pathologist gave her color printouts of the strange river of cells and she always tried to focus on those cells and mentally blast them away with her imaginary chemo weapons. It helped to know what the enemy looked like.

Once when it was her father's turn to take her for her chemo clinic visit, her father had put aside his sports magazine and stared at her.

Lying back in a lounger sipping a grape soda, Ainslie had met his gaze and said, "What?"

"You know, baby," he said, "we'll always wonder, your mother and I, whether we did or didn't do something that caused this to happen to you. I mean, we're sorry if we did. We didn't know. We still don't."

"It's not your fault, Daddy," she told him. "It's not anybody's fault. It's just a stupid thing that happened."

His face shifted in a strange way when Ainslie told him her disease was developed before she was even born, that it wasn't anything they'd done.

"How do you know this?" he asked her.

She'd shrugged as if it was something everybody knew.

All he'd said after that was, "Does your mother know?"

Ainslie said, "Yeah. But she doesn't believe it."

She was always sick for a couple of days after a chemo treatment, then she'd buck up and things would be good for a while before she had to go back and do it all over again. Her parents tried to keep everything as normal as possible. Her dad went to work and Sloan went to school. Her home-school teacher brought homework and Ainslie tried to keep up with the rest of the third grade. Afternoons were all about television and video games. Late in the day the mail would come, and there would be a few cool cards or another package from her grandparents in New Jersey.

It was in these lonely afternoons, before Sloan came home from school, that Ainslie felt sad. She would look at where her animal tanks had been and miss her little pets. The stupid doctors had made her parents get rid of all of her animals because of germs. That had been the worst part of being sick. Ainslie loved her hermit crab. She'd had Mr. Crabs for more than three years, and he had moved shells so many times that she finally lost count. Ainslie had watched his pink, squishy body trying out new shells. He was shy when he was naked, and he'd creep out, his eye stalks searching for safety, then he'd streak to another shell. Ainslie's mother said

Mr. Crabs was modest. It was a good thing her crab didn't have cancer because you couldn't be modest if you had to have your butt stuck up in the air for all the nurses and doctors and student doctors at the hospital to see. She had cried and begged to keep her old crab, so her parents had moved him into Sloan's room until Ainslie could have him back.

A couple of times during her alone time, Ainslie had considered actually writing in the journal the counselor had given her. He'd said it would help her deal with her feelings to write down her thoughts or draw pictures about how she felt. But Ainslie didn't like to write, and she couldn't draw nearly as well as Sloan. She'd scribbled a few things down, but something told her that if she wrote anything too personal, her mother would surely peek. So Ainslie just shared her problems with Sloan when she was around. Sloan always seemed to know how to make things better somehow. She wasn't like adults.

The adults were always full of advice—think positively, imagine video games, write in your journal. They were always bringing her stuffed animals and flowers and cards. Always in her face about something, but they always had that sad, almost creepy look.

At least Sloan was cool. She never said everything was going to be okay like the adults did. She just acted normal. That was one of the things about being sick, everybody acted weird around you. But Sloan just said that being sick sucked.

And it did suck. It was the biggest, most stupid sucky thing that could happen.

It sucked to have your animals taken away because of germs. It sucked that your hair fell out and your face swelled until you looked like a cartoon character. It sucked that you were constantly getting stuck with needles and poked until you just wanted to scream at people to leave you alone. It sucked to feel bad all the time and there was nothing you could do about it.

Being sick should be like school. You go for a certain number of days and do what you have to do and you get a report card and everybody says you did great and then it's all over and you get a summer vacation. But being sick wasn't like that. There didn't seem to be any end.

CHAPTER 8

Pleasure Pain

Emmett glanced over at Lauren in the passenger seat. Lines had started at the corners of her eyes, and the skin on her neck seemed tight. He noticed when she walked out to the car tonight that she was thinner; her soft round hips had dwindled until her dress hung straight down her sides. She had been quiet for the fifteen minutes it took them to drive south to Lafayette Isle.

"Sure you want to go?" he asked as they approached the guard hut.

"We have to do something normal again," she said.

Emmett pulled the car up to the security gate. A guard stepped out with a clipboard. Emmett lowered the window and sticky, moss-flavored air invaded the cool of the car, a first wave of summer in March.

"Evening, sir," the guard said as he leaned down to eye level.

"We're here for the Wannamaker party. Sullivan," Emmett said.

The guard smiled and motioned him on. "Have a nice time."

"I can't believe it's so hot already," he said to Lauren as the window slid up.

"You know it'll cool off again before summer sets in."

"I just hope it doesn't trick the trees into blooming early and then freeze them out like last year."

The smooth drive wound through dense coastal forest, land that had been owned by the Vanderbilts. Most of Georgetown County had been owned by Vanderbilts at one time, but this island had been sold and developed into a community, although still private. They drove across small causeways, and Emmett pointed out a gator languid on the bank of the salt marsh, only his tail dipping into the water. Egrets perched in craggy trees, stark white against the growing dark. They passed golf cart crossings, stables, and two pools. Giant houses became more tightly spaced, although all had a guarded measure of privacy.

They parked down the road from the Wannamakers' colossal Lowcountry home and walked past an easy million dollars worth of SUVs and sedans pulled onto manicured lawns. A dozen golf carts were clustered next to the house, neighbors who had cruised over, their early cocktails melting in drink holders. Twenty-six steps led up to a wide verandah that wrapped the pale blue house. Beach music and laughter spilled out of the open front door.

"Ready?" Emmett said.

"Yeah, I just hope I can hold it together."

"If you can't, we'll leave."

They climbed slowly. As they stepped through the entrance, their hostess met them with the high-pitched, drawn-out greeting of a certain segment of Southern women.

"Heeeyyy! We're so glad y'all could cooome," Bitsy Wannamaker sang. She was squeezed into a green-and-pink Lilly Pulitzer dress too small for her size fourteen frame. Sun-spotted bosoms blossomed from the bodice. A drink tinkled in her hand. "My goodness, Lauren, you're just skin and bones. You look just great! Come on in. Get a drink."

She steered them toward a tanned, skinny college kid standing behind a makeshift bar along one wall of the great room. Behind him, above the fireplace, loomed an oil painting, a family portrait on a windswept beach. Elsewhere, typical Lowcountry watercolors and Audubon bird prints favored by faux Southern aristocracy climbed the walls.

"This is Robert. He's a fraternity brother of our oldest, Calhoun. They've formed a little bartending enterprise to earn money. They're doing all the parties around here this summer. He'll fix you right up."

The tip jar overflowed with dollar bills.

"Calhoun's got the bar downstairs by the pool. Go introduce yourselves." Bitsy patted Emmett on the arm. "I'm so glad y'all could come. I've got to run off and see to things. We'll talk later." And she was gone.

Emmett noticed how the boy met his gaze and smiled casually, a most self-assured young man.

"Gin and tonic," Lauren said.

"Yes, ma'am," Robert said. "And you, sir?"

"Bourbon, rocks."

"Guess I'm driving home," Lauren said.

"Do you mind?"

"Zoloft, remember? One drink will be my limit."

Robert handed them their drinks.

"Well," Emmett said as he stuffed a five into the tip jar. "Let's go mingle with the beautiful people."

"You should probably keep your wit to yourself tonight."

"Who do we know here?"

"Well, there will be lots of people from Kathwood. If

you'd ever go to church with me you'd know some of them."

"I'd rather not. On both accounts."

"Don't be smart."

Glass doors opened to an expansive ocean view that faded into the night. They squeezed through the party, Lauren making little finger waves to people she knew, Emmett with his hand at the small of her back, propelling her outside. Another twenty-six steps down and they were at the pool that flickered blue light around the backyard. Beach music played softly under the conversation. Black waiters in white shirts and bow ties milled between partygoers with silver trays of miniature crab cakes and smoked tuna.

"Lauren!" a woman called from the shadows of a table umbrella. "Over here."

"Marguerite!" Lauren was drawn to the table of women like a moth to flame.

The woman patted a patio chair beside her. "Come sit and tell me how is that darling little girl of yours? How's she doing?"

Lauren slid into the chair as if under a spell. Emmett knew she believed others truly wanted to hear how their family was making out, but he could see people mentally back away when the answers got honest. Nobody wanted to know what a family goes through when their child has cancer—the fear, the worry, the piles of paperwork, the struggle to balance doctors' appointments and chemotherapy with work and school. People didn't want to hear that Emmett had switched insurance providers only months before the diagnosis so the company had yet to pay a dime for their daughter's treatment. Nobody wanted to hear about preexisting conditions. They only wanted you to tell them everything is fine, just fine.

Emmett threw back his bourbon. He wasn't going to be a part of this. He headed toward the cabana strung with hot-pepper lights. On his more cynical days, he thought people were only interested in his family for the drama, the information they could gather and pass along; but Lauren seemed to draw strength from places where Emmett found only insincerity. She'd started going to church more frequently. He'd caught her praying in the bathroom only yesterday. She was on her knees, right there on the cold tile floor, her head down on the lip on the tub as if a sudden need for solace had overwhelmed her.

He'd left her to her introspection. Instead, he'd gone for a run on the beach—seven miles to the end of Pawleys and back, a 10K. His legs still held that pleasure–pain ache of exertion.

He slid up onto a stool and rattled his glass. "Fill her up. Bourbon. The good stuff. Rocks. Use the same ice."

"Yes, sir." The young man took the glass, tossed in a couple of cubes and filled it to the rim.

"You Calhoun?"

"Yes, sir."

"Where you go to school?"

"College of Charleston."

"Like it?"

The boy grinned, and a shock of hair fell across one eye. He flipped it back with a toss of his head, but it fell forward again. He could have stepped off the pages of one of Sloan's J.Crew catalogs, all white teeth and smooth skin.

"It's okay."

"What's your major?"

"Biology."

"Med school?"

"If my parents have their way."

"What if you have your way?"

He shrugged. "I don't know. Marine biology, maybe."

"Sophomore?"

"I will be. Yes, sir."

"You sling drinks during the summer?"

"Among other things. My dad makes me earn my own money. He says it builds character."

"Well, I'd have to agree with him on that."

"Whatever."

"Top me off, would you?"

"Yes, sir."

The boy tossed a few extra cubes into the glass and filled it again. Emmett raised his drink to the underage bartender. "Good luck to you, young man," he said and walked away. He glanced back over his shoulder to find Lauren still involved in conversation. All the women there were washed in stray light from the pool, like ghouls gathered around a cauldron. Emmett smiled at his thought.

"What's so funny?"

He was startled and glad to see someone he knew. Particularly Caroline, the hottest bureaucrat he'd ever met. Her cascade of sun-streaked hair was enough to make him sweat on sight.

"Hey, Caroline. How's things at the city?"

"Same old. You know. Trying to push through that referendum so we can get a new road built. That's the only way to keep up with development."

"County and city council needs to get control of this unchecked growth or we'll end up Myrtle Beach South."

"We're working on it. It's a constant battle."

"I hear you."

"Is Lauren here?"

"Over there in that gaggle of women."

When she turned toward the table, Emmett let his eyes roam down to where her gauzy sundress draped away from the swell of her breasts. There had always been something between them, an itch Emmett knew he'd never scratch.

"You look nice tonight." The liquor was working on him.

She smiled. "How much have you had to drink?"

"Only my second." He shrugged, jiggled his glass, and sipped. This was the first time in months he'd felt loose.

"I know where the real party is."

"Oh, yeah?"

"Follow me."

Lauren was gesticulating in a way that let Emmett know exactly where she was in her story. She wouldn't miss him for a few minutes. Caroline led the way under the back deck's flying staircase into the dark. They passed showers and a dressing area, a deep, wide sink, and numerous bicycles in a jumble in the garage. Voices pulsed softly from inside a storage shed. Caroline knocked and someone opened the door a crack. A sliver of cheek appeared, then a suspicious eye.

"Hey," Caroline said. "Let us in."

Inside, sea kayaks and expensive bicycles hung the walls. Long paddles with wide, flat ends leaned in corners. Deflated rubber floats were flung in a depressing pile under a workbench. A small set of partygoers stood casually around a boogie board balanced atop two sawhorses. Six lines of coke streaked the makeshift table.

Emmett knew a few people in the room. Leaned against the workbench was Alejandro Aldrete, owner of Al's by the Creek, the steakhouse where the local moneyed crowd gathered to drink spicy South American wines and eat crab cakes and Angus steaks. Beside him was Al's wife, a criminal defense lawyer Emmett knew from the restaurant. Then there was Thomas Wannamaker, their host, whom everybody called Trip. Trip Wannamaker was one of the more influential coastal real estate developers.

"Come on in, man," Trip said.

"Shit," Emmett muttered. "All right."

"Help yourself." Trip motioned to the powder.

Emmett hesitated. "I haven't done that in a long time."

Trip shrugged. "Your call."

"I will." Caroline leaned down to sniff one of the lines up a cut straw. Her breasts fell forward heavily, and every man in the room was riveted for a moment. She jerked her head back, raised her eyebrows, and said, "Wow."

"That's some good shit," Al said. "Fresh off the boat."

Emmett stepped forward and took the other line. It hit the back of his throat like ice and trickled down into him, filling his chest with a rapid pleasurable anxiety. He had a soaring sensation in his stomach and he thought of riding a Ski-Doo over a bigass wave and dropping off the other side in midair.

Trip laid out more lines.

There was nervous laughter and lots of cigarette smoke. Emmett couldn't remember exactly when he left the shed. It couldn't have been long because the next thing he knew he was walking the beach with Lauren, party sounds fading into the low rumble of the surf. It was a full moon and they were alone on a long stretch of beach. When they were younger, they would have seen this as an opportunity to grope each other on a dune until sand scraped their skin inside their clothes. Emmett picked up errant shells and tossed them far into the surf.

"You're so hyper," Lauren said. Her high heels dangled from her fingertips. She poked her toe in the wrack line where the ocean had pushed debris as far inland as it could. Seaweed and salt foam snaked an eerie trail down the beach marking high tide.

"They were doing coke downstairs." He chucked a

piece of driftwood into the water. Ghost crabs skittered away from his feet.

"You did coke?"

"Just a couple of lines."

"Feel any better?"

Moonlight lit her hair and he thought he should kiss her, but he hesitated.

"It made me forget. For a while," he offered.

She didn't say anything else, just stared at him with the desperate eyes of a starved animal. He felt pressured to fill the void. "So, you're not mad at me are you?"

She shrugged as if all the fight had gone out of her. "Considering everything we've been through, what's a line of coke? Just don't drink anything else. I don't want you to OD on me. I can't do this alone."

"Wouldn't think of it." Emmett picked up a bulky piece of driftwood and grunted as he hefted it at the full moon. He thought it would never hit the water, that the black ocean had swallowed the wood without a sound. Finally, the breeze brought him a splash and then a hollow plunking sound as the wood was sucked under.

CHAPTER 9

Shirtsleeves to Shirtsleeves

Cal seemed cool and relaxed in his pressed khaki pants and white button-down.

"Man, you're preppy," Sloan said when he picked her up.

"It's a disease," he replied, with a crooked smile.

It had been a long two weeks waiting for Cal's call. But she was glad not to have called first. She had almost decided LaShonda was right, that Cal had just played a head game with her. But then he did call, and suddenly they were on their way to a command performance with his family at the Lowcountry Yacht Club.

She had assigned his number a special ring tone, so when Blondie's "Call Me" unexpectedly blared, she didn't jump to answer it but instead checked to make sure she wasn't mistaken. With only a few seconds to compose herself she had flipped open her phone and said in a disinterested voice, "Hello?"

He seemed to take her small games in stride. He'd asked her to dinner as she'd hoped. She had selected a sleek black dress that showed off her figure, but then Cal had called back and said that his grandfather had invited them to dinner at the club and suddenly her dress seemed shabby and her shoes all wrong.

Her mother jumped to assist, but her closet was filled with dresses Sloan thought either old or far too cheerful. Then, from the crushed depths of cloth came a dark blue dress with tags still attached, a lone ray of possibility in a palette of pastel. It was simple, straight, and short. Her mother suggested pearls, but Sloan chose a long necklace of silver loops she'd pounded out herself in a jewelry class and a stack of thin bracelets bought in the punk shop in Myrtle Beach. Shoes still presented a problem, so her mother gave her fifty dollars. She'd rushed to a boutique on the mainland and purchased a sale pair that fit her mother's instructions of "also something you'll wear to school."

Sloan was ready far in advance of Cal's arrival so she climbed into bed with Ainslie and read her a scary book they had been hiding from their parents. At the correct time, a white GMC Jimmy crawled down Atlantic Avenue and stopped at the striped single arm of the security gate. Sloan and Ainslie watched him punch in the code. As the gate rose, Sloan dashed to the bathroom to smooth her hair. She waited while her father answered the door, and was surprised to hear him greet Cal with recognition. Suddenly they were speaking loudly and as if they were old friends.

Cal talked most of the way about the College of Charleston, how he was still uncertain about his major, how he'd wanted to travel to Europe with some of his friends that summer, but his father had refused to foot the bill.

"I thought about bumming it," Cal told her, "but then I'd have to go it alone. My friends wouldn't suffer low budget along with me."

Sloan knew that a certain segment of people gave

their kids the big European adventure at some point, yet it seemed a perk his parents had thought Cal needed to skip. She'd also noticed that his SUV had more than 100,000 miles, which meant a handed-down vehicle—another indication that his family was either frugal or not as well off as she'd anticipated. Perhaps his parents were conservative when it came to handing money to their children, thus alleviating the burden of entitlement.

Sloan's parents had always stressed how many things she and Ainslie had, compared to their own meager childhoods. It wasn't that either of her parents had been deprived, it was that they had lived simply, with fewer material possessions than children had today. What they didn't understand was that every kid, even the poorer kids, had iPods and cell phones and televisions with cable in their rooms. Kids had cars, some of them nice cars and SUVs, by eighteen. Kids grew up fast, but her mother was slow to see that. Most eighteen-year-olds were totally responsible for themselves, having been latchkey kids most of their lives.

The bridge over the Cooper River arched into the sky, suspension cables streaming down in the reflection of ship masts. At the apex, Charleston appeared—the Holy City, with its scattering of church spires forming a jagged skyline. Below the bridge, cranes lifted container cars ashore at the Charleston Port Authority. Farther south, the city turned beautiful where a crescent of affluence threw soft lighting on moving water.

Down the peninsula, tony neighborhoods came to life behind wrought iron. The arms of live oaks embraced cobblestone streets. Sloan loved Charleston's architecture and her gardens all touching, crowded as if the entire city whispered secrets. She had walked the rumpled sidewalks with her father, peaking into the inner sanctums of yards and verandahs like the tourists who were both the lifeblood and the burden of the city. Pawleys Island people had bumper stickers that read Shabby Chic, but anyone would have to crown Charleston the chicest of shabby places.

When they pulled into the Lowcountry Yacht Club, the guard recognized Cal and waved him through. Along the waterfront, where the mouth of the Ashley River flowed into the Atlantic, the clubhouse rose, gleaming like a polished wood and brass ship in the harbor. Not only did the club have a sheen, all the people seemed to be of the same high gloss. Their white teeth and starched button-downs spoke of a pleasant existence. They expected the world to care about their desires. They were confident things would go their way. Of course, Sloan had seen yachts gliding by her house, some docked at the Georgetown Harbor where LaShonda's father worked. But in this world, boats cost more than homes, and some were finely-tuned athletes, swift for racing and competitive of crew.

Cal's grandfather, Joseph Wannamaker, rose from behind a well-oiled wooden table and exchanged a hearty handshake with his grandson. The family patriarch was tall, with a shock of white hair and fierce tan creases radiating from his hazel eyes. Sloan was introduced around the table to Joseph's wife, Patricia, an elegant, pale woman. Cal's mother said, "Hi, I'm Bitsy. I know your mother from church." Cal's father, Trip, was like the grandfather, tall and commanding, his navy jacket cut with precision to accentuate his broad shoulders and narrow waist. He had the same hazel eyes as the grandfather, the same as Cal. Joseph introduced a cousin from out of town who he relayed had the misfortune to marry north and become a Yankee living in Virginia. Everyone laughed politely and settled in.

Their server waited for drink orders and the grandfather nodded to his wife. In a long vowel drawl, she asked for "a glass of that Malbec I liiiike." Sloan had no idea what that was. Ordering progressed from woman to woman around the table until it reached Sloan. Cal nodded to her and she ordered a glass of the Malbec, too.

"Very good choice," the waiter said and moved on to the grandfather's order.

Conversation flowed as the waiter handed menus around. Sloan noticed no prices on the menu. Orders for snails and lobster were placed, but Sloan stuck with local flounder and shrimp, confident in her ability to eat those without embarrassing herself. As she perused the silver and glassware on the table, Sloan was suddenly grateful to her mother for forcing cotillion on her. Still, she would wait to see what utensil everyone selected before picking up her own.

Once they had ordered, Patricia leaned over and asked Sloan, "Now tell me, sweetheart, who *aaaare* your *peeeeople?*"

Sloan had always wanted to say that she was one of the Sullivans who founded Sullivan's Island, but she didn't even know if the island had ever belonged to a Sullivan at all. What she *was* certain about was that she didn't want to tell the regal Patricia Wannamaker that her family was from New Jersey.

"My mother's people are from outside of Charleston," she replied. "My mother's family owned a farm." Farm was generally a polite euphemism for plantation, only in Sloan's family's case, it really wasn't. They had truly had just a small working farm.

Patricia smiled and motioned to the waiter. Sloan's empty wine glass was replaced. She was pleasantly on the way to her first buzz and mesmerized by how the others expertly gripped decorative shells with tongs and scooped out the dark blob of escargot. Lobsters and jokes were cracked for an hour, but afterward the conversation grew sedate. The grandfather lighted a strong cigar and spoke of his father, a shrimper, a hardworking man who barely managed to keep his family above poverty level.

"I raised my own son to be productive," Cal's grandfather said, "to take risks and make sure he's worthy. Shirtsleeves. Remember shirtsleeves, Cal." Joseph smacked his grandson on the back. There was a look from Cal's grandmother, her brow ever so slightly wrinkled. He smiled and politely changed the subject.

Sloan had once studied the economic theory of shirtsleeves to shirtsleeves in three generations in a civics class. Basically, it describes how a family with nothing can spawn a family member inspired to rise above. He gains a fortune, passing it along to his heirs, but by the third generation, wealth becomes so ingrained in the family's daily life that following generations grow lackadaisical and unproductive. This slackness eats away at the fortune the elders accumulated, and a generation later, part of the family ends up as blue collar workers, back in shirtsleeves again. A simple theory on gaining and losing wealth that Sloan thought probably had validity.

But these people seemed to be a long way from turning in their white collar membership card. The women sported Louis Vuitton handbags and Chanel sunglasses. The men were comfortable in their Brooks Brothers suits and leather shoes. The marina was their home-away-from-home, and they dined here with as much ease as if they were lounging in their own living rooms. Outside, the masts of sailboats and yachts tilted with the water's motion. Occasionally, the dock under the club let out a groan, as if to shift its burden. The wine made Sloan notice all this more intensely, although her focus pulled in and out on the discussion. When she scanned from person to person around the table, there was a vapor trail before her vision solidified. She leaned into Cal and said, "I'd love to go look at the boats."

He'd smiled. "Sure," he said, then, "Grandpop, can I show Sloan your boat?"

"By all means, son. Help yourself." His grandfather

raised a swinging glass of wine his way and then turned back to the conversation.

Cal grasped her hand and led her through tables of white linen each topped by a silver candelabrum. Sloan was fascinated by one table with a candlestick of a mermaid, scales intricately twined with her hair. Along the dock, boats shone like the prized possessions they were. There was plenty of activity as people wiped down boats, rolled sails, rewound ropes, and hosed decks.

The Wannamaker boat was a Regatta. Cal told her in a way that let her know it must be important or expensive, yet it was by no means the largest craft at the club. They were surrounded by fabulous tall sailboats and shiny motor behemoths with bulbous white leather seats. The Wannamakers' sailboat was a beautiful thing made of balsam wood the color of honey and dark cherry. Sloan knew this wood because her grandfather had once pointed it out to her in their own smaller boat when he had given it to them.

The name painted in block letters on the stern of their vessel was B.O.A.T.

"Wow," Sloan said, sarcastically. "What an original name."

"You don't know what that means, do you?" Cal grinned at her.

"No."

"Everybody in the sailing world knows. It means Break Out Another Thousand." He laughed. "A boat always needs some sort of repair."

They stepped onto the polished deck and descended a delicate ladder into the galley. Belowdecks, everything was efficient and miniature. No space wasted. It had a table that could seat five, a tiny television, a couple of beds in the back.

"You like to sail?" Cal asked her. "I could take you sometime."

She scooted into the booth at the table and leaned back against a cushion.

"Oh, I think I'm drunk," she said.

He laughed. "You ever been drunk before?"

"Not really. I mean once, I guess. I didn't like it."

"What about this time?"

She opened her eyes and smiled at him. "The company is sure a lot better this time."

He grinned and slid into the seat beside her. She waited for his touch, her heart suddenly a live thing inside her. He slid his hand into her hair so smoothly that she knew he had done this many times before, but she didn't care. He was the cutest boy ever to kiss her. He was rich. What was not to like?

He brought his lips close to hers and hovered just long enough for her to think he might not kiss her, then he leaned in and his tongue ran smoothly over her lips and into her mouth. She melted into him, knowing all the while that Cal was a player.

He kissed her until her mouth was raw and then he slid his fingers lightly against her right nipple, just once. He caught her eyes as he did it, a move so bold she was frozen with delight. He leaned in for a final short kiss, then backed his way out of the seat and offered her his hand.

"I'm sure they're missing us," he said and helped her squeeze out of the tight space.

Her lips tingled in the night air, slightly raw from Cal's kiss. Back at the clubhouse, her face warmed at the thought that everyone at the table knew what she had been up to, but no one seemed to recognize they had entered the room, so involved and loud was the conversation. Apparently, the booze had flowed freely while they were gone. Perhaps the family was used to their golden boy heading out to the glorious boat for a grope session with a new love interest.

"Hey, everybody," Cal said. "We gotta go. We're driving to Pawleys."

He leaned down, and his grandmother presented her cheek, which he dutifully pecked with affection. His mother clamped his face between her diamond-encrusted hands, wrestled him down to her, and kissed him lightly on the lips. He shook hands with his father and grandfather and nodded to his cousin.

Outside, the valet brought the Jimmy around, and Cal handed him a couple of bills.

"Thank you, sir," the valet chirped as he slipped the money into a pocket of his white uniform.

"Let's drive around," Cal said and took a right onto Murray Boulevard. The avenue hugged the Ashley River until it opened up to big water at The Battery, where Charlestonians had watched the clumsy back and forth attacks of Confederate and Union forces at Fort Sumter while they enjoyed tea and bourbon on the porches of their elaborate multihued Georgian homes.

They rounded the end of the peninsula, past the Coast Guard base on Tradd Street, and headed back uptown on East Bay, meandering through side streets that Sloan had never ventured upon. Down a cobblestone lane they popped out by a worn stucco Huguenot church that each day cast her shadow upon wide, black women with deft fingers sewing sweetgrass baskets with needles made of silver spoon handles, their creations swirling like charms along Charleston's sidewalks.

It wasn't yet time for tourists to crowd the narrow lanes, boiling out of restaurants along King and Market streets. They came for the Old World romantic allure of this city steeped in history and pedigree. Cal pulled slowly around a horse and buggy, tassels and passengers swaying in union. The gray-clad guide motioned to a stately home with a flying staircase cloaked in ivy.

They cut through an upscale shopping district where

tiny boutiques and designer shops hugged the con-
stricted streets fronted by antebellum architecture. Cal
picked expertly through one-way streets, crawling gradually toward the College of Charleston.

He grabbed his cell and said, "Call Ethan."

Ethan answered on the first ring. "Zup, man?" the
thin voice said.

"Ethan, dude. Grab some people and meet me outside. I'm in the Jimmy."

"Be right there."

They were parked on the street outside a dorm for
only a few seconds before a swaying cluster of drunks
stumbled toward the SUV. As they filled the vehicle,
Sloan noticed the whiny girl from the first day at Brookgreen.

"Hey, y'all," Cal said. "This is Sloan. Say hey."

"Hey," they said in unison.

She smiled and nodded her head to the jam-packed
car. She noticed the whiny girl wedged into a corner
looking anxious and irritated.

"And that over there," Cal said, pointing to the agitated girl, "is Heather."

The red-eyed girl wiggled her fingers at Sloan.

"Heeey," Heather drawled.

All the riders crammed in the back seat jiggled and
twitched with energy. Nobody asked where they were
headed. Cal drove down toward the market and cut up
Bay. Occasionally, he would beep the horn and raise his
hand to a friend on the street. A few guys walked up to
Sloan's side of the car and talked past her to Cal about
nothing at all. "We're headed to McCormack's," he'd say,
and they would reply, "See ya there." Sloan was amazed
by how randomly happy people were. Nobody was worried about a thing.

They invaded a small Irish pub at the entrance to
Waterfront Park. Inside the warm wooden bar, they or-

dered pitchers of beer, drank freely, played darts, smoked cigarettes, and talked loudly over Irish folk songs. It gradually occurred to Sloan that since she was with Cal she had immediate rank within the circle. She didn't know the names of all the people from the car, nor the other guys who arrived later, but everybody treated her as if she were a part of them, and Sloan relaxed and just watched.

"Come here," Cal said and led her toward the tiny women's bathroom. He pulled her inside and locked the door. He took a thin silver spoon and scooped stark white powder from a brown glass vial. He put the spoon to his nose and quickly inhaled.

"Is that coke?" Sloan whispered.

"Here, little girl. It's nose candy, little girl." His voice wavered in a comical way.

"Sniff it up?"

"Just like this." He put the spoon to his nose again and snorted.

"What does it do?"

"You'll see. Trust me. You'll like it."

He held the spoon out to her and she felt a rush of adrenaline as she leaned over and inhaled the powder. A metallic taste came to her throat and a tingle washed down into her chest.

"Good?" he asked.

"I don't know. What's it supposed to feel like?"

"Take another bump. You'll see."

She repeated the process but didn't feel particularly inspired in any new way. He cleaned the spoon with this finger and then ran his finger over his gums. He returned the spoon and vial to a black velvet pouch with a drawstring and shoved it into his pocket.

Somebody paid for their beer with a gold credit card, then they all made their way next door to the park where a modern fountain spurted patterns of water. The game was to anticipate the pattern and run through without getting wet. The guys played for a while, but finally gave up and dragged the girls into the water. The girls screamed and laughed. Sloan laughed, and suddenly she felt compelled to run into the water. Cal grabbed her and pointed to a police cruiser creeping by. They all stumbled down into the park along the wide pedestrian boardwalk, snickering and checking behind them for cops.

Swinging benches were in constant movement under a row of pergolas. A couple vacated a swing and the group descended upon it, squeezing in until there was no room for Sloan and Cal.

Cal said, "Come on. Let's go see if we can spot any dolphins."

At the end of the pier they took a right turn to where the walkway widened and ran into the dark. There the water felt close, its movement apparent.

"There's usually a couple of dolphins that come around here waiting for tourists to throw some kind of food in the water," he said.

"My sister has dolphins that she swears come to see her now that she's sick. She knows their names and everything. Some researchers from Coastal Carolina named them."

"That's cool. What's their names?"

"I don't remember. Ainslie could tell you."

Ships glided silently by, dark and foreboding except for bright running lights on bows, masts, and sterns.

"So, you have a nice family," she said. "They're fun."

"Just wait until you get to know them. They're self-absorbed assholes."

They waited there for an elusive dorsal fin to slice the water, but none appeared. The night grew closer and she shivered. He pulled her to him and she trembled again, but this time without a thought to the damp fingers of ocean air.

CHAPTER 10

Storm Surge

Lauren leaned on the porch railing watching the men below manhandle the rusty trailer, groaning with the weight of their old wooden runabout. Emmett had his shirt off. The muscles in his back tensed with effort. He'd mentioned his intention to refurbish the old boat, but Lauren had hoped it was just another one of his vocalized, but never attempted ambitions. But here he was, straining and grunting as he and his buddies shoved the boat backward into the latticed carport below the house.

Her husband's bare chest made her think of the first time she saw him. It was 1989, the year Hurricane Hugo shredded South Carolina's coast. Lauren set out with a small band of her sorority sisters from USC to join thousands of volunteers cleaning up after the storm.

As they neared the coast, the chattering girls were struck dumb by the devastation. This was the place where all their family vacations had been spent. South Carolinians rarely ventured past their own state lines, preferring private vacation spots on their own shores. But the usual serenity and beauty of this area was nonexistent, replaced by a twisted, devastated scene. The world here was crushed inland. Salt-choked plants wilted westward. Trees were stripped of leaves. Even the water fowl were disoriented, flying in random patterns, unsure where it was safe to light in such a harsh and unfamiliar landscape.

Houses still standing were shoved off foundations, some collapsed into the creek, others with decks torn away and dangling. Massive heaps of boats cluttered the inland side of the creek, one suspended in a tree. There were piles of detritus so random it was impossible to recognize the origin. Fragments of lives had been whirled together in a massive blender with awe-inspiring results. The girls choked back tears as they neared Pawleys.

Chain saws whirred and shattered pines fell as they parked their car in a cleared lot near the Hammock Shops and walked toward the northern causeway, closed to vehicular traffic. The pavilion where the community barbecued and shagged into the night was a contorted mess of brine-covered lumber half jammed down into pluff mud. Everything was cloaked in a white crust of sand and salt. One of Lauren's friends recognized a house her family had rented, and they sneaked through the mangled front door where others had forced entry. The first thing they noticed was the intense smell of the mold and mildew that permeated the flooring and crawled up the walls. In the kitchen, animals desperate for food had gnawed cabinets. Crabs scurried into dark places. The house seemed alive with unseen creatures, dripping water, the wind moving torn fabric through broken windows.

Lauren walked out onto the crumpled deck that faced the ocean. She was taking in the view, the blue sky and white spots of clouds reflected in the gentle ocean. Suddenly, she heard cursing. She moved to the side of the house, where she spied three tanned young men next door attempting to wrestle a leaning pylon from the water-soaked sand. She called to her friends through a shattered window.

"Hey, come look what I found. The view's really good out here."

They spied on Emmett and his brothers for half an hour before the wind carried their giggling down to the young men's ears. By that time, Lauren had already decided which one she wanted. He was tall and lanky with smooth tanned skin and a tireless energy. Once the girls were discovered, the boys stopped their labor and waved.

"Come down here," they called, and the girls promptly spilled out of the house and squeezed through the shattered fence between the properties.

"Hey," he said to her as if she were the only girl in the world.

She brushed bangs back from her eyes, her hand lingering in her hair a moment. "Hey, yourself," she replied casually.

"You're not from around here."

"I'm from Summerville. My parents made out okay in the storm. I came down from USC to help."

He smiled. "Well, we appreciate all the help we can get around here. Place sure is a mess."

"You live here?"

"Our house is on the spit of land at the end." He pointed north.

Her gaze followed his gesture as if she would be able to see past the rubble next door. "Did your house make it?"

"Yeah. We got lucky. Not much structural damage. We stored our boat so she made it out okay too. Good thing. Road's flooded."

Lauren nodded casually as if it were an everyday event to be in the middle of what looked like a war zone.

"I'm Emmett." He offered his hand and she shook it.

"Lauren."

"We're having a cookout tonight. Big bonfire on the beach. How'd you like to come?" He gestured toward a pile of shattered wood. "We've got a lot to burn."

She made as if she were thinking over his offer and said, "That's going to take a while, I mean to burn all this."

"Yep," he agreed. "We could be up all night."

Lauren and her girlfriends never reported to the Red Cross. Instead, they helped the Sullivan boys clear the property they were working on, which turned out to be a quaint little inn. When she asked about it, Emmett told her this place was where he cleared tables and swept the beach of litter each summer in high school and college. He spoke of the good Sunday dinners they served and how his father ran away to the Sea Oats a couple of times when his parents had a fight. Emmett had answered the owner's call to clear the inn of debris. He said his friends were lucky Hugo hit after tourist season.

When they called it quits for the day, the boys led them to a sleek wooden runabout docked at the end of a shattered boardwalk on the creek. There was room for six, and Emmett skillfully guided the boat with its full load along the creek, dodging flotsam as they went.

The Sullivan home rose like a four-story dollhouse from the end of the island, ornate and frail. But her appearance was deceiving, since it was one of the few homes to escape the ravages of the hurricane, with only broken windows and cosmetic damage. Inside was musty from saltwater pooled under windows and beneath doors, but overall the house was dry and secure. The senior

Sullivans were gone, having learned from previous hurricanes that it was simply better to evacuate to their relative-laden homeland on the Jersey shore than to ride out the storm.

That weekend they grilled everything in the freezer before it spoiled. At dusk the island's air filled with the delicious smell of steak as neighbors did the same. They spent days working and late afternoons on the beach, building a bonfire fueled by wrecked fencing and boardwalk. The salty, warped boards popped and sizzled when they hit the flames, sending sparks toward the smooth onyx sky—a giant funeral pyre of the houses of Pawleys Island.

When they finally let the fire die, sometime late into the night, the group stumbled back to the house chilly and damp. The great room was scattered with sleeping bags, and everyone lay by the fireplace drinking the liquor cabinet dry. In the mornings they slept late, then had breakfasts of bread, cheese, and tepid Bloody Marys. Lunches were from cans in the pantry. All coastal families knew to fill their bathtubs with fresh water at the approach of a storm, so when the emergency water bottles ran out, they refilled them with clean water from one of the tubs. Two other tubs they used to spot bathe. The Sullivans had prepared for an eventual hurricane and they had stockpiled flashlights, batteries, candles, and matches. Even with no power, they survived quite well.

It was nearly two weeks before power was restored to the area. In that time Lauren had returned to school and made a second trip back to Pawleys. Her girlfriends hadn't connected with Emmett's brothers, so she had made the drive by herself. Rick and Judd were blissfully gone and it was only the two of them in the house that glorious weekend. Lauren had been twenty when she fell in love, Emmett, twenty-two.

So what had happened to them? How had they gone from driving hours to be together, to being unable even to talk to each other in the same room? And now the old boat, the vessel that had carried them to their first rendezvous, was getting a facelift so Emmett could sell it. If they were headed down that road, what would be next? Would it be the house? Unfortunately, they weren't the sole owners of their house. Emmett's brothers each owned a third. Even if they sold the house, she and Emmett could only recoup a third of the sales price, not even enough to pay the medical bills they owed. And they would carry forever the shame of the loss of one of the family's prized properties.

Lauren stepped softly down the front stairs and cupped her hand to shade against the sun's glare. In the twilight of the carport, she waited for her eyes to adjust. The men grunted as they connected the boat to a rudimentary pulley system so old it must have been original to the house, although Lauren had never noticed it before. The pulleys were hooked to beams underneath the house with what were apparently new ropes, their purpose exactly this. After a number of maneuvers, one that involved flipping the boat on mattresses, they had it deck-down on giant sawhorses. Success spread across their faces. They had done this before. Emmett thanked his friends. They shook hands but refused his offer of money in favor of a future beer.

Once the boat was upside down it was easy to see the waterline, where barnacles blossomed like miniature oyster banks.

"Wow," Emmett said as he ran his hand over a particularly nasty spot. "Looks like I've got my work cut out for me."

"Well," Lauren said when they were alone, "I'd say that's true. Where's the motor?"

Emmett nodded to where his friends used to stand. "They took it to down to Georgetown Harbor to overhaul it. They tinker with motors in that old falling-down fish house there."

"I can't believe you'd sell your grandfather's boat."

He poked a finger into an indentation in the hull. "Money, sweetheart. Old wooden boats are in high demand. I can't sit around and wonder what's going to happen to us next."

"Well, it just seems like an odd way to try to make money, is all I'm saying."

Anger seethed behind his eyes. She'd pushed him too far.

"Lauren, if you worked even part time it would help."

"Emmett, we've had this conversation. Ainslie needs me. I can't believe you'd bring that up again."

"So don't criticize my efforts to make money if you're not willing to make any effort yourself."

"You're so unfair. How do you expect me to do all this by myself?"

He started rasping the side of the boat, chipping off barnacles. He scraped harder and harder.

"You're not by yourself," he said as barnacles flew in all directions. "You just think you are."

She watched him chip away at the boat. Simple. Straightforward. That's how Emmett approached things. He was always physical, particularly when stressed. Every time they came home from the hospital or emergency room he'd go for a run. Even after Lauren had given him ample time to get to sleep at night before she came to bed, he'd wait up for her with the slim hope she'd be in the mood. How could he want intimacy when they were going bankrupt and their child was dying?

That part of her had vanished. Any thoughts of sex, any feelings of closeness she'd felt had been eroded each day their situation went unresolved. Why couldn't he understand? Why didn't he feel that same way—weary of mind and body and spirit? How could it not be a struggle for him to simply get up each morning?

But then maybe that's why he did go to work each day. Because just like running, just like sex, going to work was a way to forget. But she couldn't forget. She was there every minute of every day just waiting for her child to relapse. For the first time, Lauren actually envied Emmett's job. What she wouldn't give to have a job now, a reprieve from the daily drama of their lives.

Lauren stood there, numb, as she watched Emmett in his frantic scraping. She was tired of crying and tired of being strong and tired of research and just plain tired. All she had done for the past few days was sit with her daughter and stare out the window while Sponge-Bob SquarePants chuckled from the television. She was trying to be more like those palmetto trees after Hugo ripped through. Everything on the island had been indelibly scarred, but the palmetto trees stood tall, their ability to adapt and bend in all circumstances making them less vulnerable than their brittle, inflexible counterparts. Accept the new normal. That was the message.

Emmett tended to be more able to adapt, but he enjoyed a certainness she'd never had. Where everything her own family had was hard-won, Emmett had grown up with more than the material things money can buy. He'd been raised with a rare ease of life. For most people, there was always the next bill coming, always the fear of losing a job. His ease had attracted her. He'd even assured her everything would work out when she told him she was pregnant with Sloan.

They'd known each other only a couple of months, but he'd gone straight to the jewelers at the Hammock

Shops and selected a tiny diamond for her finger. They were married, and his parents took their union as a cue to head back to New Jersey to retire near extended family. Emmett's mother opted to leave nearly everything—furniture, linens, even pots and pans. His brothers followed their parents north after their grandfather offered them positions in the family greeting card company.

Emmett had said, "See? I told you everything would work out."

But cancer wasn't something that would be resolved by being laid-back and waiting to see how things panned out. Emmett's calm assurances that had once seemed attractive now simply frustrated her. Maybe he *was* trying as hard as he could and he was getting no response. How was she to know? He never offered up any information, nothing for discussion, choosing instead to leave all family decisions up to her, never speaking about even the things she had practically forced him to oversee.

He may think he's helping, that she's not carrying the burden alone, but Lauren didn't agree. She needed him to take charge. She needed him to hold her at night and not demand anything for himself. But she also felt confused by her own feelings of jealousy boiling below her despair. She'd noticed the flirtation going on between Emmett and Caroline Crawford. Other people had noticed it as well, and it was embarrassing. She'd acted as if she hadn't seen him sneak off with that woman during the Wannamakers' party, but everybody at the table had seen.

That 1989 weekend they lived on steak, bottled water, candlelight, and sex had been a bad predictor of how their life would turn out. Natural forces had joined that September off the African coast, forming a hurricane that gained momentum and power until its landfall crushed the Carolinas. That disaster had been their auspicious beginning, but what was happening to them now felt like the storm of the century.

CHAPTER 11

Hardship Cases

Without Ainslie, the ride to school quickly became lonely. Sloan had been perturbed when she got her license and her mother only allowed her to drive to school if she transported her sister. This was, of course, her mother's way of keeping her from hanging out after school at somebody's house where working parents wouldn't be home for hours.

Once home, Sloan was never allowed simply to deposit her sister. Her mother demanded homework completed, then help with dinner. But for the past few months the family's habits were off. Their days were fractured. Ainslie hadn't gone to class in months. Her mother's schedule revolved around doctors' appointments. Her father spent more and more time at the office, under the house working on the old boat and, Sloan suspected, at The Pub. Her newfound freedom had been easy to wear at first, but slowly Sloan came to miss the comfort of her family's old routine.

Past the chirpy security gate, Sloan pulled up to the mailbox, where she retrieved a bundle of envelopes and catalogs. She snapped off the rubber band and began to pick through the mail in her lap. This was acceptance-letter week, the most dreaded or most anticipated week for most high school seniors. This was the week most everyone heard from their college applications. Sloan had applied to UNC Chapel Hill, the College of Charleston, and the University of South Carolina, but when she saw a pale blue envelope from the Savannah School of the Arts, she put the Jeep in PARK and ripped open the envelope. She greedily scanned the letter, then clutched it to her chest.

She had done it. She had gotten into one of the Southeast's most prestigious art colleges. Savannah School of the Arts had a huge catalog of art classes, an awe-inspiring campus, and talented faculty who were actively selling. A four-year college, with its math and science requirements, was far less attractive than the intense study of art. Art school seemed like heaven—sculpture, photography, animation, movie production.

Her house was empty behind the cut glass door. A note in her mother's handwriting said they were at a doctor's appointment and fresh cookies lived in the jar. Sloan sat at the kitchen table looking out at the creek behind the house, picking raisins out of the oatmeal cookies. She wanted to celebrate, to run along the beach and scream where the wind would take her words and fling them out to all the world.

She'd forgotten what happiness felt like. Since Ainslie became sick, the world was gray, and Sloan stumbled through it with an even buzz of panic. But then again, she was happy when she was with Cal. He made her feel good about herself. He made her forget her home had become a war zone between her parents, a place her sister came only to rest between hospital visits, a structure to be dreaded on each approach.

She heard the crackle of the shell drive under tires.

Her father was home. She waited on the porch while he took forever to get out of his truck and climb the stairs. Her father walked as if he were tired all the time now. His aura was dull and his face seemed always distant in thought.

"You're home early," she said. Then, "Daddy, guess what?"

He stopped, one foot still down a stair, their faces even. He smiled and reached out to touch her cheek.

"What, sweetheart?"

"I got into the Savannah School of the Arts! Oh, my God, Dad. Can you believe it?"

He pulled her into his arms and kissed her head. She could feel his heartbeat as she fitted herself into him. It had been a long while since they had hugged, and she suddenly felt three years old again.

When they broke apart, he ran a hand through his hair in a tired sort of way and said, "I'm really proud of you."

"Look!" She thrust the letter at him.

He read the entire paper without looking up or showing emotion. Sloan couldn't tell if his hand trembled or if the pale paper in his grasp quivered in the wind. When he finally finished, his smile was tempered and she could see conflict in his eyes.

"You have no idea how proud I am of you," he said.

"I know, it's awesome. I can't believe I got in."

"It's a testament to your talent."

Emmett headed for the kitchen. The wind lifted Sloan's hair as she closed the door behind them and shut out the ocean's drone. In the kitchen, she watched her father get a bottle of bourbon from under the counter and pour himself a shot. He rarely drank liquor, was mostly a beer guy.

"What's wrong?" she asked her father. "Did you have a bad day?"

He shook his head. "No, baby. No worse than usual."

"Then what's the matter? You don't seem happy for me."

"I'm just . . . trying to work things out in my head. That the only school you've heard from so far?"

"I don't need to hear from any other schools. Savannah School of the Arts is the only place I want to go."

"But you'll get accepted at USC I bet and . . . what were your other choices?"

"I don't want to go anywhere else."

"I understand, but Sloan, I've got to be honest with you. I wouldn't get my hopes up if I were you. You may have to pick a less expensive college. Isn't school around twenty grand a year for tuition alone?"

Sloan crossed her arms and considered what her father had just said. Didn't they have the money for her to go to college?

"How much money is in my college fund?"

"I'm not sure. Your mother takes care of your school savings, but that sounds about right. It would only pay for one year. You could get two or more years out of that money if you went to a state school."

"This is unbelievable. Are you telling me I don't have a college fund? That I don't have enough money to go to Savannah?"

"Maybe." He hung his head like a little boy being scolded, but she wasn't moved by his display. Anger was building under her excitement.

"What about Grandmother and Grandfather? Wouldn't they help us out?"

"They haven't sent any of your cousins to college, so I don't know if they would be willing to help us or not. I mean, it would be kind of unfair to the other kids in the family."

Sloan sat at the kitchen table and began to sweep together the crumbs from the cookie she had mindlessly pinched while considering her bright future only moments before. She struggled to keep her lips from quivering when she spoke.

"You've had eighteen years to save for my college education. How could you let this happen?"

"According to your mother we saved nearly a thousand dollars each year for you, but education is just so expensive now. There are loans and grants and all sorts of things we can look into. In a school that expensive there has to be scholarships for kids in need."

"Hardship cases like me?"

Her father opened the refrigerator and leaned against the machine's door as if that were all that was keeping him upright. He finally found a beer.

"Want one?" he asked her. "Time to grow up."

She shook her head. "Mom would kill you when she got home."

"Not much more I can do to disappoint her. Guess I shouldn't take you down with me, though."

Emmett slumped into a chair and they both sat quietly. Sloan understood that he hadn't meant for things to turn out this way. She knew he wanted her to go to school in Savannah, but she couldn't find it within herself to reach across the table to touch him. She was too upset to offer him comfort.

The phone jangled them out of their stupor.

Sloan pressed the cold receiver to her ear.

"Sullivans," she said flatly.

"Sloan? It's Mom. Is your dad there?"

"He's right here."

She handed the phone to her father. Sloan could hear her mother's voice pouring into his head.

"Okay, I'll be right down," he said.

"What's wrong?" Sloan asked when he'd beeped the phone off.

"Ainslie's not doing so good. They're going to admit her again. It's apparently nothing to get alarmed about yet. Looks like they're just going to give her fluids and hold her overnight for observation. I'm going to the hospital now. You stay here. You've got class tomorrow, so don't worry about going with me. This could take all night."

Sloan watched her father drag himself through the house and out to the car without even looking in the mirror to see that his hair, long overdue for a cut, was sticking out in tufts around his ears. Sloan sat at the table until she heard the engine start, then she went up to her room where dirty clothes covered the floor and every other flat surface. Her mother no longer tidied her room or picked up her panties and crumpled jeans.

Chip bags littered her desk, her bed was unmade, a trail of discarded clothes led to her open closet. She knew the bathroom she shared with Ainslie was a disgrace. Shame caught up with her then. Her father was right; it *was* time to grow up. There would be no more mother to do her laundry or clean her room. She was eighteen and reality had just smacked her in the face. She had her entire life before her and it was possible Ainslie wouldn't even make it to eighteen. So what if Sloan didn't get to go to her hoity-toity art school? What did that matter when her little sister was lying in a hospital bed with tubes sticking out of her?

Sloan was suddenly ashamed. She'd been mean to her father, distant with both her parents really since Ainslie fell sick. She'd make it up to them, she'd be a better person, the daughter they needed her to be right now. As she bent to pick up her dirty clothes Blondie sang from her pocket and she flipped her phone open.

"Hey, Cal."

"Zup?"

"I don't know. You called me."

"You sound weird."

"Mom took Ainslie to the hospital again. Nothing serious they say, but who knows."

"I can cheer you up."

"You can try."

"You got a passport?"

CHAPTER 12

Comfort Zone

Emmett finished his run to the end of the island and was on his way back when he considered what awaited him at home. He was slightly ashamed of his decision, but he took a left over the bridge and didn't stop running until he made it to The Pub.

His heart pressed its rhythm into his ears. His intention was always to exhaust himself to the point where he was too tired to think anymore, but today there was no escape, his fears jangling between each pause in his blood's flow. Sloan called this inability to turn off thoughts monkey mind. Today, he had an orangutan bouncing around inside his head.

He wasn't supposed to stop at the bar. He was supposed to return immediately to cherish each second he had with his daughter, since each could be her last. At least that's what Lauren thought. She didn't believe the doctors who said Ainslie was getting better, and she expected him to have the same crazy obsession with Ainslie's every twinge and behavior change. But Emmett didn't think she was going to die today while he was on his run and he wasn't ashamed of that. He'd always been the more positive of the two in their marriage.

But when Emmett searched deep inside himself, he knew. Lauren was right, he was hiding from them, but not for the reasons Lauren thought. He could carry the guilt she heaped upon him for his financial failures and what she viewed as his lack of enthusiasm for the family. He could handle his older daughter's look of derision as she cut her eyes at him in her disappointment of the moment. But what he couldn't take was simply looking at Ainslie, his once robust child, now withered and pale. Each time he saw her frail limbs, each time he carried her upstairs, her body as light as when she was four, he wanted to be somewhere else. He wanted to be single again with no children at all, nobody depending on him, nobody he would miss if they were gone.

The Pub was his comfort zone now. It called to him with the chink of pool balls and the stench of stale beer. He settled onto a stool and waited for Vonda to walk his way. Behind her there were one hundred and twenty-four liquor bottles (he'd counted many times). The most expensive stayed in the same spot, a soft ring of dust growing on the shoulders of those bottles. His bar mates, friends all, sagged on their own stools. The group always kept movement and conversation to a minimum, only the occasional lift of a mug to lips or flick of a wrist as ashes settled into brown glass.

"Better quit that running," somebody said as they smoked. "I hear running'll kill you."

Emmett smiled. He felt most at home here, with these men he'd known all his life. Women seldom graced The Pub. There was nothing here for a woman, a sparse atmosphere with hard-bench booths and bar stools for leaning. There was plenty of booze, though, and a sympathetic ear if you cared to talk. But most men didn't. Most guys kept their wounds to themselves. They could sit for hours, burdens heavy on their minds, but discuss nothing but the ballgame on the screen mounted high in the corner.

"Here. This one's on me," Vonda said and slid a shot and a beer in front of Emmett. He nodded, threw the bourbon back and chased it with beer. As if on cue, Larry walked through the door and slid onto a stool next to Emmett.

"Well if it ain't Tweedledum," Vonda said.

"How do you know I'm not Tweedledee?" Larry asked.

"Just a hunch." Vonda placed a beer and a shot in front of Larry.

Larry said, "And another one for him."

Vonda refilled Emmett's stubby glass.

"How's every little thing?" Larry asked.

"Shit."

"Okay, then."

They drank for a while, contemplating the baseball game on the tube.

Emmett wiped a drop of sweat from his forehead.

"Been running?"

"Yeah, helps me think. Supposed to help me not think. I don't know. I can't tell anymore."

Nobody at the bar ever asked after Ainslie. They all gave him space, waited for him to broach the subject.

"Sloan got into Savannah," Emmett finally said.

"Sweet."

"I guess. She's pretty excited, but excited is about all she's going to get. I can't afford to send her there. That damn school's like twenty grand a year."

Larry shook his head. "Law school wasn't near that much."

"Isn't it bizarre," Emmett said, "that all my creative thoughts at work end up as every bite of food my kids put in their mouths? Every opportunity they have or don't have is based on somebody paying me to design something."

"Pretty scary. One reason I don't have kids. Couldn't handle the responsibility."

"She hates me now."

"Didn't you say she hated you before?"

"That was just speculation. Now I'm sure of it."

Larry motioned for another round.

Emmett waited until Vonda walked away, then continued.

"Lauren thinks I'm a dimwit. She thinks I should be able to just snap my fingers and fix all this. I don't know what to do. Guess I'm Tweedledum. Maybe I'll just pack up and move us to France or Canada or someplace where they have universal health care."

"You could," Larry said. "But I bet they got requirements to keep you from doing that. Or else everybody in your situation would do it."

Emmett guzzled his beer. "Hey, you remember that movie with Denzel Washington where he took a hospital hostage to force them to give his kid medical care?"

"Never saw it."

"Well, he just kept saying he had insurance, but nobody would help. His insurance was no good for some reason. I know just how he feels. I feel like taking a gun right up there to Raleigh-Durham and going on a rampage."

"That's why we have laws."

"To keep me from killing somebody?"

"To keep good people from doing stupid things they can't take back."

Emmett had to admit that at times the impulse to strike out was so physically strong he got sick to his stomach trying to control himself. Wasn't that how all men felt sometimes? You know better, but you still can't help wanting to punch something or, even better, somebody. This fruitless, wasted emotion even haunted his dreams. His unconscious had repeatedly conjured a massive building for Common Good's headquarters. In his dream world, Emmett plowed his truck through the front plate glass window and came out guns blazing like a cowboy in a Hollywood movie. He blasted his way into the boardroom where men in black suits lined a massive table. Emmett always walked up to the guy in charge and grabbed him by the tie and dragged him across the shiny surface, all the while yelling, "My daughter is not a claim number!" Emmett always awoke with his hands balled into fists, ready to strike.

This compulsion for violence was usually wild in youth and something that mellowed as you grew older. But this part of Emmett had come alive again and he'd even involuntarily formed a fist one day when Lauren was on one of her tirades. The frustration. The sheer desire to destroy. The times he'd had to check himself were becoming more frequent.

He'd held his fist and held his tongue more times than he cared to remember. Lauren had a way about her that could stab a man, undermine him with only a word. He'd never been the major breadwinner she'd wanted to marry, but now she viewed him as a miserable failure. That was Lauren's way—always setting the standard, expecting everybody to live up to her version of the perfect life. She still carried an imagined idea of what her life was supposed to be like. She'd never picked a major in college because the only degree she really wanted was an MRS. He knew Lauren had dreamed she'd marry a doctor or a lawyer and have a boy and a girl and a Labrador retriever named Scout. Why she had chosen him instead of holding out for that dream life was a mystery to him. She hadn't seemed unhappy at the time, but now, when the chips were down, she had turned on him.

Couldn't she give him at least a little credit for busting his ass building a business? Lauren didn't understand what it was to be the responsible party, at least financially. It wasn't as if he had only his own family to be concerned about. He also had employees who depended on him, so they, in turn, could take care of their own families. And it wasn't as if he spent his days in the rapture of designing beautiful public spaces. No, most of his days were spent on meetings or spreadsheets or employees who dragged their personal problems into the office. He had taxes to pay, both personal and business, and all the other business burdens that Lauren never thought about.

While Lauren only cared that their daughter had medical insurance, Emmett had to look at the larger picture and figure out how to keep insurance for both his family and his office. Every day he wondered if Common Good would raise rates beyond his ability to pay or simply dump his office and he would be on the search again for yet another insurance carrier. If that happened, he was certain no new company would take on a child in the middle of cancer treatment. If that happened, they would truly be out of luck.

Was he doing his best? Would another man have made different choices? Worked more weekends? Had a more cutthroat approach to business? Worked for big developers with deep pockets but few principles? Or perhaps he should have chucked the idea of his own company for the security of a firm where he could have traded autonomy for a steady paycheck and benefits.

Life was all about choices. Choices made you. Choices broke you.

So his choice to buy cheaper health insurance had

resulted in this financial disaster for his family. But worst of all, Emmett feared there might be a time when no money meant no help for his daughter. That was Lauren's ultimate fear.

It was a widely held belief that divorce comes to families with seriously ill children, particularly when children die. And Emmett could understand why divorce was the standard reaction to this situation. The stress was so great, the guilt so monumental, the emotional toll so heavy that nobody came out unchanged. Suddenly, the two people who gave life to a child were strangers battling to keep themselves from imploding. He'd heard that times like this were when all shortcomings were revealed and resentments came pouring out like lava, to scald and smother.

"Give us the good stuff this time," Larry said to Vonda.

Vonda poured the men another round. Emmett's vision was blurry as he raised his shot glass to her and then to Larry. The bourbon burned a swath down his throat. When had he taken to drinking in the afternoons? What did it matter? Ainslie was just a child, she'd never smoked a cigarette, never taken a drink and look where it got her.

"Ha." Emmett breathed a listless laugh into his beer mug at the thought.

"Ha?" Larry mimicked.

"I was just thinking about my grandfather who lived to the ripe old age of ninety-one. He smoked and drank right up until the state took his driver's license away. He was about eighty when that happened."

"Yeah?"

"So why is it that he got to booze it up and smoke for nearly a century, but my kid, who has never done anything bad in life, has to have cancer. There's no rhyme or reason to who lives or dies."

"No truer words were ever spoken, my friend," Larry said.

There was no talisman to ward off illness. Not good genes or religion or plain ole clean living could guarantee a long and healthy life. No. Life was just one big crap shoot.

CHAPTER 13

One More Time

Sloan had a boyfriend. This realization hit Lauren as she slid pizza into the oven. It had happened while Lauren wasn't looking. Thank goodness he was a good boy from a good family. He wasn't sporting face piercings or black disks in his ears, so he seemed much safer than some of Sloan's previous choices. Lauren felt as if these prior paramours had only been play acting, trying on a tough façade for the effect it had on adults. Sloan always insisted that these boys were only friends and that they were strongly antidrugs, but then what else would she say?

Cal Wannamaker had the oily smoothness money cultivates, a façade of its own, but he was still preferable to kids who looked as if they hadn't bathed in three days.

Lauren stepped into the laundry and began to fold clothes. She found that Sloan's clothing choices had become more refined since she started seeing the Wannamaker boy. He'd invited her to the Lowcountry Yacht Club and to Al's by the Creek, so she'd necessarily had to take more care with her appearance. Lauren folded a couple of blouses and cute short skirts she had purchased for birthdays and holidays, clothes that had previously languished in the back of Sloan's closet in favor of paint-stained T-shirts and ratty jeans.

This new boyfriend had shocked her out of her malaise over her sister's illness. Sloan was quick to point out that they were just dating, that they were not a couple. It had only been a few weeks, and Lauren was sure this boy kept other love interests, but he seemed content to spend his weekends with Sloan.

Lauren also got the distinct feeling Sloan was going to sleep with him if she hadn't already. She suspected Sloan had been with a couple of boys from school, but it had all been very quiet and had never resulted in anything, so Lauren had held her tongue. Lauren believed Sloan suffered from a confidence deficit, which probably stemmed from a suspicion that her father had more interest in her younger sister.

And it was the truth, in Lauren's opinion as well, that Emmett had a distinct preference for Ainslie's wild ways. Sloan and her father had unaddressed issues. Conventional thinking was that a girl would find either a boy to fill Daddy's shoes or somebody so very different and inappropriate it would shock the father into paying attention. Cal Wannamaker seemed to be neither, but Lauren wasn't completely taken in. She'd dated enough rich boys in college to have a feel for the games those types played. She just hoped Sloan was smart enough to keep the upper hand.

Hormones poured off those two when they were around each other, a physical connection Lauren recognized from the first time she set eyes on Emmett. It happened, and when it did, it was hard to ignore, so there would be no fighting the Sloan–Cal connection. That situation was going to run its course.

Last week, Lauren had walked into the girls' bathroom when Sloan was getting ready for a date. There were still a few things Lauren could do to establish a physical bond with her daughter, and brushing her hair was one of those things. Lauren held up a brush.

"Okay," Sloan said and sat at the vanity. Lauren made long strokes. Sloan's hair fell in waves like a 1940s movie star. After a while, Lauren asked her, only once, if she knew what to do when it came to protection.

Sloan rolled her eyes and said, "Yeah, Mom, I learned that in, like, seventh grade."

It was insane how quickly children were growing up today. That music channel was so saturated with sex it was basically soft porn—women in hot pants and string bikinis grinding their asses into the laps of rappers and rock stars. And the female rock stars were no better, basically strippers themselves.

How had society changed so much so rapidly? Lauren had been shocked to see her first transvestite in college. But now they attended public high school just like the rest of the students. How anyone could know they wanted to be a transvestite at that age was just one of the things that stunned Lauren. But people didn't fall in line anymore, do the expected thing, play by the rules. Nobody wanted to be the overachiever, the band leader, or the president of the student council. Perhaps it seemed obsolete to care too much in a time when students passed through metal detectors to get into school, businesses required urine samples, and road rage could end your drive home in the hospital or worse.

Lauren finished folding clothes and took the pizza from the oven, sliding the tray onto the eyes of the gas stove. She heard the mailman's boxy vehicle pull into their drive and went to meet him. Some days he couldn't fit their mail into their box, so he brought it to the front door.

Lauren saw his figure swim in the cut glass and opened it before he had a chance to knock. Today, his arms appeared to contain more happiness than misery.

"Good morning," he said. "Got another big load for you today."

He thrust a thick pile of colorful cards at Lauren.

"How's she doing?" the postman asked.

"Pretty good right now. Thank you for asking."

"She must be a popular little girl."

"It's nice people care."

"Yes, ma'am. You have a good day now."

Inside, Lauren separated bills from pastel envelopes and made a pile for Ainslie. Forty-two cards and a couple of packages for her. This all started a few months after Ainslie became ill. First it was the church, with all the children making cards. Then there was the Nintendo GameCube and games the congregation provided. Of course, there had been food at first. Lauren had served grits casseroles and barbecue to her family until they cried for fresh vegetables. She'd frozen the rest, but too soon even the frozen food had dwindled. There was still the occasional vat of soup that came their way, but mostly people had stopped with the food.

What had become strong was the flow of cards and gifts into their home. Someone posted Ainslie's story on the Internet and people began to flood them with attention. Every day cards arrived, sometimes toys or nail polish or stickers, frequently photographs of other children who survived this illness. Lauren had to be careful that letters from bereaved, slightly off-kilter parents didn't make it into Ainslie's hands. The doctors said keeping positive was the most important part of treatment. The whole family had to believe in the treatments. Everybody had to be upbeat. Well, none of them had been exactly stellar on that account. Still, although Ainslie was tired and sad, she hadn't had a strong reaction to anything that had happened to her so far. It was almost eerie how calm she had been.

This day's haul seemed safe, mostly children's scrawl on the envelopes. Lauren climbed the stairs and knocked lightly on Ainslie's door.

"Hey, Miss Popular. You've got another pile of mail," Lauren said.

"Just put it over there on the table," Ainslie said. She was playing a game called Animal Crossing on her Game-Cube. "Mommy, do you think somebody would give me a Wii if I asked?"

"Probably, baby. Do you really need a Wii?"

"Exercise."

"I see. Well, we'll talk about it." She slid onto the bed beside her daughter and ran her fingers through Ainslie's fine, reemerging hair. It seemed like such a small thing, so inconsequential in the grand scheme of things, but she prayed her daughter's hair would grow back straight and shiny like before. She'd heard chemotherapy changed the composition of some people's hair, straight hair became curly, blonde hair became brown. Ainslie stopped playing and leaned into her mother for comfort.

"It's growing back in," Lauren said.

"I know," Ainslie said. "But it's still all over the bathroom from before." How long had it been since she had touched the girls' bathroom? She'd cleaned up after sickness, but she couldn't remember the last time she had scrubbed the tub or swept the floor. A swift moment of anger flashed her mind when she realized Sloan should have offered to clean her own space, but she quickly dismissed this thought. What kid, even a teenager, would voluntarily scrub a tub?

"That's okay. I'll clean it up."

Ainslie turned back to her video game and was immediately immersed. Lauren watched her and thought about what she'd heard from this room last night.

She'd been passing by on her way to bed and she heard soft voices.

"Are we poor now?" Ainslie had asked.

Sloan sighed. "I don't know. I guess we're lots more poor than before."

"I'm sorry."

"Ains, stop it. None of this is your fault. I mean, seriously, it could have been any one of us. Nobody blames you."

"But if it wasn't for me, then everything would be okay."

"You get well and everything'll be fine. Mom and Dad always take care of us. You're going to be okay. I just know it."

Lauren had slipped away then. She couldn't stand to hear more. Downstairs she washed dishes with a vengeance. Not actually washed, but loaded the dishwasher so violently she dared dishes to break. She slammed them in, not bothering to line them up for maximum capacity. She stopped when she realized that if she broke her plates there was no money for more. She'd be digging her old college crap from a box in the attic. She stopped and assessed as she so often did now. She could make it to the end of this day and then she would close her eyes and go to sleep and get up in the morning and face life all over again. But right now, right now she had to get control of herself. One. More. Time.

CHAPTER 14

New Friends

The direct flight from Atlanta to Cancún International Airport would take only a couple of hours, but the party had already started. The cabin pulsed. The flight attendants were gay, cracking jokes over the intercom. There was a loud couple who sounded as if they'd enjoyed cocktails along with breakfast. There were other groups of college students like theirs, but also families going on vacation and others who appeared to be returning home. A handsome Mexican guy smiled at Sloan and she returned his gesture. She had been on a number of airplane trips, but people on their way to New Jersey were never this happy.

Cal was scrunched forward, peering out the oval window of the opposite aisle. His buddies hugged their girls in anticipation of the action they would be getting. Sloan quickly realized she had filled the position of necessary female friend in Cal's vacation plans. She also realized that by coming on this trip she had agreed to sleep with him. She intended to anyway but had been putting him off, assessing him.

And he did seem to like her. He'd taken her to Charleston to meet his family on their first date. That day she learned he knew her father from a party. Since then, he'd picked her up from school on the Fridays he was home from college. He'd been everything a boyfriend could be without actually asking the big question. And Sloan knew he wasn't going to shut down his options for a high school girl.

The intrepid travelers finally stepped from the airplane into the colorful, sleek airport. Outside the terminal, the kids stood mesmerized by throngs of people, all nationalities, jammed together, horns blaring, vans and cabs jockeying for position. A man with a pleasantly round face and skin like good leather held a sign Cal recognized. Once they were loaded into the Imagine Resort shuttle van everyone grew quiet.

Their driver felt it necessary to fill the void of conversation by giving his riders a free history lesson. He told them that thirty-five years ago the peninsula of Cancún had only six hundred residents. He said that in August of 2007, Hurricane Dean had demolished most of the area, but they were used to repairing after storm damage, and most of the hotels were open for business in only a few months.

There seemed to be little lasting effects of Dean. The peninsula was a palm splattered ribbon where upscale resorts grew from white sidewalk, like brilliant Lands of Oz, and shoppers strolled under festive market lights, fingering native textiles and jewelry. As they drove south, hotels turned gaudy and the clientele became smoothly tanned young adults who draped themselves from stools at open-air bars, silver shining on their tawny arms.

At the resort, a bellhop opened the taxi door. "Welcome to Cancún Imagine Resort, our friends from South Carolina," he sang. "Would you like a glass of champagne or perhaps a beer?"

The resort rose like a stone-stacked Mayan temple. Inside, artwork was contemporary. Sloan's father would have admired the simple Mexican architecture. Their rooms were on the top floor, off the center corridor of a five-story triangular breezeway. This hotel, though immense, reminded her of Charleston shotgun homes with their sides open to the sea for ventilation.

The bellman situated their luggage and bowed out of the room. Sloan stepped over the high threshold onto the balcony. The Caribbean spread out before her, blue and clear, water she had never experienced. It called to her with intensity, engendering a longing to submerge beneath its silky motion. The breeze was perfect. She noticed tile beneath her feet and she thought of the hurricane last year and wondered if this room had been flooded. She stepped back inside.

"Are we supposed to tip the bellhop?" Heather asked.

"No. This is an all-inclusive resort. Tips are built into the price," Ethan said.

"So we don't ever tip anybody?" she asked.

"Nope. And we can eat all the food we want and drink all we want."

"Awesome," Heather said.

"Hey, guys," Cal said, "I hate to interrupt, but let's go get drunk."

The four couples lined up at a right angle around two sides of the thatched-roof bar on the beach. Sloan took one of the rope swings with wooden seats that dangled around the cabana. Her white legs were bright against the blue of her sarong. Her eyes fell upon the brightly polished nails of the other girls and Sloan realized with horror that her toes were ragged and unkept. The guys ordered beers, but Heather and her friends ordered margaritas on the rocks. Not a big fan of beer, Sloan ordered the same. They toasted each other and stared out at the crystal clear water.

Sloan sipped her yellow-green drink and wondered what her parents would say if they could see her here in Mexico with a bunch of college students. Probably they wouldn't say a thing. Cal had bought Sloan's airline ticket and the room was already covered, as well as food and drinks. Sloan had her own spending money, but Cal had taken care of nearly everything so far. When she told her parents she was going to Mexico with girlfriends, she had seen their disbelief, but they hadn't questioned her. She had been poised for a confrontation or at least for some inquiry. She had wanted them to care that she was doing this crazy thing, to show any reaction at all, and she wasn't sure they even heard her accurately. All she got was the same disconnected void she always encountered when they were occupied with her sister's health issues.

"Where are you getting the money?" her mother had asked. Money was one of the few things that registered with them.

"It's already paid for. Somebody dropped out," Sloan had said. And it was nearly true. True enough to get her here.

Her mother had said, "We'll talk about this later." But they never did.

Sloan wondered why she had even bothered with such a thin lie, but it was somehow comforting to all of them that she keep up pretenses, not make them confront her and put more strain on the family. Sloan had never been terribly wild, and when she did choose to do something questionable, she had always been careful to shield her parents. She'd never gotten herself into a situation she couldn't handle, but she'd also never been this far from home before, with people she barely knew, and as she sat there, a little ball of fear leaped into her throat. They were sharing a room with another couple. What if Heather and Ethan started having sex right there with them in the room? What if Cal wanted to do the same? Or, worst of all, what if they decided it would be fun to mix it up a little? Sloan had some sexual experience, but nothing that would qualify her to take on that.

The thickly shellacked bar was embedded with shells and starfish. Cal leaned across this frozen sea and motioned to the bartender.

"Barkeep," he called, "another beer and a margarita for my lady."

He turned his megawatt smile on her.

"Here you go, little darlin'," he said. "Cheers."

The group wandered the hotel grounds, up and back down the beach where tanned locals jumped from white boats to hawk snorkeling trips and hang gliding. Dark banks of seaweed moved in the white sand and water. People lay immobile on lounge chairs, their skin shining in the sun. The breeze meant that the sun's burning rays fell like silk against skin, so Sloan reminded herself about sunscreen. On a few white vacationers, the sun's burn was already pink in Sloan's polarized sunglasses. Others were hardened by exposure, dark as polished wood and healthy-looking despite a future of sun damage.

That night, with her shoulders slightly sun-kissed, Sloan considered her clothes. Everybody had decided on dancing, but as Sloan sorted through her suitcase she rejected nearly everything as too high school or too dark. There was a knock on their door. Heather answered, and suddenly the two other girls appeared, rolling suitcases into the room.

"Grab your shit," one of them said to Cal. "Guys are watching soccer in our room."

The boys obeyed and went to the other room, towels in hand. The girls cracked open suitcases and began a fashion show on the beds. They stripped down, pulling on skirts and tanks, handing clothing around as communal property.

"I'll order us some margaritas," Kristin said.

"Room service!" Emma screamed. Emma was usually the quiet one.

Heather said, "Sloan, come here and try this on. I bet you can rock this look."

Sloan allowed herself to be dressed. A short red skirt and a black tank only made her look more pale.

"You really should have gone to the tanning bed before you came," one of the girls said in a critical tone.

"I don't tan," Sloan said, almost apologetically. "I mean, I can't."

"Here, try this self-tanner." The girl pitched a bottle to her. "It works fast. Go in the bathroom and don't get it on your clothes. It dries in, like, ten minutes."

Sloan shut herself in the bathroom and unfurled the towel from her head. She stripped naked in front of a wall-length mirror. She was pale, with no bathing suit stripe. For a second she wondered if she were dreaming. Would the others come bursting into the bathroom any moment to laugh at her, pale and heavy-breasted, her hair unruly? She squirted a dab of tanner into her hand and per instructions began gingerly and thoroughly smoothing it over her face. The change was immediate, and she smoothed and smoothed until an even glow came to her, a goddess before her own eyes.

When she stepped from the bathroom, the girls squealed.

"Oh, I get to do her hair," Kristin said.

As they blow-dried her hair straight with skills she had only passing acquaintance with, Sloan was thrilled. They brushed and discussed and considered small bottles of goo. Sloan was mesmerized by their intensity with appearance. When Kristin was through with her flatiron, Sloan's hair was as straight and silky as a shampoo commercial. After an intense thirty-minute makeup job and borrowed shoes and jewelry, Sloan was shocked to see a twenty-five-year-old woman staring back at her from the mirror.

She couldn't help admiring herself. Her figure looked great bursting from the tank top. Her tan legs looked longer and more lean.

"You're hot," Kristin said.

"Take it from me," Heather said, walking up to the mirror and adjusting her own bra. "It's all about the cleavage."

And Heather was right, because Cal touched her continually on their way to the club. He'd kissed her and had his arm around her neck in the elevator. He'd been the Southern gentleman, opening doors and shielding her from weaving pedestrians as they walked the bars and hotels that littered the strip. The girls were drawn into a jewelry shop. Inside, Mexican silver of all shapes and styles spoke of commerce, a small fraction was true art that appealed to Sloan's eye. The other girls were slipping bracelets onto their hands and trying on necklaces. On a wall of earrings and bracelets, Sloan spied a modern metal cuff.

"Try it on." The way Cal said it made Sloan's heart catch.

She slid the bracelet onto her wrist. He ran a hand down her arm and threaded his fingers through hers. He held her arm out so they could look at the jewelry.

His other hand was at her waist. He pulled her to him and whispered softly in her ear. "Beautiful. Let me buy it for you."

They commandeered a tall cocktail table at La Fiesta, an open-air bar where a large banner advertised one-dollar beers. While the guys seemed content to suck beer bottles and watch the wide screen, the girls buzzed with excitement to move down the strip. The thump of Crazy Town's song "Butterfly" called to them from a disco across the street. Sloan, still in jewelry glow, could have been anywhere with Cal and she would have been happy, but the other girls were more demanding.

"Come on. We didn't come to Cancún to watch sports and drink cheap beer. Let's go dance." They complained and postured, trying to draw the boys away from the bar.

"We'll meet you over there in a minute, baby," Ethan told Heather. "You girls go ahead and scare up a little attention from the local boys."

All the guys laughed, and Heather said, "Fine. I think I will."

The three girls headed toward the disco without a second glance at Sloan. Cal shrugged and nodded his head that she should go with them. Reluctantly, Sloan darted across the road to catch up with her new friends.

"He just didn't want to pay my way in," Heather told Kristin.

Inside, a disco ball cast frantic light around the room. It crawled across them as they made their way to the bar.

"Margaritas all around?"

Sloan nodded and handed her friend a ten. The girls maneuvered through the writhing sea of pheromones, tanned dancers crushed together, a throng of movement. On the other side of the dance floor they found an empty ledge where they could lean and watch. They barely had time to set their drinks down before Heather was squeezed against a guy at the edge of the dancing crowd, immediate intimacy.

Sloan had been to raves before inside warehouses in Myrtle Beach, but this was something different. Where the raves had been about music and costumes and craziness and, Sloan had to admit, sometimes drugs, this was altogether different. Here, the air was heavy with lust, ripe and oily with sex. Breasts surged from spaghetti straps, belly buttons flashed, silver glinted from tongues. Sloan was enthralled by the near-orgy on the dance floor, a mass of writhing arms and hair. Her gaze traveled to the bar and there she saw, only a dozen feet away, the Mexican guy from the airplane. His sleek printed shirt was open at the collar, but unlike the vacationing white boys in their jams, he wore a pair of slacks, and a thin belt encircled his trim waist. He was good-looking and, you could tell, buff under his rolled-up sleeves. He raised his glass to her.

She turned back to watch Kristin and found all her friends grinding to the beat, eyes closed, arms and hands pushing upward, raising the roof to a Nelly song. Everybody seemed to know the lyrics and the crowd sang of how hot it was and how they were going to take off all their clothes.

A crescendo swept the crowd with the lyric: *"I got secrets can't leave Cancún."*

Sloan shifted her eyes to steal another glance at the guy from the plane. She was startled to see him making his way toward her, drink in hand.

"Margarita? Right?"

"Oh, thank you," she said. Was she so obvious? Had her one glance been an open invitation? She suddenly wanted Cal. And no sooner had she that thought than she felt his familiar touch on her shoulder. Cal's face was sunburned and his eyes were ringed white from sunglasses. He smiled and reached forward to shake the guy's hand.

"Hey, man," Cal said. "You're the dude from the plane. Right?"

"Verulo," the guy said and shook Cal's hand.

"You from here?" Cal asked.

"Yes. But I live in Miami."

"UM?"

He nodded.

Cal motioned to the bartender, then said, "You need a beer, man?"

Verulo held his bottle of beer sideways to check the contents and drained it.

"Sure. Hook me up."

"Excellent," Cal said. "How about you, darlin'? You need me to freshen your drink?"

Sloan held up her new glass. "I'm all set."

The blackout curtains were certainly misnamed because the Mexican sun easily cut through into their room, a slice falling across Sloan's eyes. She moaned and rolled over to see her roommates, arms and legs tangled in tousled bed sheets, faces buried, hair mussed. The memory of their lovemaking came to her in a rush. As soon as they'd hit the hotel room, Cal had been on her, his tongue in her mouth, his hands on her body under her skirt, then between her legs. Over Cal's shoulder she could see Heather's bare breasts jiggling as she moved on top of Ethan. Desire flooded Sloan and she reached for Cal. Her hands found his muscled ass and she drew him against her. When they came together, a sensation of abandon shot through her. Her mind went blank as her body took over and she traveled to sweet tremulous territory.

Sloan felt pressure behind her eyes and then the explosion of a headache. Her first hangover. In the bathroom, Sloan downed a fizzy headache drink, brushed her teeth, and cleaned the previous night's makeup from her face. She slowly made her way downstairs in a dirty pair of shorts and one of Cal's T-shirts.

The cabana bartender smiled a knowing smile at her and she knew she must look as bad as she felt. "Vodka and orange juice?" he offered.

Sloan had tried not to drink too much the night before, had drunk a glass of water for every glass of alcohol, but bottled water was expensive in Cancún, and soon she'd forgotten her caution, and after a couple of tequila shots she hadn't remembered much of anything. She did recall the trouble they had getting their card to scan in their room door, how everyone laughed and how it took three people to figure out how the thing worked. She remembered thinking they were loud and that surely someone would come to warn them to be quiet.

She pondered the glassy blue water, recalling Cal's touch. It had been beyond her expectations. He knew what he was doing. She finished off her drink, and headed back to the room. There, everybody was up and hustling to get their clothes on. Heather was cramming things into a backpack.

"Come on. That Mexican guy we met at the bar last night called and we're going zip-lining in the jungle," Cal said. "Put on some shoes that won't fly off your feet. No flip flops."

Sloan took a moment to absorb what was going on. She had started the day with a screwdriver on a beach in Mexico by herself. Why not go into the jungle with a stranger and dangle by a cable in the canopy of a rainforest?

They traveled inland on the Yucatán Peninsula, toward Chichen Itza, on a rough secondary road threading past squat dwellings snugged up to the jungle's edge. The thought occurred to Sloan that they didn't know these people, but everybody else seemed relaxed so she said nothing. There were, after all, eight of them. They bumped along and Sloan felt nauseous. They traveled only an hour to their destination, an elaborate tree-house tourist business like the Swiss Family Robinson's at Disneyland. Behind the wooden structure, cables ran into the distance and disappeared into the jungle, zip-lines to who knew where.

"Cram together!" Ethan demanded. He held his cell phone in front of him ready to snap a shot.

"No, wait," Verulo said. "Stand with your friends. I'll take it."

Verulo took the shot, release papers were signed, money was exchanged, and each person was fitted with a harness. The first guy brave enough climbed onto a platform and zoomed away into the trees, the cable singing like a giant zipper. He hooted a Rebel yell on his way out of sight. The two other couples went.

Kristin's scream was muffled by the crush of plant life and birdcalls.

Sloan crawled to the platform, her enthusiasm suddenly drained. She looked down and Verulo was smiling at her. Cal, Heather, and Ethan all looked up at her expectantly.

"Jump!" Verulo said. "You will be fine."

"Jump," Cal said. "I'm up next."

Sloan closed her eyes, and when the bottom fell out she had the most wonderful sense of weightlessness. She was frightened, dangling up there by herself, but she slid smoothly through the canopy, wind in her ears. She turned, frantic to find Cal behind her, but the forest had closed like a wall and he was an indiscernible spot in the mass of vegetation like a *Where's Waldo?* storybook she had as a child.

CHAPTER 15

Death Knocks

"**E**verything's under control," Emmett assured her.

"Keep an eye on her. She's been acting funny," Lauren said. "Like she doesn't feel good. She has a headache."

"Go have lunch with your friends. Have a good time. You need a break."

Emmett could see the hesitation in Lauren's eyes. She walked over to Ainslie, who was sitting at the dining room table with her tutor. Lauren kissed her child's hair.

"Is there anything you need while I'm out?"

Ainslie shook her head and turned her attention back on her books. Third grade wasn't supposed to be that hard, but Ainslie was struggling to keep up with the other kids. Still, she wanted to go back to school. All she said she wanted was for life to be normal again.

After Lauren left, Emmett sneaked a peek as the home school teacher leaned into studies with his daughter, and then he slipped away. He'd agreed to work from home today so Lauren could meet some of her old college friends who were in town vacationing with their families. These were some of the same girls who had been with her that first weekend they met after Hugo. That's how everybody in South Carolina generally divided time now. Before Hugo and After Hugo. Now his family would always think of the world in terms of Before Cancer and After Cancer, although the After Cancer chapters had yet to be written.

Before Cancer, he and Lauren had been going through the usual ups and downs of married life. He had to admit that things had cooled from the early days of marriage when they couldn't wait to get Sloan down so they could get into their own bed. But their sex life had long ago evolved from the drawn-out, sweaty lovemaking of youth. Now, for Emmett at least, when they came together, it was more an affirmation that his wife still loved him, that he was doing a good job as husband and father. He knew Lauren questioned why the heat had gone out of their marriage bed, but for Emmett, he liked their comfortable ways now. He was more absorbed with running his business and doing what was required of him to keep their house from falling apart. In some ways, he liked that they had become more friends than lovers; it took away some of the pressure to perform.

But the woman he'd been living with for the past few months was not his wife, nor his lover and certainly not his friend. This woman didn't even see him. He was invisible unless he was doing something to further the cause of their daughter's health. Had he picked up the medications? Would he drive her to the doctor? Where did they stand with the insurance?

When Emmett approached Lauren for confirmation that he was meeting her expectations, that she still thought he was a good father and husband, she turned away from him. He wanted to touch her and to feel her soft skin against him again. In passion, Emmett could forget the tragedy their lives had become. But that part of his wife had shut down, and now when he tried to seduce her she shrank from him as if he had leprosy.

Lauren had lost a lot of weight, and one day it dawned on Emmett that she looked like a younger version of herself. This rekindled a desire he hadn't felt in years. It wasn't that he hadn't found her attractive before the weight loss, but suddenly she seemed like the college girl who responded to his touch, who couldn't wait for him to come home from the office, whose face lit up at the sight of him. This younger version of Lauren had always approved of him, affirmed him in so many ways.

But Lauren seemed insulted by his renewed interest, and rather than welcoming his advances she pushed him away. He wasn't surprised the day she asked him to move into the guest bedroom. He'd read lots of couples slept apart, but surely this wasn't a permanent situation. He definitely intended to get back into his own bed.

Emmett sat at his drafting table, the master plan for a monumental development spread out before him—Wannamaker and Pinckney's plan for a tract of land along the Waccamaw River. W&P had purchased the property for a song with the intention of developing it into a multi-use property. *Upscale living! A shell's throw from the coast!* W&P was staging the first sortie on objections to their plans, but it was only a matter of time.

The parcel in question had originally been a rice plantation, so elevation was low and soggy. W&P was fighting wetlands restrictions. They argued economic hardship, job creation and tourism dollars as if all the locals wanted strangers moving in on them.

Emmett had wondered if he should solicit for the job. His company certainly needed the money. And while Emmett despised working on these types of projects with massive developers, he was a realist. He knew some landscape architect would get the job and while his sustainable designs were often altered for quick turn-around on a property, he found more and more people were considering impact. Emmett found ways to contain sites, save trees, encourage recycling, and devise outdoor activity.

Emmett shoved the W&P proposal aside and began to design a landscape plan for a 1950s home on the mainland. That's what he preferred, renovating existing properties, bringing infill to dying towns, rejuvenating run-down parks. Emmett was a romantic.

In the other room, Emmett could hear his Ainslie's frustration as she tried to decipher a worksheet of clock faces. Telling time was frustrating her. The teacher's voice was patient and soft, but Ainslie's whine wasn't. Emmett wondered how she would be doing if she hadn't gotten sick. Would she be breezing through this or would it have always presented a challenge for her?

Emmett was getting ready to go give Ainslie a little encouragement when her complaining stopped. He waited, poised on the edge of his seat, ready for her grumbling to commence. Suddenly, Ainslie cried out, a strange guttural sound, followed by a dull thud. Had she knocked something to the floor?

"Oh, Mr. Sullivan! Mr. Sullivan! Come quick!"

Emmett sprinted from his office. The glare of the dining room light filled an empty room. He was confused. That was when he saw the overturned chair. On the floor, nearly under the table, his daughter convulsed. The teacher fluttered near her, afraid to touch her, paralyzed by fear.

"What do we do? What do we do?" the teacher cried.

Emmett jumped to action.

"Call 911!" he yelled.

She ran to the kitchen. Emmett knelt beside his rigid daughter and grabbed her hand.

"Ainslie, Ainslie, it's Daddy."

Ainslie jerked repeatedly, her hand unable to grasp. Her teeth snapped.

"Oh, God, do I put something in her mouth?" he cried.

Ainslie's eyes faded and she gasped without air.

The teacher came to the doorway. "What's the address here?" she barked.

Emmett told her, all the while never letting go of his daughter's hand. There was a blue tint to Ainslie's skin. Was she even breathing?

"Ask them if I can put something in her mouth!"

Ainslie stopped vibrating and fell slack, her head to the side, her eyes wide and dilated.

"She's stopped! She's stopped!" he cried.

"They're on their way. Cover her with a blanket and get her feet elevated to keep her from going into shock. They said don't put anything in her mouth."

Emmett ran into the den and grabbed an afghan and pillows from the sofa. He arranged one pillow under her feet and the other under her head and covered her with the spread.

"Ainslie? Can you hear me? Ainslie? It's Daddy. I'm here, baby." He turned to the teacher for help. "How long before they can come? Should we take her to the hospital ourselves?"

"They said stay calm."

"Is it okay to move her?"

"Can we move her off the floor?" the teacher asked into the phone. "They said don't move her."

"Ains, look at me. Ains, can you hear me? Baby, wake up." He touched her lightly on the cheek. "Baby, please wake up."

The wait was too long. Too long.

"The gate," Emmett said with sudden realization. "The ambulance can't get through the security gate. Screw this, I'm taking her to the hospital." He swept Ainslie into his arms. She was limp, but she whimpered, which he took as a good sign.

"Get the door," he said to the teacher. And on the way out, "Grab my cell phone." The teacher did as she was told, scurrying behind him. Emmett carried Ainslie down the front steps to the truck. The teacher opened the back of the cab and they gently laid her in the second seat. The teacher got in, and positioned Ainslie's head in her lap.

Emmett drove toward the mainland like a madman. A few times he registered a caught breath from the teacher, but he paid no heed. As they crossed the bridge the ambulance came screaming toward them. Emmett flashed headlights and waved as they rushed by. The ambulance slowed and made a U-turn. Emmett made it into The Pub's parking lot and opened the back door to check on Ainslie.

"Here! Here!" he yelled and motioned as the ambulance pulled up beside him. "She's in here."

Emmett knew all three EMS guys who jumped from the vehicle.

"She's not breathing right," he said. They quickly placed Ainslie on a stretcher, strapped her down and positioned an oxygen mask over her nose. Locals from The Pub gathered at a respectable distance. One EMT, who had played ball with Emmett in high school, fired questions as he loaded Ainslie into the ambulance.

Ainslie became more conscious, and she tried to scratch the mask away from her face. When her eyes registered on her father she clawed frantically for him.

"I want to ride with her," Emmett said.

His friend hesitated, then nodded.

Emmett climbed in the back.

"Hey." Larry stuck his head in before they closed the doors. "Give me your truck keys. I'll meet you at the hospital."

"Here, take my phone, too," Emmett said as he tossed his keys and phone. "Call Lauren."

Through the small back window Emmett glimpsed his worried friends as the ambulance plunged onto the highway, its siren scattering traffic.

By the time they arrived at the Waccamaw County Hospital's ER, Ainslie was talking.

"Ow, my neck hurts," she complained from behind the oxygen mask as she was rushed to the ER. Emmett was left with a pale doctor who asked questions he couldn't answer. She asked if Ainslie had ever had a seizure before. Had she complained of headaches? Had she been vomiting?

"She's been vomiting on and off for a couple of weeks, but I thought that was because of the chemo," Lauren said from behind him. She'd gotten to the hospital quickly and Emmett had never been so relieved to see her.

The doctor turned her attention to Lauren. "What time of the day would this happen?"

"Usually at night."

The doctor peppered her with questions. They threw around words Emmett didn't understand, names of procedures and medicines like electrolyte imbalance and CT scan and meningitis. He felt faint when the doctor said, "Spinal tap." Lauren understood her and answered with certainty.

"Once she's stable we'll do an EEG and blood work," the doctor said. She didn't look old enough to be out of college, but she was confident and in control.

Lauren nodded.

"EEG?" Emmett asked.

"Electroencephalogram. It measures electrical activity in the brain," the doctor said. "It tests for epilepsy."

Epilepsy? How in the world could Ainslie have epilepsy?

"She's awake now, so there was no sustained loss of consciousness, which is good. Your husband said there was some respiratory distress, but she seems to be breathing fine right now. Was there a fall of any sort? Anything that could cause brain injury?"

Emmett shrugged helplessly.

"No. She was just sitting at the table doing homework."

The doctor continued. "Had she been experiencing headaches?"

"Yes," Lauren answered.

"Considering her history, we'll need to do a CT on her, just to rule out a brain tumor."

Lauren's hand flew to her mouth.

"Brain tumor?" Emmett whispered.

The doctor nodded. "It is a possibility, but we're not going there just yet. We're stabilizing her and then we're moving her to the Children's Hospital at MUSC. They'll do the CT there."

Emmett had expected Ainslie to be transported to the Medical University of South Carolina in Charleston by ambulance, so he was shocked when the doctor said, "You need to start driving soon. I've already called for the helicopter. It is specially equipped to handle pediatric cases like this. It'll be here soon."

"I need to see her," Lauren said.

"Of course. Let me check on her."

Helicopter blades whirled fiercely on the helipad. Emmett had been stunned when the young doctor sedated and paralyzed Ainslie. She was hooked up to a breathing machine and strapped down for the ride. Lauren was wide-eyed and frantic.

"I want my husband to go with her," she cried.

"Ma'am, we don't usually do that," the doctor said.

"Never?"

"Well . . . there is room."

"Please, please. Somebody has to be there with her when she gets to the hospital. I can't do it," she said. "Emmett, you have to go."

"Let's go!" someone yelled.

"Are you okay to drive down?" he asked.

"Larry can bring me. I'll be fine. You go with Ainslie. Please, do this for me."

They loaded Ainslie into the back of the transport vehicle through a drop-down door in the rear. Emmett took a tiny seat mounted behind the pilot. They were accompanied by two pediatric trauma specialists who constantly checked her blood pressure, heart rate, eye dilation, oxygen saturation. Emmett knew this because they explained to him what they were doing, apparently their way of reassuring him. He wasn't sure if he was grateful to them for this or not.

The rescue transport lifted into the air and Emmett felt a flush of terror as the hospital dropped away below them. They skimmed the tops of long-leaf pines. Ainslie began to convulse.

"Don't panic," one said to him. "We're giving her antiseizure medication. Sometimes this happens when they lie flat."

For the second time Emmett felt terrified, and he fought to hold himself together as he watched his child struggle for life.

The airlift took twenty minutes pad to pad, but it seemed like both a second and an hour had elapsed when they touched down on the roof of the parking deck beside the Children's Hospital. A waiting crew rushed to roll her out on a stretcher, the breathing machine trailing along. They took a wide elevator down, then transferred Ainslie to yet another ambulance for the short ride to the emergency entrance. They rolled her inside the hospital and brought her up to the eighth floor to the pediatric intensive care unit. All this was accomplished in swift order, with each medical professional along the way assuring him Ainslie was in good hands.

On the way, a doctor tried to take Ainslie's history by firing questions at Emmett, but Emmett was unable to answer as Lauren had. "I don't know," he answered so many times he wanted to cry. He was so woefully inept at medical things. Why hadn't he listened? Why hadn't he researched and participated in her health decisions? Now all he wanted was to understand, to assist her, and yet he was helpless, useless.

A nurse laid a calming hand on his arm as he watched his daughter disappear down a corridor. "It's okay," she said. "Anyone in your situation would be stressed and a little flustered."

"No, you don't understand," Emmett cried. "I can't help her. I can't help her at all."

"You have to wait here," a nurse said. "You can't go in the PICU."

Emmett sank into a waiting room chair, leaned over with his head in his hands, and for the first time since the start of his daughter's medical nightmare he cried. He wept without shame or even a thought to the few people there with their own dramas unfolding. Emmett cried out of frustration and anger and fear and exhaustion. And when the adrenaline rush began to wear off, he slumped back into his seat, limp and confused. His heart leapt again when he saw his wife and Larry coming around the corner on a dead run.

"Good God, how fast did you drive?" he asked them.

"You don't want to know," Larry said. "How is she?"

Lauren peered through the windows of broad double doors back into the restricted area as if her daughter were waiting on the other side to wave at her.

"How was she when you left her?" Lauren asked.

"They still had her sedated. Everything's going to be okay," Emmett told her. He didn't tell her Ainslie had experienced another seizure in the helicopter. He didn't see how that would be a good thing to share right now.

One side of the door swished open and a serious doctor in a knee-length white coat approached them.

"Are you the Sullivans?" he asked.

"Yes," they said together.

"I'm Dr. Hart. I've got some good news."

"Good news, please," Emmett said.

"Ainslie is stable now and she's off the respirator. Her neuroexam and CT were clean."

"What does that mean?" Emmett asked.

"It means she doesn't have a brain tumor."

"Thank God," Lauren said, but she still stared at the doctor with dread-filled anticipation.

The physician continued. "We've called her oncologist and she'll be here momentarily. We have some answers about Ainslie's seizures. The reason she was vomiting at night is that when she's in a reclined position, cerebrospinal fluid accumulates, causing increased intracranial pressure from a tumor on her spine."

"Hydrocephalus," Lauren said.

"Yes," the doctor nodded.

"What?" Emmett was confused.

"Ainslie has a small tumor on her spine and it is causing fluid to collect in her brain. The first thing we have to do is put a shunt in to drain the fluid and relieve the pressure on her brain."

"You're going to do brain surgery on her?" Lauren whispered. His wife was so pale Emmett thought she was going to pass out. He put his arm around her shoulders.

"It's not as bad as it sounds. Recovery time is quick.

There are many people walking around with shunts and you never know. They lead very normal lives."

"What about the tumor on her spine?" Lauren asked.

"We're still assessing that. As I said, her oncologist is on the way. I will say it looks small. We'll know more soon."

"So she'll have to have spinal surgery, too?" Larry said.

The doctor nodded. "I'm afraid so. Although that's not our most immediate concern."

CHAPTER 16

Homecoming

The plane was filled with sunburned, exhausted passengers. The flight home was subdued compared to the trip down to Cancún. Cal had slept through the last inflight drinks service, and Sloan watched him, his eyes moving with dreams. Cal's hair had more blond streaks than before Mexico and his skin was tan and smooth. Sloan hummed with desire and smiled to herself. No more fumbling high school boys who couldn't even roll on a condom. Cal made it all quite clear how sex should be.

Cancún had been a drunken sex fest, and Sloan had no regrets. Their chemistry was undeniable. They spent nights grinding against each other on the dance floor. Cal would pull Sloan against him and she would ride his leg until her whole body buzzed. But by early morning, when they got back to their room, they were too exhausted to make love, and they usually fell into bed in a drunken stupor.

Afternoons were another story. Sloan would be lying under an umbrella, reading a steamy novel one of the other girls had discarded. Cal would walk out of the surf, water trickling down his flat stomach, and she wouldn't even have to voice her desire. He always sensed her cravings as if they were his own. So they would leave their friends on the beach and spend the next hour rolling in the cool white hotel sheets. Cal brought her to orgasm that first night and he continued to hit her high notes, leaving Sloan in a constant sexual stupor.

Back on the tarmac in Atlanta, the plane erupted with the click of opening cell phones. Sloan waited for her phone to boot and then called voice mail. Her mother's voice came on, as she had expected, but what followed made panic carve a piece of her heart.

"Sloan, it's Mom. Honey, I'm not sure if you'll get this message or not, but Ainslie's back in the hospital and it's pretty bad. She's really sick, but don't freak out. Just come to the hospital as soon as you can. I'll call you back if things change."

"What hospital?" Sloan said. "Mom, what hospital?"

She checked and there were no other messages from her mother.

Sloan checked the time of her call and realized it had been placed only twenty minutes before. Whatever was happening with Ainslie was still in process. If Sloan called, she would only be adding to the tension her parents now faced. Sloan's impulse was to dial her mother, or perhaps her father, since he tended to be more calm in these situations, but she didn't. She needed to check to make sure her connecting flight was going to get her home on time. They had only a short amount of time to get from one terminal to the other before their flight left. The last thing she wanted was to make contact with her parents, find out things were terrible, and then end up getting stuck in the Atlanta airport all night. Sloan decided to wait before she called.

Everyone in their party was weary, and as they waited

in the stuffy cabin to disembark Sloan felt a rise of emotion she knew was going to bring about a scene, but she couldn't help it. She choked back tears as long as she could, but when Cal saw her face, he said, "Sloan, what's the matter?"

She cried then, silently, as she hunched forward against the window. Other passengers watched her in silence, embarrassed by her grief. Sloan hunkered toward the tiny window to hide her face. Cal held her for several minutes. When the center aisle began to move, Cal gathered their things from the overhead compartment and motioned her out into the aisle ahead of him.

On their arrival into Charleston, Sloan checked, and her message indicator was blinking again.

"Sloan, it's Dad. They're airlifting Ainslie to MUSC's Children's Hospital. Where are you? I thought you would be back by now. If you get this message call me. You probably need to meet us at MUSC. I love you."

Sloan snapped her phone shut.

"Can you take me to Children's Hospital?"

"Sure. Anywhere you want to go."

Thirty minutes later, Cal drove into the parking garage.

"What're you doing? You can just let me off at the entrance."

"I'm coming with you."

"That's not necessary."

"I want to. Although I will say it usually takes longer than this for me to get on the parental shit list."

They parked and walked through a small courtyard with shaggy palms that made Mexico flash to Sloan's mind. The hospital was cold, much colder than outside and Sloan, in her flimsy tropical clothes, immediately wished for a wrap. She was familiar with the hospital. She knew where to find radiation and chemotherapy and emergency, but today MUSC seemed the most foreign place in the world.

Sloan found the information desk and learned that Ainslie had been moved to the pediatric intensive care unit, a new place for Sloan to find.

As they rounded the corner toward the PICU waiting room, Sloan stopped short and Cal nearly ran into her. Her mother and father sat on straight chairs. Her father stared up and out of Sloan's line of vision at what was probably a television, but her mother stared at the floor. Makeup pooled under her mother's swollen eyes and her hair was limp and unkept, but she had on a pretty dress as if she were getting ready to go to a luncheon party.

"Mom?"

Both her parents turned blank eyes on her as if they didn't recognize her. Neither rose to greet her. They sat with their arms slack at their sides.

"Sloan," her father finally said, and he reached toward her. To her surprise, her mother returned to her vacant expression without even acknowledging her presence.

"She's out of surgery," her father said. "She's going to be okay."

"What does that mean?" Sloan asked.

"I don't know specifics," he said. "It means she's going to live and that's what's important."

"What's wrong with her?"

"A tumor on her spine. That caused fluid on her brain. They had to put in a shunt."

"What's a shunt?"

"A drain type of thing."

"They did surgery on her brain?" Sloan felt sick.

"It's not as bad as it sounds," her mother said. "It's not as bad as it sounds."

Sloan felt the bottom drop out, a sinking like the zipline without the thrill, only anxiety holding on at the bottom, the old dread creeping back into her stomach.

"Does she have a brain tumor?"

Her father stood there with his arms still limp at his sides. "No. She doesn't have a brain tumor. It was fluid pressure. We're waiting until they tell us we can see her. She's been out of surgery for about an hour now. They say she woke right up. They say that's a good thing."

Her father's eyes wandered up to Cal's face.

"Son," he said. "What are you doing here?"

"Sir," Cal said. "I'm sorry about Ainslie. If there's anything I can do, please don't hesitate to ask."

Her father studied Cal, and Sloan could see him summing up the situation—their clothes, the shiny new bracelet. Sloan so wanted to cover the bracelet with her other hand, but instead she followed a sudden need to feel her father's reassuring pulse against her. She stepped forward and clung to him. He raised his arms to enclose her and they stood there, without moving for a long time while her heart ached beyond belief.

"Did you say she has a tumor?" Sloan whispered.

"On her spine," her dad said into her hair. "We're just waiting. That's all we can do now. Just wait."

CHAPTER 17

Collapse

Ainslie's veins had collapsed.

"Honey, I just can't find a good one. I'm sorry. I know it hurts," the nurse said as she flicked the top of Ainslie's hand to try and raise a pale blue path for her needle.

"I want Miss Vivian!" Ainslie cried and jerked her hand away.

"Vivian?" the nurse said, a look of relief washing her face. "She comes on right about now. I'll go get her."

Her vein stick had been red and burning for hours. Her mother had insisted that a new location for the IV be found, but Ainslie was so thin her veins were rolling. Nurses had tried to flush Ainslie's chest port numerous times and finally concluded that it needed to be replaced. The nurse had stuck her three times before Ainslie finally lost her patience and cried for Miss Vivian.

"What are you doing back here?" Vivian said from the doorway. "I'm off for a couple of days and I come back to find my favorite girl's come to see me."

Ainslie was pressed into the pillow, her head swathed in

gauze. She touched her bandaged head and tried to smile.

"That is not a good look for you," Vivian said. "Oh hey, I got me some new Crocs." She walked beside Ainslie's bed, kicked off a shoe, and held up her psychedelic Mary Janes.

"Cool," Ainslie whispered.

"Yeah, so why *are* you back here?" She raised an eyebrow to Ainslie's mother.

"You want the long version or the short version?" her mother said in an odd tone that implied no answer would be a good answer.

"How about the happy version?" Vivian said.

"You sound funny," Ainslie whispered.

Vivian smiled wide and her mouth flashed silver.

"I got braces!"

"Do they hurt?"

"Nah, nothing I can't handle. We're tough girls, right? Give me your arm, I want to find a good vein." She walked cautious fingers over on Ainslie's hand and inside her elbows searching for a place not bruised. "You're too skinny. You need to eat something. After I get this thing in you, how about an ice cream sandwich?"

"Okay."

Vivian wrapped the rubber tourniquet around Ainslie's arm and handed her a red stress ball.

"You know the routine," she said.

Ainslie squeezed and Vivian slid the needle in with the softest touch.

They both sighed relief.

"I'm on tonight." Vivian moved smoothly, hooking up a new bag, adjusting the flow. "You need to rest, so I'll try to make sure you get some sleep, okay? I'll try not to wake you up any more than I have to."

It was nearly impossible to sleep in the hospital. Nurses woke her up all night long to check her temperature and take her blood pressure and give her meds. Most of them were quiet and efficient, not fun like Vivian. Sometimes, Ainslie would pretend to be asleep, hoping the parade of white lab coats would just leave her alone. She slept with the covers over her head so nurses would leave instead of getting her vital signs. But Vivian protected her, and she slept better those nights Vivian was on. She was the only one who always pulled the drape around her bed before she gave an injection, just in case people were passing in the halls. She seemed to know what Ainslie needed before she did.

Vivian's husband was in the National Guard and she talked about the Iraq War. How her husband was over there building bridges and just as soon as they built one it would get blown up. Ainslie started thinking about Vivian's husband as the cartoon character who was blasting away cancer cells, a little guy in camo with a big gun mowing down unwanted cells.

Days in the hospital dragged by. After the shunt surgery, there had been more tests and then, when she was strong enough, they had operated on her to remove the spinal tumor that had been making her legs tingle. She'd come out of that surgery with more scars and a new port in her chest so they could draw blood and give fluids without having to stick her every time.

Ainslie had declined to talk with the hospital chaplain or therapist, but she had found a good use for the journal the counselor left her. She'd had Vivian roll her wheelchair down to the lobby where they catalogued all the tropical fish in the lobby tanks. A book from the hospital library helped them identify every fish and crustacean in the colorful underwater world.

"That one's a trigger fish." Ainslie pointed to fish the color of one of her sister's graphite sticks. The dark gray fish looked as if he had been spray-painted with thin strips of blue, yellow, and black. He slowly opened and closed pursed lips. "He eats other fish, so they have to be careful what fish they put into the tank with him."

Vivian leaned down on the back of Ainslie's wheelchair to take a closer look.

"But he's so pretty. How could he be so mean?"

"That's just nature. He's a hunter. He can't help it. It's just natural."

"He sure is a good-looking son-of-a-gun."

Ainslie sighed and pressed her finger to the glass. Fish darted away from her, except for the trigger fish, which stood his ground.

"I didn't tell Mommy my butt hurt."

"What do you mean?"

"Before I had to go to the emergency room. Before they flew me here in the helicopter. My butt hurt really bad."

"And you didn't tell anybody?"

"No."

"Why not?"

"Because I didn't want to come back here."

"I understand."

"I just want it all to be over."

"I guess you know now it's not a good idea to keep secrets like that, right?"

Ainslie shrugged.

"When do I get to go home?"

"Soon."

Vivian wheeled Ainslie back to her room and eased her into bed.

"Can I have a blanket?" Ainslie asked.

"Sure. I'll get you a warm one."

Since the last surgery, Ainslie couldn't stay warm. Her body weight had dropped so low she was getting supplements, but she still shivered most of the time. Vivian came back with a heated blanket and tucked it all around her until Ainslie was snug.

"There, like a butterfly in a cocoon."

"Moth."

"What?"

"Butterflies have a chrysalis. Moths have cocoons."

"Aren't you just the smartest girl I've ever met? Do you want some TV?"

"No. I want to sleep."

"Okay, hon."

Vivian put on an ocean wave sound machine Sloan had brought and Ainslie closed her eyes and tried to relax. But her mind kept wandering back to what Vivian said about not keeping secrets. Ainslie hadn't told about the shooting pain in her tailbone because every time she mentioned anything new, her mother rushed her off to the doctor again. So she thought, just maybe, if she didn't say anything the pain would stop on its own.

And her headaches. She'd had those since the first time she did chemo, so she hadn't thought it was anything new to mention. She had wanted it all to be over, but everything had just gotten worse.

Ainslie touched the bulging place on her skull where the shunt was inserted and traced its path that snaked down the back of her neck. It was still sensitive, but at least now her headaches were gone.

She rolled onto her side and touched the incision on her back where they had taken her kidney out in her first surgery. It was healing over, a scar with ruffled edges and a smooth center right above her left hip. She had thought it would make a huge scar, but it was only about four inches long, not nearly as scary as she had thought it would be.

She reached closer to her spine and felt the pads where the surgery incision lived. She'd have to wait and see how bad that scar would be. She knew it had been much larger than the first incision. It really hurt. She wished it was like a jellyfish sting where her mother could rub meat tenderizer on it and make it go away. No, this was a throbbing that made her eyes water, but some days she'd rather have the pain than be drunk on meds. At least the ache let her know she was alive.

Tomorrow would be painful. She hated physical therapy and they would be taking her to physical therapy instead of the therapist coming to her room. So far he'd massaged her arms and legs and had her squeeze a ball, but tomorrow she would probably have to lift some weights or walk for a while. Ainslie's right hand didn't want to cooperate with her. Her doctor said some kids had to learn how to write with their left hands, but he thought she would recover if she tried. She was supposed to write in her journal, but her hand was so weak that Vivian had to help her catalog the fish. They would probably make her write in therapy the next day. Their theory was the more you used it, the faster it would come back. They said it was probably only a matter of time. When you're sick, everything is always a matter of time.

There was a plain round clock on her bedside table and she watched the hands move, ticking off the seconds and minutes in her head. Telling time wasn't so hard after all. She played games with herself to see how long she could hold her breath, if she could guess when a nurse would walk in. She always let her visitors know when they were a few minutes late.

Sloan seemed to always be late. She was supposed to come today but called to say she couldn't make it. She'd gone to Charleston to see her boyfriend. She said he wasn't her boyfriend, but that was just because he'd never asked. Sloan liked him so much it was scary. Ainslie wanted to be with Sloan every day, since she was leaving for college in August. But with Cal around, that wasn't going to happen. As soon as school was out they would be together all the time. Sloan would be driving to Charleston if he stayed down there.

Cal was always nice to her, but still Ainslie wanted to poke him in the eye. He came to see her in the hospital and brought her a manicure kit. A weird reaction to the chemo caused Ainslie's fingernails to grow incredibly strong. Sloan had shaped and polished them for her, alternating pink and blue. Ainslie had to admit the manicure kit was an awesome gift, but that didn't make her like Cal any better.

Ainslie lay back and gazed past the window clings of cartoon characters at the black night sky. The best part about mornings was that the sky was such a pretty blue. It made you feel good to look at it. She reached for the bed controls, lowered herself flat, and closed her eyes. She needed to sleep while she could. They always came to get you early in the morning for tests, and she was not a morning person.

Ainslie turned onto her side and shoved a pillow under her chin. Her eyes immediately fell on her bedside table and her sea monkey habitat. Luckily, since they were in a contained environment, the doctor had let her have them. Ainslie watched the scrawny little brine shrimp jerking aimlessly through the clear, plastic tank. They were a simple, dumb animal, but she thought that just somehow, in their tiny little brains, that they knew she was there.

"Somebody named you wrong," she said. "You don't look like monkeys to me."

One bounced against the side of the tank again and again. Ainslie sighed as she watched him.

"You poor thing," she whispered. "I know just how you feel."

CHAPTER 18

Wings

"Hey, Mom," Sloan said as she walked past her mother into the kitchen to get a glass of tea.

Her mother raised red-rimmed eyes and gave her a weak smile. She had the phone pressed to her ear. She seemed to be on hold. She was constantly on the phone. Sloan couldn't imagine all the people she must be talking to, reeling off long names of medicines and procedures. She had her notebook beside her, her security blanket where she scribbled every minor medical thing ever uttered about Ainslie. Sloan worried that her mother had been on overdrive for so long that she might have a mental breakdown. If that happened, what would they do? Who would hold them all together?

Apparently their father had been worried about the same thing because he arranged for them to go to a counselor, something so unlike him. He always balked at the idea that any of them needed emotional help. He cracked jokes about therapists and counselors, but he must have felt they were at the breaking point because yesterday her parents had solemnly left the house and come home two hours later in one of their most agitated states yet. They continued their heated therapy session and for once they didn't hide behind bedroom doors or walk to the end of their dock out of earshot.

Sloan had been instructed to "Go upstairs!" but their parents' argument traveled up the staircase. Sloan had tried to distract her sister with video games, but Ainslie refused to play and finally muted the sound, and they had lain in bed listening to the argument raging below.

"What if I make a mistake?" their mother had hissed. "I need more participation from you."

"I try to participate, but no matter what I think, you tell me I'm wrong and you ultimately make the decision. What's the point?"

"See, we didn't get anywhere. I don't want to go back to counseling anymore. All we do is dredge up more things that distract from what's most important, taking care of Ainslie."

"Fine. I didn't want to go in the first place. But we can't go on like this. You're agitated all the time. Is there no happiness in you at all anymore?"

"Happiness? How am I supposed to be happy when everything is falling down around us? You want me to take care of everything, and, by God, be happy while I'm doing it so you don't have to be inconvenienced by my emotions."

"You're unreasonable."

"Why is it always about me? It's not my attitude that's the problem here. Let's talk about you, you're distracted and disconnected from everything going on here."

"I am not! I'm working as hard as I can to resolve this. You have no faith in me at all. I'm just your whipping boy now. Oh, let's blame Emmett for everything!"

"This whole fiasco isn't my fault!"

"I'm doing the best I can."

"Well, that's not good enough."

"That's the real issue. I've never been good enough for you, have I? You've always thought we should have a different life. Drive nicer cars. Belong to the country club."

"I don't want to belong to the fucking country club! Now you're projecting your own feelings of inadequacy onto me. Deal with your own problems."

There was a lull in the argument, an impasse. Then a door slammed and there was silence.

"Mom said the F-word," Ainslie whispered slowly.

Sloan said, "They're just scared."

"I know."

"We're all scared."

"Don't they love each other anymore?"

Sloan sighed. "I read somewhere that we're the most cruel to people we love, people we know love us."

"Why?"

"Because other people, like friends, can go away."

"I know about that."

"Right. But family, we stick it out. We put up with all the bad parts of each other, the frustrating things and the things that hurt. I just hope Mom and Dad don't say anything they can't take back."

Sloan heard her mother's slow footsteps on the stairs, so she silently pushed Ainslie's bedroom door closed, hoping she would pass on by. Their mother stopped on the other side and they anticipated her knock but none came. She moved on to her own bedroom and closed the door, and the girls breathed a sigh of relief.

Sloan hoped they wouldn't go back to counseling. If therapy exposed so many pent up feelings, then she hoped they never went back. Denial seemed a less painful route.

* * *

Sloan passed her mother, who had her head down, pencil behind her ear, notebook open in front of her. With two plastic glasses of lemonade, Sloan headed to the porch to sit with her sister. Outside, the salty breeze was smooth and soft on her arms. Sloan set the lemonade down on an end table where her sister could reach it from her rocker, but Ainslie made no move to drink.

Miraculously, Ainslie had come home less than two weeks after her operations. They had inserted the shunt in her head and removed the tumor from her spine and she had been rebounding at a decent rate. But this last medical disaster had fueled their parents' fight. Their bickering had escalated after their last visit to the hospital's financial office, where they had signed away the rest of their lives, promising to do everything they could to repay the medical expenses that kept accumulating.

The front door opened and their mother stepped out.

"I'm making supper. What do you feel like eating?" she asked Ainslie, then waited patiently for a reply. The doctors had said to engage Ainslie in conversation, and seeing her mother wasn't going to leave without an answer, Ainslie finally said, "Pizza maybe." Her speech was deliberate, something doctors said might come and go as her brain adjusted.

"Okay," their mother said. "Um, look girls." She squatted down and took Ainslie's hand in hers. "I'm real sorry you girls had to hear that last night. Your father and I . . . well . . . we're trying to work things out. It's all going to be okay. I promise we'll get through this and everything will be fine."

Ainslie had no expression. There was a moment of hesitation between Ainslie and their mother, a second when Sloan thought her sister might turn away. Sloan was ready to step in, to comfort her, when Ainslie raised her frail arms and her mother melted into her fragile embrace.

When they finally moved apart, their mother wiped her eyes and said, "Okay. Pizza." She headed back inside.

Sloan lowered herself down on the top step at Ainslie's feet. Her sister stared out at the ocean, the day's last light settling on the surface. Ainslie hadn't said much, but there had been wisdom and compassion in her fragile embrace. She was so young and yet so weary and wise. It was all too serious for somebody only nine. Ainslie's head was wrapped with gauze like a monster in a cheesy movie and Sloan thought to lighten the mood. The doctors all said she didn't need gauze anymore, but Ainslie insisted on this bit of drama. The counselor said it couldn't hurt to indulge this quirk. Besides, Sloan found it amusing.

"Hey, mummy head," she said.

"What?"

"Maybe we can get a bunch of rolls of that gauze the next time you're at the hospital and I can wrap you up like a real mummy for Halloween. Wouldn't that be cool?"

"A mummy in a wheelchair."

"You won't be in a wheelchair then."

Ainslie pulled her parched lips into a thin smile. The soft light of the clouds at day's close pressed into her skin. Sloan let the conversation drop. They watched the ocean's give and take with the shore. A bird perched on the railing and flitted away.

"They know," Ainslie said.

"Who knows what?"

"They know about Mexico."

Sloan nodded. "I figured as much. Am I in huge trouble?"

Ainslie shrugged. "I don't think so."

"I guess they're too busy fighting about other stuff. Thanks for telling me."

They fell quiet again.

A butterfly, a whisper of a being, lit on Ainslie's hand. She didn't flinch, only watched the small creature's wings move gracefully together and apart. A second butterfly found her shoulder. To Sloan's amazement seven butterflies arrived, their wiry legs clinging precariously to her sister, two on the gauze that hugged her head.

Ainslie turned weary eyes on their fragile wings.

"They missed me," she said.

CHAPTER 19

New Normal

Neat stacks of bills and invoices covered the dining room table. Part of the table held household expenses, the other half medical bills and statements, many with red slashes across the first page. Lauren and Emmett had sorted these into piles that had to be paid versus those that could be put off for another thirty or sixty days. Property taxes were due.

There were other, much smaller piles made of investments, college funds, savings bonds, CDs, and insurance policies. There was about eighteen thousand dollars in Sloan's college fund, a thousand in Ainslie's. These assets were achingly meager next to the looming mounds of payables.

The hospital bills totaled nearly three hundred thousand dollars, and they owed more than a hundred thousand dollars to surgeons, anesthesiologists, pathologists, physical therapists, and counselors. Still, they were unsure exactly what they owed since the same bills kept coming each month, sometimes with late fees or interest added.

The hospital's billing statements seemed particularly confusing, with innocuous descriptions like cough support device, thermal therapy, and cotton professional, descriptions Lauren suspected were merely cough drops, ice packs and cotton swabs. These things showed up numerous times on various bills, raising the question of erroneous multiple billings. How were they to tell if Ainslie had actually received the treatments and the medical supplies listed on the bills?

Larry said not to be overwhelmed, that the bills they were receiving were pretty standard and he would help them get everything worked out. He said the hospital had been unusually willing to work with them, and while the relationship between a hospital and patient was based on trust, he had requested an itemized set of statements for his own files. He intended to hire a medical saving specialist who understood diagnosing and coding to reconcile the statements. This person would make sure everything was in order and, in the end, that everyone got paid.

Another part of the table held the insurance policy quagmire—all of Larry's letters on their behalf and Common Good's replies. Of course, every procedure Ainslie had received, every medicine she had taken was not pre-approved by the insurance company, so for every statement there was a letter of denial. All these lived next to their lengthy Common Good policy that hadn't paid a claim in eight months, and the accompanying massive coverage catalog.

"Let's decide what we're going to pay," Emmett said. They'd stopped renovations like painting and repairs that were chronic with old houses. They had a plumbing issue that would have to wait. They didn't have to worry about a mortgage, but they did have to keep the lights on and water pumping through their pipes. Cable could go, but Lauren argued against it as necessary for Ainslie. She'd said surely, in the bigger picture, cable wasn't what was going to do them in.

Lauren and Emmett both had calculators whirring. They flipped through paper, adding, subtracting. They didn't talk, but kept at it, their heads down, fingers tapping keys and scribbling notes.

Lauren sighed, pushed away from the table, and went to the kitchen. She returned with two of their best wine stems and a bottle of red with a gold label.

"I thought we were saving that for a special occasion," Emmett said.

"I say no time like the present." She waited for his response.

"Break it open."

The bottle made a happy pop when uncorked, and Lauren filled their bulbous glasses a quarter full. She handed one to Emmett and eased herself back into a dining room chair.

"So," she said. "Are we bankrupt?"

He took a sip and scanned the organized mess of their financial life. "It would appear quite possible in the next two months."

She nodded as if to say she expected as much.

"It's not just the big bills, but trips to Charleston and missed work. Stuff adds up. There's no way to account for all the incidental expenses."

"How much longer does Larry say this can take?"

"We've jumped through all the insurance company's hoops. Our next step is to sue them. He's drafting the papers."

"Lawsuits take forever. How much longer will the doctors and hospital wait to get paid?"

"Larry said they're used to this sort of thing. He said he'd talk to them for us. They won't deny basic treatment. As long as we make payments of some sort on our bills they probably won't refuse us outright, but of course that means nothing experimental or out of the norm. Basic services."

Lauren sighed. "No new hospitals or doctors will touch us right now, so Duke is out for the time being."

"She's getting good care in Charleston."

"True. But what if they want to refer her?"

"We'll cross that bridge when we come to it."

"What are we paying Larry?"

"Right now, nothing. But if we get a settlement I'll expect him to take part of it."

"And what if they just pay the bills they're supposed to pay and there's no extra. What do we owe Larry then?"

"I have no idea. Expenses at a minimum."

"Well, thank God for Larry."

"He swears we'll win, Lauren. He says it's just a game of tenacity. That only people committed to the long haul manage to get their claims paid. It's their 'we have enough money to wait you out' game."

"And yet you're still paying premiums?"

"The entire office is insured with those sons-of-bitches."

Lauren took a long drink of wine and held it in her mouth.

"We're screwed," she finally said.

Emmett swirled the dark red liquid in his glass as he perused his house. It was not that large a house really; there were lots of rooms but they were small, as was the case with most Victorians. The ceilings were high, the windows long and narrow. The woodwork and floors were honeyed, and slightly warped with age and dampness.

"We're sitting in our biggest asset," he said.

"So we sell the house?"

"No. But what if we rent it? Beach houses of this size can rent for up to five thousand dollars per week. We could rent a smaller house inland for less than a thousand, I'm sure. If we could keep this house rented all summer, we could gross, maybe, I don't know, forty thousand dollars."

"Would we hire a management firm?"

"Have to. I wouldn't know how to keep the place rented myself."

"So we subtract the rental on our new place, and the fee for the rental company. Would the management firm provide a cleaning service or would we clean the house?"

"I guess we would clean it and save the money."

"What about repairs? You know there are a bunch of repairs we'd need to make before we could rent it."

"Maybe people will buy into the rustic charm."

"So between now and high season we have to find a new place to live, move, find a rental management firm, make repairs, and then hope the house rents. Assuming we accomplish all of that, do we have to give Judd and Rick their two-thirds cut of the income?"

"No. They wouldn't expect it, considering our situation."

"Okay. I hate to always be Ms. Negative, but what about the creek dredging and the beach renourishment? When's that all scheduled to begin? Doesn't it keep getting delayed? What if we move and rent and then have to refund money because big machines are grinding away cordgrass in the creek or spewing wet sand all over the beach?"

He contemplated this. "You've got a point. I'll have to check with the city and see if they have a definite start date."

She sighed. "I don't know, Emmett. It all seems pretty complicated."

It was true. How could they move their sick child to a less comfortable place and rearrange their lives all in hopes of netting thirty thousand dollars? It would help, but truly, that amount wouldn't begin to touch their huge debt. He'd have to find a storage area for all their personal belongings and store them for the summer. They'd be packing and cleaning for weeks without the assurance that any of it would pay off. And how could he ask his exhausted wife to clean this house for strangers each week when she could barely keep it in order for their own family? It did seem like a huge gamble, but Lauren seemed to be seriously considering his proposal, or perhaps she was too tired to put up a fight.

"So," she finally said, "next problem. What about the Savannah School of the Arts?"

"Sloan may have to delay college."

"Emmett, we can't do that to her. Who knows what will happen to her in a year or two? Do you want her waiting tables or working in a bar and losing all that enthusiasm she has about going to school?"

"We all have to make sacrifices."

"You know she's drifting away from us. I don't even want to think about how she paid for that Mexico trip."

"She's pretty frugal. She probably had money saved."

"I don't think for one minute she went with girlfriends. That Wannamaker boy paid for everything. I still think we should confront her."

"What good would it do? It's already a done deal. She's technically an adult. I'm not willing to get into a fight with her over it now. I say let it go."

"You would."

"What does that mean?"

"Nothing."

"Go on. Say what you mean."

"You know what I mean. It's the easy way out."

"You're right. It's not the best choice. It is the easy way out, but I say we take it. We've got too many other problems to worry about."

"We've always told her not to worry about college. We told her that all she had to do was get in and we'd pay for it. Now we're reneging. Can't we at least send in the money for her deposit? Things might change between now and the time school starts. I mean, surely to God the insurance will come through before then."

Emmett gestured over the table. "Where do you see a thousand dollars here? I don't see any extra. I don't even see gas money or food money here."

"She's our child, too."

"I've talked to her about this. She's looking into financial aid. She understands."

"Didn't she need to apply for financial aid long before now?"

"Surely she can still apply for January."

Lauren lowered her voice then. She didn't sound accusatory when she said, "So that's it then. She's on her own."

He hated to broach the subject again, but there was another option that would put money in their pockets quickly. "You know, you could get a job."

Bitterness reanimated her tired face and Emmett realized he had said the wrong thing. He watched her formulating words, organizing her thoughts, weighing how she should respond. When she spoke she was angry, but also defeated.

"Really? And what would I do? I didn't even have a major when I dropped out of college. So should I go down to the market and get a job as a checkout girl? Well, maybe then we could get a discount on groceries. Oh, no wait, I know. I can . . ."

"Stop it. Don't demean yourself." He stood and paced toward the bay window. Outside, white-crested wavelets dissolved into the mouth of the creek, slender reeds trembling at their gentle touch.

On the verge of tears, her voice quivered. "I've never had a job. What do you suggest I say I'm qualified to do?"

"You're good at organizing things." He came back to her. "You're always on those nonprofit committees. I bet you could get on with one of the catering companies or wedding planners or nonprofits as a project coordinator."

She stopped her downward emotional spiral then. "You think I'd be good at that?" she asked weakly.

"Sure, I mean look at how many things you juggle all the time. You're always balancing a bunch of stuff. More now, but you know what I mean."

"Still, Emmett. I can't do it. Not with Ainslie so sick. She needs me. Every day is different. Every day could be critical and I couldn't be a reliable employee. Would you hire somebody with a child with cancer?"

Emmett sighed. She had a point. She always seemed to have a valid point.

"No. Probably not."

"Well."

"But she is getting better."

"That's true. She is getting better."

"And she's going to go back to school eventually."

"Right."

"So you'll think about it."

"I'll think about it."

"Remember what all those books you're always reading say. This is our new normal."

Lauren wandered into the living room and flopped down on the sofa. "There's nothing else we can do tonight. Let's watch a movie." She clicked on the television and Animal Planet blipped to life.

Emmett slowly settled beside his wife. Suddenly his joints ached and he felt old and weary. He found her hand and slid his fingers through hers. When was the last time they just sat and held hands? Probably not since the first year they were married. She stared at the television, but Emmett could tell she wasn't seeing the screen. She lowered her head onto his shoulder and closed her eyes.

"I'm sorry," Emmett said as he brushed her hair away from her eyes. "I'm so sorry for everything."

CHAPTER 20

The Swing of Things

The doctors suggested they all go out for pizza. "Get back into the swing of things," was how he put it. Ainslie suspected he chose pizza because then she could use both hands and wouldn't have to use a fork. Although her right hand strength had been getting better she was still only a few weeks out of surgery. They recommended another round of chemo, but she would have to get some meat on her bones before they would even consider it.

Ainslie wore a ball cap with a star on the bill, but she was aware that the back of her head was bare. This was the second time she'd lost enough hair to feel a breeze on her scalp. Sloan came in, flopped down on Ainslie's bed, and grabbed the controls for the video game.

"You about ready to go?" she asked as she booted up Super Mario Brothers.

"It's not like I have to put on makeup or fix my hair," Ainslie replied. "Are you going out with Cal tonight?"

"After we eat. Grab a control. I'm gonna kick your butt."

"I don't feel like playing. Don't go out with him tonight. Stay here with me."

"Do you really want to make me feel bad about this?"

"Yes."

"Well, it's working. But I'm still going out with Cal. So now I'll go but I won't have a good time. Is that what you want?"

"Yes."

"Shut up."

Their father called from downstairs. "Girls, let's go!"

Pizza King had good handicap access. Inside, a birthday party was going on. The kids were about Ainslie's age, but she didn't know any of them. They seemed so happy with their stupid hats and colorful birthday cake. She had a friend who always had a birthday party this time of year, but she hadn't received her invitation yet. She thought for sure she'd be invited. Every day Ainslie went through the stacks of cards she still received, but she hadn't found the invite. Maybe she'd been forgotten since she hadn't been to school in so long.

They found a table in the corner perfect for the wheelchair. As they approached, the loud family at the next table stopped talking and began to eat in silence. At their table, a boy about four rested his unblinking eyes on Ainslie. He stared at her when they came in. He stared at her while she was ordering. He never stopped staring as his red-smeared, open mouth moved around and around a wad of dough.

Ainslie put up with it for a while, but his shameless gawk finally made her say, "Dad, please, make that dumb little boy stop staring at me."

Emmett frowned at the situation. This type of behavior from other people was annoying. Her father always told her that while other people shouldn't be rude, that he couldn't exactly pick a fight.

"I can come over there and sit between you two so he can't see you," he suggested.

"Just make him stop."

"His parents should control his behavior," Emmett said loud enough for them to hear, "but let's just ignore it a while longer."

The adults at the other table stole guilty glances at one another.

"I'm tired of it," Ainslie said. She scrunched up her face and leaned toward the child in a menacing way. She stuck out her tongue and snarled like an angry dog. The boy's eyes grew large and he reached for his mother. His lower lip puckered and he dissolved into tears. Ainslie watched his little face turn red as he imploded into a bawling mess. She glanced over at Sloan, who raised her eyebrows, paused in mock disgust, then burst into laughter. Their father opened his mouth to scold both girls, but there was a sudden change in his eyes as well. He started laughing. Their mother just stared at them all with a grin on her face.

"Nicely done, Ainslie," she said. "Very nice." And then she too fell to laughing.

And they were all laughing. The people at the other table were hesitantly staring at them, as if wondering what their table might do next. They gathered their things and the father motioned for the check. The Sullivans continued to laugh while the other people shuffled for the door. The father threw a few bills on the table and followed them out. Even after the other family was gone, everybody at their table snickered and wiped tears. Ainslie's side began to cramp from laughter and it felt so good, so good.

*   *   *

On the way home their father drove slowly along Atlantic Avenue and Ainslie read all the signs marking each house. She loved that the homes on Pawleys had names even though they weren't grand like ranches out West or horse farms in Kentucky. *Idle Awhile, Lost Weekend, The Sandcastle, Safe Harbor.* Ainslie used to know all the people who lived in these houses, but not anymore. Many of the gravel drives had a different SUV each weekend of the summer. When school started back, the strange vehicles stopped coming and it was just natives again. In Ainslie's opinion, this was the best time to be on the beach. Sloan said it was lonely in the fall, but Ainslie liked the chill of the water and the blue-gray haze that tinted the land and sky. Maybe by fall things would be better and she would be allowed out on the beach again.

Ainslie closed her eyes and rested her head against the cold window of her mother's car. Tired. She was so tired of all the things she had to do and all the things she wasn't allowed to do anymore. Her doctor had recommended low-stress events like attending church, but that was a joke. Low stress? What that doctor didn't know was that church people could really get in your face. She hated to be stuck in the congregation traffic jam after the service. She felt as if she were swimming in a sea of butts and knees. Somebody always popped their big head right into your personal space and then you'd have to act all happy to see some stranger, somebody who only ever talked to your parents before. Ainslie had gone to church twice in her wheelchair. The second Sunday, she had asked her mother to head for the elevator as soon as the service was over so she could avoid the crush. Everything just took so much more effort with the wheelchair.

And then there were the kids who stared at you, like that stupid little boy tonight. Sometimes it just didn't seem worth it to leave the house. But that, her mother said, was exactly what the doctor didn't want them to do. Just stay home and hide. But she had shown that little boy. Maybe she had let her good manners slip, but her mother wouldn't punish her. She never got punished anymore. Besides, Sloan and her father had laughed until the people at the other table got in a hurry to pay their bill. The little boy had whimpered all the way out the door. Well, that was just too bad. Maybe he would think again before he gawked at somebody else.

Home appeared at the end of the road and Ainslie squinted to read their sign in the distance. *Painted Lady,* it read in the same script as her grandfather's card business. Maybe the doctor didn't want her hanging out at home, but that had always been her favorite place, so why shouldn't she want to be here? All the doctors, everybody really, was just so full of advice when really, if everybody would just leave her alone, she'd be happier. Ainslie had her own list, mostly things she didn't want to do. Going back to the hospital was definitely at the top of her list of things to avoid. But her parents wanted to drag her back to the hospital for another scan, an MRI. Ainslie was trying to psyche herself up for it, but just the thought of that hospital smell, the cold machines and skimpy green hospital gowns, was enough to make her sick to her stomach.

At home, Ainslie slowly climbed the stairs, brushing off her mother's hand at her elbow. Sloan zipped by her, taking the steps two at a time.

Ainslie knocked softly and pushed open Sloan's door when she said come in. Sloan was seated at her vanity applying makeup.

"You're not supposed to come in here."

"I've been playing with Mr. Crabs every day when Mommy's not looking and I haven't died yet."

Sloan applied mascara.

"Well, if you get sick, don't say I didn't warn you."

"Wanna watch a movie with me?"

"I told you. I'm going out with Cal tonight."

Ainslie picked up her sister's lip gloss and smoothed the tube across her lips.

"I don't want to have that MRI test."

"Well, you don't have a choice. You pretty much have to have that test, so figure out how to use it."

"Use it?"

"Sure. Tell them you won't get the test unless they give you something you really want. What's something you really want? Something they wouldn't ever get you."

"A dog."

"I want a dog too. So let's guilt-trip the parental units into getting us a dog. Why don't you want to have that test?"

"Because it's like a big white cave and it's real loud and scary."

"So tell them that. Tell them it's like totally scary and stuff. Cry if you have to. Then when you've got them all guilty, tell them you'd do it for a dog."

"A real live dog. No more stuffed animals."

"Sounds like a plan to me."

CHAPTER 21

Emancipation

"So that's the deal." Cal was assured of the plan. "All you do is drive my Jimmy. We drop the rental car at that truck stop off 95 near Florence and we're done."

"What's in the car?"

"You don't need to know. See, that's the beauty of the plan. The less you know, the better. You make a thousand dollars. I make four thousand dollars. We're both happy and we drive home."

"So I just drive your car from Miami to Florence and then you drive back home?"

"Yeah. Easy."

"How long a drive is it?"

"It'll take us all weekend. We'll leave Friday and drive through the night. Lie on the beach on Saturday. Pick up the car late Saturday night and drive through to Florence. We'll be back home by late Sunday afternoon with money in our pockets."

Sloan considered his offer. Money in her pocket was something Sloan desperately needed. But people didn't pay that kind of money just to transport a car. It was the something in the car that carried the high price of transportation.

Sloan lowered herself down onto the picnic blanket beside Cal. The stone walls of Atalaya grew around them, crumbly and gray. Palms scratched in the ocean breeze. An old oak cast patterns of shade against their bodies.

"Cal, you're not telling me the whole story. Who asked you to do this?"

He was on his back with his eyes closed. His arms cradled his head. "You don't have to know every single thing. It's just a road trip and I need your help."

He rolled over and stared into her eyes. "Look, you need the money, right? Well, I need the money, too. It's too easy to pass up. A weekend road trip. That's all I'm asking. Two days. Can't you give me two days?"

"It's kind of scary is all."

"Kind of exciting, you mean?"

"No. I mean I don't like doing things and not knowing why. I know this has to do with something illegal."

"Look, I can't tell you anything. I want to leave on Friday. You're not going to let me down, are you?"

"What will I tell my parents?"

"Tell them you're going camping in the mountains. That way you can say there isn't any cell phone reception."

"Why would that matter?"

"Trust me. I'll take care of you. I'll take care of everything. It'll be fun. I just really need you to do this for me." He pulled her close. His lips brushed hers as he whispered, "Come on, Sloan. This is a sweet deal. Like free money."

But, she thought, *nothing is free.*

Still, she could use the cash for the deposit for school. Of course, the tuition was eighteen thousand dollars and it had to be paid by July. She was hoping things would change with her family, that the insurance company would pay, that her college fund would have enough for them to squeak by. She'd thought about calling her grandfather in Jersey to ask for help, but her mother had said no, to be patient and her father would take care of everything. That's what her mother always contended in front of the girls, that their father was strong and in control, that he would solve their problems. But behind her parents' bedroom door Sloan heard the tone of her mother's remarks. And she'd seen her father's reaction over the past few months as he pulled away from them, into himself, spending more time at The Pub and on the beach running, always running.

Sloan had kept silent to Cal about her parents' financial situation, partly from embarrassment and partly, she knew, because she didn't want him to see her flaws. Sloan felt that each day Cal chose to be with her was somehow a gift. She was never as happy as she was with him. Still, something in her made her cautious. It was his swagger, his self-assurance, his ability to manipulate people that Sloan both admired and fell victim to in short order. She hated it and yet was completely unable to stop herself. It was with difficulty that she said, "I don't know, Cal. I'll have to think about it."

"Trust me." He grinned at her. "It'll be fun."

At home, the lights were on for her and she always felt comforted to know her parents thought of her in this small way. Sloan let Cal kiss her, his hands strong in her hair, pulling her toward him in that masculine way that made her forget her name. Their lips moved together, smooth and swollen. She pushed him away.

"I have to go in. It's late."

"God, you're a good kisser."

"I've really got to go in."

"Hey, wait. What about what we talked about?"

"I told you I'd think about it."

He let the SUV idle as she ascended the stairs. Her phone vibrated in her pocket and she snapped it open. The text message envelope was blinking.

U got a grt ass

She waved to him from the front door, and he backed the Jimmy out to the gravel road and took off. She watched his vehicle move away down Atlantic and she felt light as a feather. Energy radiated from her in waves.

She softly clicked open the door and slipped inside the foyer. The television mumbled low. The call of hunger came to her and she remembered fried chicken a lady from a church had brought earlier in the day.

In the den, she stopped short. Her parents were asleep on the sofa, her mother's head against her father's shoulder. Empty wine glasses with pennies of dark red pooled in the bottom. Things seemed different, and then Sloan realized why. They seemed normal. Normal was something she hadn't seen in so long between her parents. Her father twitched and jerked as he was inclined to do when asleep. In the morning, the harsh reality of life would etch their faces, but at least for now, they had peace.

Sloan made her way toward the sympathy food, but in the dining room she was stopped again, this time by looming piles of papers. Very slowly, she walked around the table, leaning over to read. On a pad, her father had written medical expenses. The bottom line made Sloan catch her breath.

Suddenly, she understood. She had a general idea of how much money her father made, and if the insurance didn't come through, her parents would be paying Ainslie's medical bills for the rest of their lives. This was what adults called stark reality. Her father wasn't bluff-

ing when he said she might have to choose a cheaper
college. The truth was, she would be lucky if she got to
go to any school.

And what about Ainslie? Would doctors just stop seeing
her if her parents didn't pay? Would they end up being
a charity case? Would Ainslie have to go to that hospital
for children in Tennessee her father had researched?

Sloan didn't feel hungry anymore. She climbed the
stairs and saw Ainslie's light on. She stopped with her
hand on the railing and considered her sister. Sometimes she wished so strongly for Ainslie to get better
that she ached physically, a hollow pull in her chest that
a writer would describe as despair but which she viewed
as an oddly sucking adrenaline rush.

"Hey, Ains, what are you still doing up?"

"I can't sleep. Sometimes I can't. Mommy doesn't
know."

"Okay."

"Tell me a story. The one about the dolphin in
Charleston."

Sloan climbed into bed beside her sister. They pressed
their bodies together. "Okay." They settled back against
the pillows and Ainslie tucked her hands beneath her
chin and pulled in to her sister.

"So once there was this woman in Charleston who
came back to her house after Hurricane Hugo and her
house was, like, totally destroyed, like moved off the foundation and stuff. She had a hard time getting the front
door open and she pushed and pushed and when she
finally did get the door open she heard this sound. At first
she didn't know what it was, so she followed the sound and
then she's like, oh my God. There was a dolphin thrash-
ing around in three feet of water in the living room."

Ainslie wiggled with delight. "So then the neighbors
come and get the dolphin."

"That's right. It took about ten people to get a tarp

around the dolphin. He was heavy and it took a long time for those people to drag and carry him back out to the ocean. But the people did it right away, before they worried about their smashed houses or anything else. They all went down to the beach and they dragged that dolphin back out into deep water."

"So then he's confused."

"Right. The people were all upset because he was disoriented and they didn't know how to help him."

"And then . . ."

"And then he sort of perked up. He snapped to. He went out a ways and just sat there like he was thinking about which way was the best way to go. They said everybody just stood there silent waiting to see what he would do."

"Then he swam off."

"Then he swam off. And they were all happy."

"I bet that dolphin's still alive. You know, dolphins live to be, like, thirty years old. That's why they get so attached to their pods."

"I bet he's still out there, too."

"He could be one of my dolphins."

"And he could be one of your dolphins. Hey, how are your dolphins?"

"They're good. They come to see me."

"No way. Do you wave to them?"

"No. But they know I'm here. Hey, did you hear Grandma's story about that guy playing golf who had cancer and he was going to die and he got hit by lightning and it fried the cancer?"

"I heard that. And now that guy has lived, like, ten years or something without any cancer."

"That's cool."

"That's supercool."

Chapter 22

Charity

Emmett strained as he hoisted Ainslie's wheelchair onto the boardwalk. His daughter's situation had given him a newfound respect for the guidelines set down by the Americans with Disabilities Act. He used to grumble about the guidelines, but now every place he went, accessibility was the first thing he noticed. Life in a wheelchair would be a challenge; thank goodness that wasn't his daughter's future.

Emmett pushed her down the lumpy, bumpy pier toward The Bait Shop. She sang, "Ahhhhhhh," and her voice vibrated. Sometimes they brought their fishing poles, but today was just a candy run. Emmett was instructed to get as many calories into Ainslie as possible, and he thought a trip to The Bait Shop's old candy counter would do the trick.

The door opened outward, which always presented a problem for wheelchairs, but Ainslie wouldn't need it much longer. She walked around the house on her own. It was only when they were manipulating unfamiliar territory that the doctor wanted Ainslie to still be chaired around, as she called it.

The candy aisle at The Bait Shop was a thing of beauty. Boston Baked Beans, Pixy Stix, and bubble gum hard as a rock until about the fifth chew, when it became a sugar explosion. Emmett remembered the childhood rush of pleasure he used to get from candy. He handed Ainslie a bag and said, "I'll fill one for your sister."

At the counter, Emmett paid for their heavy cache of refined sugar. The doorbell jingled and a young voice said, "Hey, Ainslie."

"Hey, LaShonda."

"What's up?"

"Nothing much."

"When you getting out of that wheelchair?"

"I'm out now. It's just a precaution."

"Oh," LaShonda said. "Well, right on then." She took a Coke from the cooler and grabbed a bag of boiled peanuts before stepping into line behind Emmett.

"Oh, we're finished," Emmett said and stepped aside so she could check out, but he continued his conversation with Bert, the shop owner.

"Look here, girl, you're on this jar," LaShonda said. "Did you know that?"

"No." Ainslie strained to look up on the counter, so LaShonda handed Ainslie the glass pickle jar with her name and photo on the front.

Emmett was silent as he waited for Ainslie's reaction. The child stared at herself. Not one of her most becoming photos, but still a cute one. She glanced up to her father, confused, and then returned to the jar with a look of sorrow so profound he was immediately moved to explain, but how he couldn't fathom.

"It's like you're homecoming queen," LaShonda chirped. "And I'm going to be one of the first people to vote for you. I'm sure you'll win." With that the girl plunked all her change into the jar where it chinked past a couple of dollar bills to join a thin layer of coins at the bottom.

There was a sea change then, a shift in his daughter Emmett recognized, a decision to always accept the slightest nudge in a positive direction. It was one of the reasons he loved her so.

Emmett took the jar and read the small print before Ainslie had the chance. It was a sincere, if inaccurate account of what was happening to his family. The jar said Ainslie needed an operation but their family had no insurance. Well, in effect, the part about the insurance was true at the moment, although the spinal operation was behind them. The jar seemed like a cruel joke, such an impotent act that made him feel all the more impotent in the face of the looming invoices for Ainslie's operation, another round of chemo, more physical therapy.

And now Emmett had to tell Lauren, and what would she think of this? This intended kindness would become a source of pain for them, as everything that happened to them now seemed to.

"Who's responsible for this?" Emmett asked.

"Some church, I don't know," Bert replied.

"I've got to find out."

"Take that number there. I'd call that."

Back in the car, Emmett called the number from the jar and it rang so many times he was ready to hang up, when a woman answered with a soothing voice.

"Oh, Mr. Sullivan," she said. "I was going to call you today. If you could come by the church, I'd like to give you a check for all the donations that have come in."

"A check."

"Yes. About eight thousand dollars."

"What?"

"Donations for Ainslie are about eight thousand dollars, so far. We expect a little more to come in, of course."

"What is it, Daddy?" Ainslie said. She touched him on the arm. "Daddy, what?"

Emmett was in a daze. How had his life become so unreal?

"Oh, okay, well, thank you. Uh, can you tell me how to get to your church?"

Emmett waited patiently as Ainslie pulled herself up the stairs to their porch. Doctors said it would be good exercise, but it was difficult to watch, and Emmett hovered behind her every step. Before they reached the top, Lauren was outside.

Ainslie pushed past her mother's proffered hand and walked into the house.

"Emmett," Lauren said when their daughter had gone. "We have to talk."

"I agree."

"Some reporter called. He asked about the insurance issue. I guess word got out. I mean, I don't know how long we can really keep this to ourselves."

"Everybody knows."

"How do you know that?"

Emmett held up the check.

"What's that for?"

"From a church. To help us out."

"Do we know these people?"

"No. It's the whole community. There are pickle jars with Ainslie's photo on them all over town."

Her eyes grew frantic and wide. "No. What are we going to do?"

Emmett had expected this. "How about we take the money and we say thank you and we use it to pay off some of our bills?"

"Think we should?"

"If we don't take it, the money will just end up donated to a charity of some sort and let's face it, we're a damn good charity right now."

"No. We're not a charity. We're not. We can take care of things. I don't want any charity money. You have to make it stop."

"There's no way I can do that. And even if I could stop it, what's wrong with letting the community help us? Lord knows, you've spent enough time volunteering and raising money for the less fortunate. Well, guess what, babe? Those less fortunate people are us."

"Stop it! That's not true! Don't you have any pride?"

"I've got plenty of pride, but this isn't just about us anymore. This has turned into something larger than us. People care about Ainslie and we shouldn't deprive her of knowing how much other people care."

"I don't want people feeling sorry for us. Just make the insurance pay and make her get better. I don't want charity money. I don't want to talk to reporters. I don't want to act like everything's okay when it's not! Everything is definitely not okay!"

She was shaking and he touched her hand, but she pulled away. She wasn't ready to accept even this, his small gesture of comfort. Had he really expected that she would warm to this money quickly?

She said, "I'm sorry. I'm sorry. I'm just not doing so well today."

Emmett folded her into his arms and pulled her tightly against his chest.

"Everybody has their bad days. You're allowed a few. This can be one of yours."

Lauren pushed away and swiped her eyes with a shirt sleeve.

"I don't want Ainslie to see me like this. It might scare her."

"Shit, Lauren, don't you think she knows we cry? Surely she expects everybody who loves her to cry about this."

Right now he wanted to cry, too. He wanted to weep out of gratitude for the check that would help them last another month. Hopefully by then Larry would have forced the hand of almighty commercial greed to reason. If not, then Larry said their next step was to go public, but now that door had been opened for them. Emmett was going to call that reporter back and start generating interest in Ainslie's case. Lauren would fight him on this, but Emmett had decided. He would do it, even though it was going to be a fresh hell.

CHAPTER 23

Road Trip

How many beaches would Sloan sit on in her life? She hadn't realized until this year just how different beaches could be. At home, the beach was flat, no trees, a highly reflective surface with lots of smooth edges where heavy sand blended into an earthy sea. In Mexico, the sand was white and the water was transparent and alive. And although the atmosphere here in Miami Beach was as beautiful as in Cancún, most of the wildlife was stretched out on the sand and slathered in SPF 8.

Sloan loved it here. The strip sparkled with Art Deco architecture. Palms pressed against pastel hotels. Chrome-trimmed towers with round lettered neon signs had a glamour that made her happy. Sloan had read there were more than four hundred renovated buildings in the Art Deco District of Old Miami Beach, and Cal had acquiesced when she asked to drive around sightseeing last night. He'd let her select a hotel she liked and they'd lucked into a room. She noticed that Cal paid cash for gas, food, and now their room. He'd given a false name to guest services and produced a fake ID to the same effect. All these things Sloan did not comment upon. Questions from her would do nothing but disrupt Cal's apparently well-oiled plan.

And Sloan had to admit that so far everything had been wonderful, the way things always were with Cal. He lived a lifestyle filled with possibilities Sloan never considered. He roamed freely from one excitement to the next.

Sloan was stomach down on one of the hotel's lounge chairs. Clad in a black bikini Cal had bought her in Mexico, Sloan was one of the more modest women on the beach. Cal sat beside her, cross-legged in the sand. He sipped beer under his forward tipped hat. Sloan noticed an almost imperceptible turn of Cal's head with the passing of each slender, tanned woman.

"I need another beer," he announced. "You want anything?"

"No, thanks."

When he had gone, Sloan lowered her head onto her forearms. A heat sensation crawled along her back and she wondered if her mother would ask how she'd gotten sunburned in the mountains. Sunburn was just one of those things she'd stop worrying about so much since she'd met Cal. She kept expecting her phone to ring, for it to be her mother and she would be busted. But Cal made her turn her phone off. He'd gotten them both disposable phones and instructed her to call him and only him. "No phone records," he had said. And she had felt her stomach tighten.

The sun was intense. A bead of sweat trickled down her side.

"Hello, chica." Sloan shielded her eyes as she twisted to look up at a dark figure against the dazzling sun. What she could see were Hawaiian print boards and a UM shirt.

"Verulo."

"What a surprise to see you."

"I could say the same."

"Where's Calhoun?"

"Cal went to get a beer. Are we meeting you?"

Verulo sat in the sand beside her. His skin glistened with sweat. His reflective sunglasses made Sloan uncomfortable.

"Let's talk about something else," Verulo said.

Sloan wanted to sit up, but she didn't want to fumble with her bathing suit top in front of him. She'd never felt so completely undressed by a man, and she couldn't even see his eyes.

"Are you enjoying your vacation in Miami?" Verulo asked.

"It's wonderful here. Just beautiful."

"As beautiful as Mexico?"

"Yes. But in a different way."

"Okay. Now I'm asking you. How are you involved in our business?"

Sloan held her breath.

"Um, I don't know anything about your business," she said. "I'm just helping Cal drive a car somewhere."

"Don't play stupid, chica. You weren't supposed to come."

"Why?"

"There was no need for you to become involved."

"I'm not involved in anything."

"Yes. You are now."

Sloan felt relief when she saw Cal approaching with a beer in hand.

"Hey man, you need a drink?" Cal said to Verulo.

"No, thank you. I bring you this." He handed Cal a black leather pouch. "There are keys and instructions and your due."

Cal took it. "Thank you."

"Don't read it here. Read it in your room. We have two rules. You touch anything, you die."

"Damn. That's harsh. What's the second rule?"

"No drugs. Think clearly. Understand?"

"Got it."

"Leave now."

"Right now?"

"Yes."

Sloan struggled to her feet as the men stood. She tied her top and then drew Cal's shirt around her.

"It was wrong to involve her."

"I can take care of my own business," Cal said.

Verulo turned to her, his body language blocking out Cal. She could feel his eyes behind his shades. "If you ever get tired of him . . ."

Cal made a tight laugh. Sloan simply stared at Verulo, her face, she hoped, expressionless. She knew her own sunglasses masked her strange twinge of pleasure at Verulo's aggressive act. Still, she didn't answer, and he walked away down the beach parallel with the ocean until he blended in with the shiny beach throng and dissolved into the distance.

"Well, that was just a creepy buzz kill," she said, as if she hadn't felt the slightest thrill.

"Get your shit and let's get out of here."

"Are we leaving now? Aren't we going to stay for dinner?"

"No. What the fuck, Sloan? Don't you see? They expect us to get out of town."

Sloan gathered her things and they wove their way between sunbathers until they reached the sidewalk and crossed the street to their lustrous hotel. The smell of oily beach bodies lingered in the lobby and wrapped around them in the elevator. Sloan tingled at the thought of Verulo's attention, and Cal was still fuming with his own reaction to it, although he tried not to let it show.

In their room, Sloan walked out onto the balcony to take a last look down on the pale strip of beach. She leaned over the railing, taking in all the activity, the shoppers and skaters and ripped guys with glistening bodies. She could smell the spice of ethnic food and hear the laughter from a party four stories below. She could live here. Florida was artistic and exciting and free. Like Cancún, only closer to home.

Cal stepped onto the balcony behind her. She thought it was to fuss at her for procrastinating, but instead, his hands found her hips and he moved up behind her. She felt him hard against her through her thin bikini bottom. He wrapped his arms around her and slid a hand down her front into her bathing suit bottom and into her. Their smells mingled, musky and strong—sun and oil and sex. She held the railing and pushed back into him. He ripped her suit to the side and entered her and they made love as she watched the world pass below them.

"We've got to leave soon," he said when they were sated. "You can jump in the shower first." He stretched out on the bed and clicked on the television. Sloan showered quickly, using the hotel's sweet-smelling body wash. She twisted her hair up and pinned it under a floppy hat. Once she dressed and put her sunglasses on, she was again that twenty-five-year-old she had been in Cancún.

Sloan was packing the guest bottles of shampoo and soaps into her bag when Cal said, "Don't take those. Don't take anything from here."

Cal paid cash at checkout. They retrieved his SUV from a garage a block away from their hotel. He was cautious about everything and Sloan felt ill with anticipation at what they were about to do. Cal directed her to the parking lot of a gay bar where buff, tanned guys in baggy madras shorts and tight T-shirts smoked and flirted.

"There it is," he said, pointing to a nondescript midsize car. "Just be cool and follow me." He swiftly started the car and pulled away.

She followed close behind in the Jimmy, fearful she would lose sight of him. She wasn't used to driving in large cities, so she switched off the radio and concentrated on the road. They merged onto the interstate and soon began to pass plant nurseries and citrus groves. Her phone rang and she fumbled to answer it.

"How you doing?" Cal asked.

"I'm fine. I think."

"We're on the interstate now. Don't tail too close. Stay back a few cars and keep your eyes on me. We're not going to leave this road until we reach Florence, so just relax. The hard part's over."

"Okay."

"If I should get pulled over, you know to drive straight on home, right?"

"Right."

"No hesitation. You go straight home. Say you understand."

"I understand."

"Okay, call me if you need me."

CHAPTER 24

Holding Hands

Ainslie should have been ashamed. But she wasn't. It hadn't taken long to extract the promise of a puppy if she would only submit to the MRI. When her parents said yes, Sloan had taken her to Litchfield Books and bought her an awesome dog book. They'd been discussing things and they couldn't decide between a cute lap dog to sleep with them or a big lab to play with.

The day of the MRI, Miss Vivian came to see her. Ainslie had shown her pictures of the dogs she liked. Once Ainslie was loaded into the giant rumbling machine, she started going over dog photos in her mind. She could see their well-formed noses and alert ears. She imagined what their fur felt like and how they would smell. She went over the pros and cons of each type of dog until she drifted into a dog-induced trance, and before she knew it, the MRI was over and she was on her way home.

Good results meant she got to avoid another round of

chemo and the time to get her puppy was all that much closer. A bad test meant more chemo and a longer wait while her white blood cell counts recovered. She wasn't even allowed to have Mr. Crabs back yet. The doctor said nothing that poops.

Sloan stayed with her while their mother went to the hospital's financial office. She told Ainslie that every time the hospital or a doctor did anything their parents had to sign papers promising to pay.

"So what about the insurance?" Ainslie asked.

"Dad says Larry's all over it. He says to trust Larry."

"I don't think Mommy trusts Larry."

"Larry's a lush."

"What's that mean?"

"It means he drinks."

"Is he an alcoholic?"

"Geez, Ains. I don't know."

"Do you think we'll get the dog?"

"We'll get the dog."

That night, their family grilled steaks and celebrated the possibility of a clean scan. After dinner, they all went for a walk on the beach. Ainslie struggled with the shifting sand, her balance still a challenge, until they reached the hard-packed foundation closer to the water. Ainslie thought to herself that if she had a dog, she could let it run. There were no leash laws observed on the beach and familiar pets often greeted you long before their owners appeared in the distance.

Their parents walked in front of them along the shoreline's curve. A new moon shimmered full on the water, round and bright, which meant high tides. Their parents used to hold hands when they walked, but they hadn't done that in a while. Did worry make you forget things? Things like how much you love somebody? Like that somebody wanted to hold your hand?

Ainslie walked between her parents and took each of their hands. Sloan was off to the water's edge and they all three stopped to watch her move something in the wet sand with her toe.

"What is it?" Ainslie called, but her sister didn't hear her.

They walked to where she stood.

"It's gone. I felt something move under my foot."

"Mole crab," Ainslie said. She dug her toes into the sand and wiggled her feet around. In only a few seconds, she reached below her foot and found a grumpy little mole crab, a tiny armadillo curled in on itself.

"Here, you can hold it, but watch out for its spike," Ainslie said.

"No, thank you," Sloan said. "Are those creepy little things all under the beach?"

"Pretty much."

"Gross."

"Ainslie, put that thing down," her mother said as she walked on. "I'm sure it's just crawling with germs."

They went on down the beach, the tide washing in so quickly that if they walked too far they would have to cut through houses and take the road back home. But it didn't matter, they simply walked. Ainslie held her crab, stopping occasionally when she thought she felt another one underfoot.

"Hey," Sloan said. "Check it out."

Ainslie tore her attention away from her crab search.

"Wow," she whispered.

Their parents were growing dimmer in the distance of

the night. As they strolled, their mother's hair blew around her head in a fantastic swirl. Their father's shirt billowed against his lean body. They walked slowly, talking. They held hands.

CHAPTER 25

Making Waves

LaShonda locked the café door behind the last two lunch guests and cleared the tables. The only remaining person was Sloan, who had college catalogs spread out on the table before her. Her friend stared at her laptop, a perturbed expression on her face. LaShonda set two cappuccinos down, picked up one of the heavy catalogs and flipped through its colorful pages.

Swirls of graphic designs crawled the pages. Photographs popped of students chatting on a tree-lined campus, staring at giant computer screens, forming massive blocks of clay, painting huge canvases. Everything at this school seemed larger than life.

"Wow. This looks like a cool place," LaShonda said as she perused the thick publication. "I see why you want to go here."

LaShonda had agreed to help Sloan slog through financial aid applications. LaShonda had been through the entire lengthy process herself a few months before, so she was somewhat of an expert on financial aid. She knew they were too late to apply for aid for the upcoming fall semester. They were looking to the January session now.

The first thing Sloan had to do, before any other aid option would be available to her, was fill out the Free Application for Federal Student Aid, but she was stalled by the part about her parents' financial situation.

"I have no idea how to fill this out," Sloan complained. "How much property do we own? Does that mean my dad's office, too? We don't own our whole house, so how do I tell them that? I can get my dad's tax information, but how do I explain that my parents are hundreds of thousands of dollars in debt and that I need financial aid for everything because we have no money. And I mean *no money*."

"I didn't have all those complications you have, but seriously, they're not going to give you every penny you need anyway. I mean, even with my dad reporting less than thirty thousand dollars a year, I couldn't get all the money I needed. That's why I'm working here and why I help out selling shrimp on weekends. You need to find out about student work programs."

Sloan started as if LaShonda had just slapped her. Her heart was set on this fancy art school, but she didn't seem particularly skilled at making things happen in that direction. She had been floating along, just expecting everything to turn out for her. LaShonda had heard people say artists were dreamy sorts of folks, people who had a hard time with deadlines and forms and things everybody else took for granted. Maybe there was some truth to that theory.

"Hey," LaShonda said. "Do you even know what the bottom line is on Savannah?"

"What do you mean?"

"I mean, once you pay tuition, books, room and board, activity fees, computer lab fees, all kinds of extra stuff they tack on, what's the bottom line for a year at your fancy school?"

"I don't know."

"Well, look here." LaShonda flipped to the back of the thick catalog to a section marked Schedule of Tuition and Fees. She set about writing everything down and soon had a figure. She whistled.

"You won't like this." LaShonda slid her figures across the table to Sloan. The bottom line was more than thirty-five thousand dollars per year.

"Shit. I thought it was like eighteen."

"Then you didn't add in all the fees and all your living expenses."

Tears edged Sloan's eyes. She stuck out her bottom lip in a pout. LaShonda always walked a thin line when it came to her friendship with Sloan. While Sloan was one of the few girls at school willing to cross the color line, she was also somebody who didn't really seem to need friends. So when Sloan went away into her own world LaShonda tried not to take it personally.

But for all her independence, Sloan was weak. She was one of those girls who had always been taken care of, never made to work. What was that word for it? Sheltered. Even LaShonda, who lived on a remote island, sometimes knew more about the world than Sloan.

"So what were the other schools you applied to? Have you heard back from them?" LaShonda asked her.

"Yeah, I got into all of them but UNC. I got accepted at USC and the College of Charleston."

"I checked into the College of Charleston. It's like thirty grand a year too if you live in the dorms, but at least then you could use in-state scholarship money. The Palmetto Scholarship is nearly seven thousand and you've got the grades for that."

"That leaves more than twenty grand."

"Charleston's an expensive place to live. You could live at home and drive."

"Wow. What fun."

"You're way past the point where fun is what's important. What about USC? You could use the Palmetto Scholarship and go there practically for free. Why didn't you apply last year?"

"Because my sister was going through chemotherapy and my parents didn't have time to think about me."

"So why didn't you do it?"

"Because I assumed I'd be going out of state."

"In-state might be the place for you to start and then you could transfer."

"Charleston does have a good art department," she said without enthusiasm. "But I don't want to take English 101 and History of the Civil War. I want computer animation and illustration and digital photography."

"I thought you wanted to do sculpture."

"I want studio classes, too, but I need to be able to use the latest technology. I want all art, all the time. I don't want to waste my time doing something mundane just to get a degree."

Sloan's attitude was wearing thin. It was time for a little tough love.

"Maybe you should get a job. Live with your parents for a year and save your money."

"Are you kidding me? There's no way. I'd have to live at home and save money for two, maybe three years before I'd be able to go to Savannah."

"Okay, then. Let's look at that application again. So, just guess. About how much money does your dad make?"

"I think about a hundred and fifty a year."

LaShonda sucked in a little breath. "Really? He makes *that much* money?"

"Yeah, really. That's why I didn't apply for financial aid before. My parents thought my dad made too much money." She held up an application. "Expected family contribution? Right now, that would be a big fat zero."

"Maybe you should go to the community college."

"LaShonda, come on. Community college is great if you want to be a teacher like you do, but there's nothing there for me. No art classes that'll transfer for me. It would be a waste of my time."

"Maybe you can move to Georgia and establish residency there. That way you can qualify for in-state tuition."

"That won't help. Savannah isn't a state school. It's private, so I don't think they care where their students are from."

LaShonda threw up her hands. "What do you want from me? I can't help you if every time I suggest something you tell me why it won't work."

"I'm sorry, but things are just more simple for you."

"And just how's that? Why do you think things are so easy for me?"

"I didn't say easy. I said simple. Your life's not so complicated. You want to be a teacher. You have a lot of places you can go to school. What I want to do is very specialized. Not many schools teach it, so I have limited choices."

"Poor you. Maybe you need to go ask your boyfriend to help you pay for school."

"Cal doesn't have any money. People don't have as much money as you think they do. People have stuff like houses and cars and things, but not money."

"Why would you date him if he didn't have money?"

"I like him."

LaShonda studied her.

"I think," Sloan said. "I don't know . . . I think I might love him."

"You got no business falling in love with Cal Wanna-maker."

"Why not?"

"I'm just saying."

"You're just saying what? You're not saying much of anything except you don't like him. Well, you know what? His parents don't give him very much money. He's a smart guy and makes most of his own money."

"He has a job?"

"He's got ways."

"Sounds like my stupid cousin Ronald to me. There are always ways to make money. That don't mean a thing."

Sloan was silent.

"Girl, I don't care what you say. There are those people and then there's the rest of us. We're pretty much on our own, so get used to it. You're just in their club right now. You won't be staying. They're not really your friends. I don't see you asking any of them to help you with your financial aid."

Once again, LaShonda had hit the mark. Sloan had never admitted to any of Cal's friends that her parents were going bankrupt.

"That's a shitty thing to say. You are *so* wrong."

"I call it like I see it. Money makes it easy to get what you want. Makes it easy to want too much. Easy to walk away from mistakes. A little bit of money can make you think you deserve things you don't necessarily deserve."

Sloan cut her eyes at her but curbed some submerged impulse. She took a sip of her coffee and said, "Look, LaShonda. I don't think I'm better than you."

LaShonda smirked. "You're the only one."

"Why do you say that?"

"Shit, girl. Every weekend I sit out by the side of the road with my daddy selling shrimp and all them women from Lafayette Isle come buy our catch. They pull up and let those big SUVs idle and belch fumes all over us while they talk us down on the price of a pound of shrimp. They flit around in those little tennis skirts gossiping about all their neighbors like we're deaf-mutes. Like what we think about their people don't count."

"I'm sorry."

"Why you apologizing? It's not your fault."

Sloan looked out at the lawn where sprinkler heads had popped up, spewing dandelions of mist.

"I do find out all kinds of stuff that way," LaShonda said. "I heard something about your boyfriend's mom just the other day."

This tweaked Sloan's interest and she cocked an eyebrow.

"There was two Isle women talking about her. Her name's Bitsy Wannamaker, right?"

"Right."

"They said she's got a drinking problem. They said she was being shipped off to one of those spa rehabs out in Arizona or some place."

"Really?"

"Yeah, they talked about how they saw her out at Al's by the Creek sound asleep in one of the booths. They said soon as her husband saw she nodded off he jerked her up and dragged her out to their car. Pretty funny, huh?"

"No. I don't think it's funny at all."

"Why? It's not like she's your mother-in-law or something."

"She's been nice to me."

"Well, she never was nice to me. Guess maybe it makes me feel better to know those people ain't so perfect."

"Is that what you think? That people in big houses have perfect lives?"

"I'd trade problems. Think about it. If you had your

boyfriend's money, you wouldn't be sitting here wondering about financial aid."

"You know, I don't want to talk about this anymore. That's their private business." Sloan started packing up her books, shoving her laptop back into its case. "And I've got a little bit of advice for you. You need to learn to mind your own business."

CHAPTER 26

The Way Home

A few miles south of Pawleys lay Georgetown, a fishing village generally spared the coast's influx of tourists with their demanding ways and tired, unruly children. Emmett drove across the highway bridge, turned left, and worked his way through a neighborhood of low-slung Lowcountry houses, Georgians with wide verandahs, and a sprinkling of tall Victorians. Along Front Street, restaurants and bars opened back decks to a handsome boardwalk along the Sampit River. Among the pleasure boats, a tour boat rigged to look like a pirate ship was docked and from her deck Blackbeard called to the thin tourist crowds of summer. Diners sipped wine beneath hanging baskets of festive flowers. Emmett frequently brought his family here for Sunday brunch. That was, of course, before they'd started pinching pennies.

Emmett parked across the street from the town hall and courthouse in a lot under a giant oak. It was his habit to always find the shady spot. Emmett was here to catch up on issues that affected his company and home, like beach renourishment, growing development, and increasing traffic problems. Today, the South Carolina Department of Transportation was meeting with locals to discuss the growth and traffic increase along Highway 17. Emmett had a number of projects in the works that could be affected. His daughter was also interested to learn about the county's plan for beach renourishment, since scientists theorized that drastic beach change could confuse mother turtles returning to familiar spots to lay their clutches of golf-ball eggs.

He stopped on his way in to read the historic marker in front, stalling to avoid conversation with a gathering of men in seersucker suits and bow ties at the top of the stairs. The marker said the yellow building with white trim was Classical Revival, designed in the early 1800s by Robert Mills, who also designed the Washington Monument.

Inside, a board on an easel directed him to the room for the DOT meeting. The board also had directions to chambers for a case pending between the Southern Environmental Law Center, which represented conservationists and residents, against Wannamaker & Pinckney, one of the area's biggest developers. Emmett had never worked for W&P. His was a small shop with only five employees, including himself, so Emmett had never gone after one of the enormous jobs that kept pushing natives into the interior of the country while the superrich ringed the coastline.

But there was another reason he hadn't approached Trip Wannamaker and his massive W&P. They had what Emmett considered a scorched-earth policy when it came to development. They'd take a pristine site, completely denude it of native trees and plant water-thirsty ornamentals that withered in the punishing Carolina sun. To compensate, they'd irrigate like crazy. But Emmett worked toward sustainable design with more drought tolerance, mostly native plants and collection ponds and cisterns that provided free water independent of the city.

Another issue was run-off control. When buildings and parking lots took the place of land that held water, there was the problem of where the displaced water would go. Once again, holding ponds were an answer, unless, of course, the area was so saturated the excess couldn't be contained. That was the reason wetlands were not appropriate for construction projects. But tell that to W&P. Their lawyers were fighting to allow construction of a mega upscale community along the Waccamaw River. They had purchased 5,000 acres with the intention of capitalizing on what they thought was a loophole in restrictions concerning man-made sites. The land they purchased was wetlands formed by rice farmers flooding fields for cultivation before the Civil War. W&P wanted to call their new development Waccamaw Plantation Pointe, but conservationists wanted to call it an animal sanctuary.

Of course, there were design guidelines and ordinances in place on a local level, but those were routinely ignored by council members who didn't understand them or didn't care. That's where Caroline Crawford came in. She was a good city manager. She understood things, knew how to get things done, as well as how to prevent things from happening. Caroline tried to guide the council in the right direction. She had supported a tax break on infill projects, but the council had voted it down. So there was no incentive for developers to contain sprawl and DOT was struggling to keep up with the road improvements needed to handle the extra traffic. To Emmett, local government, state government, and developers were all one big cluster fuck.

Still, there was no stopping developers. The deepest pockets eventually won. Even if the tree huggers defeated W&P this time, the company would merely wait another three years and launch another attack, hoping for a change of bench in chambers or new town leadership that could be bought.

And sometimes larger companies went ahead with their plans—fines, penalties and negative newspaper coverage be hanged. Most people had short memories, and a few years down the road, nobody would remember or even care that a few thousand animals were rendered homeless, that unlucky neighbors were flooded, or that the floodplain corridor was permanently scarred.

Through a glass door at the end of the hall, Emmett saw Caroline on a cast iron bench in the courtyard, her smooth legs ending in four-inch heels. Her hair fell around her face in that way that made Emmett swallow hard. He pushed through the door into the inner courtyard. She smiled upon seeing him and swung her hair behind a shoulder.

"Well, hey, stranger. Long time no see," she purred.

"How's city life?"

"Been better. Been worse." She took a drag on her cigarette, a habit Emmett found appalling. How he could be so attracted to somebody who smoked was a mystery to him, but Caroline's danger vibe was what he liked. She was all business on the surface, but underneath lived a woman who drank too much and danced when she felt like it. She was a woman who embraced desires. She smoked and ate chocolate and slept with any man she wanted.

He let his guard down then, only for a fleeting moment. *Damn.* She'd seen him scanning her. A fleeting second of desire, but she'd recognized it as quickly as if he'd spilled his guts onto the ground at her glossy shoes.

"You'd never cheat," she teased.

"No."

"So why do we go through this every time we're around each other?"

"I don't know. Maybe I just like to think about it."

"Well, maybe you shouldn't just think about it."

"I can't."

"You can. You just won't."

He shrugged and shoved his hands into his pockets.

"Suit yourself." She pitched her cigarette down on the walk and ground it out. Another habit Emmett found unacceptable, but he really liked her shoes.

"You sitting in on the hearing on the Wannamaker deal?" he asked.

"I am, but it won't be decided today."

"You and I both know it's just a waiting game."

"Oh, I don't know. They walked away from Sandy Island."

"For now."

"Right. For now."

"But this is a much bigger deal."

"True. What do you care? You should hope they get it, then you could get the job."

"I won't work for W&P."

"Why not? Too pure? You could make them better corporate citizens."

He snorted. "Don't make me laugh."

"It's going to happen, Emmett. You may as well get on the gravy train."

He frowned.

"Stop it with the look. I just work here. I don't make the rules." She stood and smoothed her skirt, running her hands down her sides. She stopped at the door before she made her exit and turned to him.

"Wannamaker's going to run for county council," she said.

"You're shitting me."

She grinned. "I shit you not."

They paused another second.

She said, "The offer stands."

He just nodded.

The door swished shut behind her. Emmett considered her invitation. It was attractive. He'd thought about it many times. He'd thought about it many, many times. He'd imagined throwing her down on her desk in the corner of this building and turning those spiked heels to the sky. He'd pull her silky hair until she arched up to him and he'd taste her neck and that deep valley between her breasts and he'd make her say his name. She'd say, "Emmett" in her throaty smoker's voice. He wanted her. His entire body ached for her. He could do it. Just once he'd hold her in his arms; she'd cradle him in the curve of her hips and he'd fuck her and then he'd be done with her. He could do it and get past this fantasy and move on. It was doable.

His brain abandoned him then. He focused on her office, hoping he could catch just another second with her before she moved into chambers. He wanted to tell her he accepted her proposal. The carpeting hushed his steps and made his stride easy as he rounded the corner and saw her, just a sliver of her in her office. At the last second before the door shut, Trip Wannamaker stepped into sight and rested his hand on the curve of Caroline's ass.

Profound clarity rushed him. Anger crawled his body like a heat wave. Shame seared his heart. He checked behind him, but there was no one else in the corridor. *Stupid. Stupid.* Had he really thought her interest sincere? There was no way he could sit through a boring municipal meeting now. He was opening his cell phone ready to pretend he was in deep conversation as he made for the exit, but he was recognized by a huddle of citizen property tax watchers. In the South, it was bad form not to acknowledge your neighbors. He had no choice but to stop.

"How's that little girl of yours?"

"Ainslie's doing fine, thank you."

"I see her picture in the stores and all around."

"Yes. Everybody's been just wonderful. Thank you for asking."

Blah, blah, blah. Emmett couldn't deal with this. He nodded and made polite replies until he saw his chance and ducked out. Finally at his truck, he was ready to drive off when the passenger door opened and Caroline jumped in.

"What's this?" Emmett said.

"Look. I don't know exactly what you saw back there," she started.

"Caroline, get out of my truck."

"But it's not what you think."

"He had his hand on your ass. It is definitely what I think."

This was a new tension that buzzed between them. He stared ahead while she searched for the right thing to say.

"Can you keep your mouth shut for me?" she finally asked, her eyes darting back across the road where people were beginning to leave the building.

"Why? Scared your little tryst will go public? Well, fear not. I won't be the one to blow your deal with Wannamaker. Just tell me, what's he paying you to help out with his little project?"

"It's not like that."

"It's either that or you're going to tell me you're in love and then I'm going to call you a liar to your face. So go ahead. Tell me you're in love right after you propositioned me in the courtyard."

"It's just sex."

"You're a whore. Get out of my truck."

"Emmett, don't do this. We're friends."

"We're nothing of the sort. Fuck you and fuck Wannamaker. Now get out of my truck before I cause a scene."

"Please don't do something you'll regret."

"What does that mean? Are you threatening me?"

"No. Don't misunderstand."

"So *you* don't misunderstand, I'll speak real slow. Get. Out. Right. Now."

She stepped out and when she closed the passenger door she placed her palm flat against the window in a pleading gesture. Emmett wanted to slam his truck into DRIVE and peel out of the parking lot. Instead he drove away calmly to avoid drawing attention. Shame and anger muddled his thoughts. What was he thinking? Whatever made him consider knocking around with Caroline Crawford a good idea?

He was such an idiot. She was just a politician playing all the angles, and apparently everybody. But who was he? He wasn't powerful. He wouldn't be able to help her in any way, so perhaps her interest in him was a sincere attraction. No. Women like Caroline weren't sincere. They were predatory. Maybe she got a kick taking another woman's man. Who knew what her game was?

Thank God he hadn't done it. Thank God he'd escaped before he made the worst mistake of his life. So this was the architecture of immorality—one part desire, one part neediness, one part stupidity.

Emmett found himself back at his office but he couldn't remember the drive there. He hoped none of his employees could see him sitting in his truck, staring at his concrete building jutting from the middle of this hardwood forest. Birds called. Squirrels jumped from one tree to another, sending a limb rattling down to land soundlessly in the thick blanket of long-leaf pine needles.

He reached in his shirt pocket and removed a five-thousand-dollar check, his second installment of community goodwill. He'd forgotten to take it to the bank. Who forgets to deposit money like that? This was a literal reality check and he needed it right now. He needed to be reminded there were still good people in the world. This money was a sign that not everyone was greedy and unprincipled.

The guys at The Pub, all hard-working, hourly paid men, had handed him five one-hundred dollar bills and then they all went back to drinking beer as if nothing had transpired. They didn't ask questions. All they knew was his family needed help. But instead of helping his own family, Emmett had been ready to bring them shame, to add to their already horrible life by doing something selfish and destructive. And for what? For an orgasm? For a stolen moment of personal pleasure?

Emmett pulled the bills from his pocket. Cash money. He should take the family out tonight. They needed a little reprieve. Larry was getting ready to file the lawsuit against Common Good and things were only going to get more complicated for everyone from this point forward. He'd take his girls out to eat and maybe to a movie. He'd help them forget, if only for a while, that they were an unhappy crew. He'd recommit himself to fighting the insurance company. He'd be home more. He'd make amends. Things would turn out okay.

Still sitting in his truck, Emmett called home. Lauren answered.

"Hey," he said, more lively than he felt.

"How'd your meeting or whatever go?" she asked. He could hear exhaustion in her voice. It made him feel even more guilty.

"Fine. Everything's fine. Let's go out to eat tonight. I think we need to have a little fun."

"Do we have the money for that?"

"Let me take care of it, okay?"

"Okay."

"Fancy or low key?"

"Chicken and Waffles?" she said. It was Ainslie's favorite place. And cheap.

"Low key it is. I'll be home around six to get y'all."

Emmett clicked off the phone and considered what he would tell his daughter when she asked about beach renourishment efforts. He thought of the cumbersome sea turtle mothers and their struggles up the beach to familiar nesting territory. If something were amiss, they would return to the sea without laying their eggs. He understood the creatures' plight. All he wanted to do was lay his burdens down, but his home had become so strange that he found it hard to recognize.

CHAPTER 27

Invisible

Sloan had purchased a gift certificate to Al's and movie tickets for Mother's Day. It was strange to have a thousand dollars hidden in her closet. She'd never had so much money, and while it should have made her giddy, it only made her feel selfish and dirty. So she had purchased the gifts and Ainslie had drawn a card and much to Sloan's relief, her parents hadn't asked questions.

"Look," she told them. "I'll stay with Ainslie. I never get to stay with her anymore. We'll be fine."

"Yeah, Mommy," Ainslie said. "Please go do something with Daddy. We need a break from each other."

Sloan urged her mother to dress sexier.

"You look so pretty now," she said, and the expression that came to her mother's face was strange and distant.

"I do look more like I did when I was younger." She peered into the mirror over the dresser and leaned in to examine herself more closely. She pulled the skin on

her face up and away. "Now, I'm thirty." She let go. "Forty."
Up again. "Thirty." Down. "Forty."

"Mommy, you're weird," Ainslie said.

She sighed then and said, "I guess losing weight does
have benefits. Your dad said I looked nice the other
day."

"You always look nice, Mom." Ainslie hung on her
mother's shoulder like a toddler.

Sloan knew that somewhere beneath that perfect-
mother façade lurked a woman wild at heart. She suspected her mother of different ways in youth. After all,
Sloan could count and she knew she'd been conceived
before her parents were married. But this woman didn't
seem like her mother anymore, more a dull shell of a
mother, a robot who said the right things and did the
right things, but whose every movement was passion-
less.

As soon as her parents left, Ainslie settled into the
sofa for her dolphin show. Sloan made a huge bowl of
popcorn. They had all the get-well cards spread out on
the floor where they made a collage during commercial
breaks. For weeks Ainslie had anticipated this bottlenose
dolphin show about strand feeding. Apparently, in Carolina tidal creeks, dolphins herd fish ashore onto exposed mud banks with a bow wave.

Ainslie sat mesmerized as dolphins rushed fish onto
shore. Gulls and egrets dropped from the sky to com-
pete for the catch. The announcer said, "Dolphins avoid
oyster beds, since the sharp edges lacerate their smooth
hide."

"They strand on their right side, and their teeth on
that side wear down," Ainslie said, touching her own
mouth absentmindedly.

The predators thrashed their tails and wiggled onto
the bank, snapping up writhing fish, then they slid back

into water. They rapidly clicked, one squeaked, and then they regrouped for a second attack.

"Hey, what's up with your dolphins?" Sloan asked.

"They come to see me sometimes."

"Really?"

"They know something's wrong."

Lightning flashed white outside and they grew quiet as rain thrummed against the porch and windows. The hammock on the screened-in back porch began to shudder.

"Come on. Let's watch TV upstairs so we can listen to it rain," Sloan suggested.

In Ainslie's room, Sloan checked out her sister's treasure shelves. "Do you have anything new?" she asked. She picked up a contorted shard of glass. "I love this," Sloan said. "It's so dark and twisted."

"That's fulgurite. It's what happens when lightning hits sand. They're hard to find."

"Interesting."

"Can I have a grilled cheese?"

"Sure. I'll make you one." This was what they both wanted when they were sick, the comfort of a warm, soft cheesy sandwich. Downstairs, Sloan waited for butter to melt in the skillet and her mind wandered to Cal and then to Cal's new proposal. She had been sucked in so easily. Cal had asked her if she knew anyone who could read the Waccamaw up to the school-boat landing. She told him Mr. Washington and Ronald could both navigate that area. Cal had said, "Not the old man. Don't tell him anything. But Ronald, can you introduce me to him?"

And so she had and before she knew what was happening, the two men were hatching a scheme out of touch with reality. She still didn't know the finer details, but she did know she wasn't going to have any part of their arrangement. Prison was not in her plans for the future.

Sloan cut the cheesy sandwich at an angle and made the food tray look as fancy as she could. As she climbed the stairs, water hit hard and cold against her face. Stunned, it took her a moment to realize the steps were slick. She looked up the stairwell. The hatch of the widow's walk was open to black sky. Sloan quickly climbed the ladder, her hands slipping around the rungs. Rain stung her cheeks as she crawled atop the opening and frantically scanned the tight space. There was her sister, clothing plastered to her thin frame, hair whipping in the wind, arms extended to the sky.

"Ainslie!" Sloan screamed. "What are you doing?"

Her sister didn't move or turn to acknowledge her.

"Hey! Ains, hey!" Lightning flayed the sky. "Come down here right now!" she yelled at her sister. "Cut this shit out!" She grabbed her arm and pulled her off the bench. Sloan dragged Ainslie to the top of the ladder and pointed down. "Now!"

Ainslie crawled slowly backward down the ladder. Sloan followed and pulled the hatch closed behind them.

When they hit the landing Ainslie stopped and waited for her sister. She shivered. Water streamed off her onto the floor. Sloan grabbed her by the shoulders and shook her, flinging droplets from Ainslie's hair onto the walls.

"What, are you nuts? What are you doing? Do you think if you get hit by lightning you'll be cured?"

Ainslie stared at her own feet. Sloan pulled Ainslie's face up to her own.

"Hey." Sloan got down on her knees and grasped her sister's arms hard. "Look at me. Listen to me when I tell you none of this is your fault. Do you want to die?"

"No."

"Lightning can kill you. You know that. This is not

the way to cure cancer. Even if that old guy was cured it was just a freak accident. You're more likely to die from getting hit by lightning or get blown off the top of the house and plunge to your death in the yard than to be cured of cancer. Ains, promise me you won't try something like this again."

Ainslie drew in a hitching breath and let out an extended, mournful wail. She collapsed into Sloan's arms and they sank to the landing, where they held each other. Ainslie cried great wracking sobs until she was limp as a rag doll.

When she thought it was safe, Sloan said, "Come on. Let's take a hot bubble bath. That'll make you feel better. You can use my fancy expensive stuff."

In the tub, warm and thick with bubbles, Ainslie slumped forward, her arms around her knees while Sloan poured water down her back.

"I'm sick of being sick," Ainslie whispered. "I'm sick of hospitals and doctors and people feeling sorry for me. I hate presents from strangers and I hate missing school and hate it Mommy and Daddy are always mad at each other."

"I know. I know."

"Everybody talks about me around me but not *to* me. Nobody ever asks me what I think."

"I hear you."

"I hate being poor. We're poor now because of me."

"Please, don't feel guilty about being sick. It could have been any one of us."

Her sister stared at the bubbles massed like glaciers against the side of the tub. Sloan couldn't tell if Ainslie was crying or if rainwater still trickled from her thin, drooping hair. And then she saw something in her sister she had never seen before. Ainslie's eyes shifted as if someone suddenly told her a horrible secret. There was hardness to those eyes, a resignation of hope. Her sister was tired of fighting, and this scared Sloan more than anything that had happened so far. But it wasn't just Ainslie who was like the desperate clinging rider astride the crazy granite stallion statue at Brookgreen. Everyone in their family was just holding on for dear life.

CHAPTER 28

Wrack Line

Lauren ran into the Litchfield Food Lion to grab a bag of rice for supper. She'd been vigilant about shopping at the less expensive inland markets and only stopped occasionally to get a few groceries along the coast.

Outside again, she checked her watch and realized she had forty-five minutes before she could retrieve Ainslie from physical therapy. She wandered down the strip mall toward Litchfield Books. Although she'd been frequenting the library now that things were tight, Lauren enjoyed wandering around this bookstore. It took her mind off her problems, if only for a short while. They had a wonderful section on travel, and Lauren loved to look through the photography books on Italy and France with their cottage flower gardens and artfully crumbling architecture. Someday, she'd always tell herself when she flipped through these books, someday she and Emmett would take that honeymoon they'd never had.

The aroma of coffee wafted over her as she entered.

Lauren stopped to check out the new releases. A couple of dust jackets appealed to her and she made a mental note to request a couple of these new books from the library. She remembered that she still had a few thank-you notes to write, and she made her way over to the stationery section. The coffee smelled so good, and while it was against her current frugal ways to spend three dollars on a cup of coffee, she was considering doing just that, when familiar voices floated over the stationery display. It was Marguerite and a couple of other women from church.

Lauren was trying to shove a box of envelopes back into its slot and step around the end to say hello, when she heard Emmett's name come up.

Lauren didn't even realize she was holding her breath, but she froze, one hand poised in midair, all her senses homed on the voices.

Marguerite said, "I would never have suspected Emmett Sullivan of the like. There they were, in broad daylight. Granted they were back under a tree and all, but they were fighting right there in his truck. You should have seen them, yelling at each other."

"In the parking lot across from town hall?" another woman said.

"I saw it with my own eyes. And you know people don't get all emotional like that unless they're . . . well, you know what I mean."

The women hummed knowing replies. They knew exactly what Marguerite was talking about, and it wasn't a savory situation.

"Poor Lauren," one of them said. "You think she has any idea?"

"Probably not," Marguerite said. "She's just been at her wit's end trying to take care of that poor little girl. I swear, that child just gets sicker every day and that husband of hers just doesn't seem to be any help at all. Well, I mean, you can tell Lauren's just run ragged and there he is practically making out with that Caroline Crawford right there for God and everybody to see."

Lauren set the envelopes down at her feet, clutched her purse to her chest, and ducked out as quickly as possible. In the car, she felt sick and shaken. Suddenly, the door to Litchfield Books opened and the women walked out, their heads down in discussion, expensive handbags dangling from their elbows. Lauren caught her breath when she realized she was parked beside Marguerite's car. She fumbled her keys, crammed them in the ignition and nearly backed into the approaching women, still deep in conversation. Lauren didn't stop as she tore out of the parking lot and gunned her way onto the highway. She headed toward home and then realized that Ainslie was with her physical therapist in the opposite direction. She pulled into a parking space at the Hammock Shops and let the engine idle.

Lauren sat there, numbly looking at the resort wear in the windows of a swanky women's shop. What was she going to do? Her suspicions had been warranted. Emmett was cheating on her. That explained a lot. Maybe he wasn't always at The Pub or the office or running. Maybe some of those times when he'd gone unaccounted for he'd been otherwise occupied with the city manager. If Marguerite was spreading the word, then half of the town would know by tonight. Lauren flung open her door and gagged. Nothing came up, but a line of drool escaped her mouth and she felt faint. She pulled herself upright and cranked the air conditioner to full blast, directing the vents toward her face, pulling her hair back and leaning close. Something crawled at the edges of her memory, and she suddenly remembered her bag of rice still on a ledge in the bookstore. That was when she burst into tears.

* * *

Lauren collected Ainslie from physical therapy, barely registering his assessment of her daughter's progress and his instructions for the week. Back home, Lauren gave Ainslie ice cream and distracted her with Cartoon Network.

In front of her closet now, Lauren yanked up her slacks, but they slipped down again until they were hip huggers and the crotch seemed halfway to her knees. She hadn't been this thin since college. Somewhere in the back of her closet was a box of clothes she'd kept from that time in her life. She pushed into the depths of the closet hunting for the box of sorority shirts and skinny jeans.

Even though she'd been only twenty when Sloan was born, she'd never returned to her svelte size four. She gained two full dress sizes during her first pregnancy and ended up at a curvaceous size eight. After Ainslie was born she'd gone from an eight to a large-size ten, which still looked good on her frame. She'd fussed and starved on occasion trying to get back into single-digit dresses, but until now, she had been unsuccessful. Emmett had never complained. He had always assured her that he found her womanly, but Lauren had never grown accustomed to the fat pockets that rode the crest of her hips, nor the extra flesh that rounded out her face.

Now she had no more baby weight on her, but along with her new body came thin hair, sallow skin and deep hollows beneath her eyes. She was slender, but she didn't look or feel healthy. She'd have to take care of that. She was still attractive. She'd start taking vitamins. She'd exercise again. She'd show that bastard Emmett that two could play his game.

Over the course of their marriage, their sex life had gone from four or five times per week to four or five per month, and then finally she could count on both hands the times they made love in a year. It was as if Emmett's libido went on permanent vacation. His lack of interest had worried and hurt her, but she'd never been the type to initiate sex. Their love-making had become so sparse that Lauren considered herself basically celibate.

But when Ainslie became ill, Lauren started losing weight, and Emmett woke up. For the first time in years, he told her she was beautiful, he touched her more. Suddenly, he wanted intimacy. But rather than being able to enjoy her husband's advances, Lauren felt betrayed by his sudden interest in her. She was shocked he could even think about pleasure when things were so wrong in the family, that he would ask one more thing of her at a time when she was so utterly exhausted. Now that she was ready to have a nervous breakdown, now that she was emaciated, she'd suddenly become interesting to him.

So maybe he'd been waking up to more than just her. Maybe when she turned him away he'd sought out Caroline Crawford. So what? That didn't make this her fault. She'd always been aware of the flirtation between her husband and the city manager, but Lauren thought Emmett had enough character not to cheat. And even if he was going to cheat, surely he had enough brains to pick somebody besides this woman. But he hadn't. He'd picked one of the most high-profile women in town, a woman everybody had an opinion about. Was he in love with her? What had they been fighting about?

Lauren found the box of clothing marked COLLEGE. On the floor of her bedroom she arranged her life before—before marriage, before babies. She arranged a pair of jeans flat and bent one leg out at the knee. She topped the jeans with her pink-and-white Chi Omega baseball jersey and raised the arms at cheerful angles. She took one of her big pink bows and placed it where her head would be. She'd been the consummate sorority girl—hair bows, duck shoes, and kelly green pants. Her clothes still smelled faintly of Chloé perfume. She found photos in the bottom of the box and she slipped out an eight by ten headshot of herself, all hair and smile. Here she was, the girl Lauren had been years ago. Before cancer. Before divorce.

Tears burned the back of Lauren's throat, but she pushed them down. She had worked so hard to be in the sorority. Had held two part-time jobs to pay the dues and all the fees. In the box, she found her pledge pin, a ratty brown corsage still in its clear plastic box, concert tickets, and her garnet-and-black gamecock pompoms. She'd loved to go to football games, loved the spectacle of the massive cheering crowd.

Lauren shed her clothes and pulled on her old jeans. They zipped smoothly over her hips but were snug in the waist. Next she pulled on her Chi O shirt and found a black hat with USC on the bill. She stood in front of the mirror examining herself from all angles.

There was a whistle from the doorway and Emmett was there. He still held his satchel from work, his tie was askew. He had the bleary-eyed look she now associated with his post-office stops at The Pub.

"You look hot."

Lauren had expected to scream at him when she saw him, but instead she felt sick on the words caught inside her.

He moved toward her and slid his hands around her waist. She stiffened at his touch but her husband didn't seem to notice. "You look good, babe," he said as he bent to kiss her on the neck. "Like the day we met."

Lauren quickly sidestepped him.

"I'm not the girl you remember," she hissed.

A puzzled expression washed his face. "Well, hey, whatever. Come here."

She pushed him away. "Don't you dare come near me."

His drunken smile disappeared. "Lauren, what's wrong?"

"I know about Caroline Crawford."

His eyes widened and his mouth hung open.

"You must think I'm pretty stupid. How long has this been going on?"

"What are you talking about?"

"Don't play stupid. I know you're fucking her."

"What? No. I don't know why you'd think that."

"People saw you. Together."

"Where? When? I've never been with Caroline Crawford."

"You're lying."

"I'm not lying. I've never been with Caroline Crawford. I've never touched the woman."

"Don't lie to me! People saw you."

"Who saw me?"

"It doesn't matter."

"It does matter. I deserve to know who my accuser is."

"You don't have an accuser. Nobody told me anything. I found out on my own."

"Considering the fact I haven't done a goddamn thing wrong, why don't you just tell me what you think you found out so we can get it all out in the open and talk about it?"

"Don't you dare be condescending to me, Emmett Sullivan. You're practically a damn drunk! You're never around when the children need you."

"That is not true."

"You can't even keep us in the black financially."

"There! That's what this is really about. It's about money."

"How dare you! Don't try to turn this around on me. This is not about money. This is about loving your family and doing the right thing. Something you don't seem to be able to do."

"Stop." Emmett held up his hand. "Stop, just stop, Lauren. This is crazy. I know what you are referring to now. I was sitting in the parking lot of the courthouse last week and we were in a heated discussion about zoning ordinances."

"Zoning ordinances."

"That's right. I think she's in bed with Trip Wannamaker. She's helping him push his agenda through on a project that affects this entire area."

Lauren folded her arms across her chest and made her stand.

"That's not the only time you've been seen in the company of Caroline Crawford. Everybody at the Wannamakers' party saw you go under the stairs with her. What were the two of you doing back there?"

"I didn't do a goddamn thing with her."

"If I recall correctly, you were doing coke with her."

"There were about a dozen people there that night. I wasn't with her by myself."

"Get your stuff and get out. I don't care where you go. You can go shack up with her for all I care. I'm done with you."

"Lauren, I'm begging you to listen to reason. Give me a chance to explain."

"Get your stuff and get out or I'm calling the cops to remove you. I'll think of something to tell the girls. You're here so little anyway, I doubt they'll even notice you're gone."

Emmett opened his mouth as if to protest, but words seemed to escape him. He reached for her.

"Listen to me," he pleaded.

"Don't touch me!"

"Lauren, listen to me."

"No. You listen to me. You've been drinking down at The Pub with your cronies and finding all sorts of excuses so you don't have to be home and now I find out you've been messing around with Caroline Crawford. You get your shit and you get out of here."

"You're right." He held his hand to his forehead. "I need to leave before this goes any further and we end up saying things we'll regret later."

"You do that."

"I'm going to Larry's."

"I don't care where you go."

But that wasn't true. From the upstairs window seat Lauren watched her husband throw his bags into the truck bed. He paused and glanced up at the window where she was, but she knew from experience he couldn't see her when the lights were off. He looked forlorn and tired. As tired as she felt. She watched Emmett drive away. She went into her bedroom and cried until she could cry no more and then, for the first time in months, Lauren slept through the night.

CHAPTER 29

Bluffing

Common Good Insurance was headquartered in Raleigh-Durham. It was a half day's drive from Pawleys Island. Emmett felt lucky their insurance company wasn't in California or Michigan, where it would be harder and more expensive to arrive on their doorstep. As Larry had advised, they had accepted Common Good's offer of mediation, another delay tactic and a way of negotiating with desperate policyholders. But Larry's plan was not to mediate, but rather to use this audience to launch their attack against the company.

Emmett had been giddy the night before, eager to tell his wife that he and Larry would be butting heads with the enemy today, but Larry had advised him to keep quiet until they were through.

"You just never know how things are going to turn out," Larry said. "It's better not to get her hopes up."

Larry had planned their strategic attack for months, and yesterday, for the first time since this whole ordeal began, Emmett felt hopeful. He had gone home fully intending to go against Larry's advice and tell Lauren what they had planned the next day. But Lauren had been crazy when he arrived home. Who had been gossiping about him and Caroline? People were always interested in their neighbors' business, good or bad, but this was just an outright lie. This whole blow-up was his fault. He should have been more careful. No. He should never have flirted with Caroline or responded to her advances. Then they wouldn't have been fighting in his truck and there would never have been anything for anybody to see and report on.

"Lauren's going to divorce me if this doesn't work," Emmett said.

"Did you tell her we were doing this today?"

"I'd told her last week it was a possibility, but I think she was so pissed off last night she forgot."

"You're in sad shape, my friend."

"It would be different if I'd actually done something wrong, but I didn't do anything."

"I believe you, but I'm not the one you've got to convince."

"I mean, shit. It wasn't like I hadn't thought about it. I had. But I'm not guilty of actually doing a damn thing. And I resent being accused of something I didn't do."

"That's not the avenue to take. I think contrition might be a better move."

"God, why did I get married in the first place?"

"Tried it once. Didn't like it."

Tall, slender pines blurred by in Emmett's peripheral vision. A headache threatened, and Emmett lay against the headrest of Larry's car and closed his eyes. He had to be calm, take one thing at a time. Lauren would come around. Or not. But after everything that had transpired between them over the past few months, after enduring her disappointment and derision, this accusation just might be the last straw. Emmett wasn't exactly sure he wanted to work things out. Right now he needed to focus on one thing—getting these insurance bastards to pay for Ainslie's treatment. Then he could worry about everything else.

"They're just trying to wait us out until Ainslie dies," Emmett said as they drove north on I-95. "Now that she's had a spinal tumor they really won't want to pay. How could they do this to her?"

"Don't make it personal," Larry advised.

"How can I not make it personal?"

"When you let things get personal you lose perspective. This is a big-picture situation where the squeaky wheel gets the grease. And today, we're going to be the squeakiest fucking wheel they've ever seen."

"Mike's going to meet us there?"

"He'll be there."

"That should scare the shit out of them."

"That's the plan."

Larry's old college buddy Mike, a producer for CNN, had experienced a similar situation with a different insurance company years ago. Mike's son had struggled with an unusual type of lymphoma, and while the company debated the benefits of what they considered experimental treatment, Mike's son had died. Later, the treatment the insurance had denied was found effective. It was now standard protocol. Emmett had never had an occasion to be grateful for the loss of others, but today he was glad to have Mike on his side.

"Would CNN actually do a story on Ainslie?"

"No. We're just running a bluff."

"Really."

"It doesn't take much media attention to get the ball rolling in the right direction. Mike's pitching a series on the insurance industry at CNN. He's waiting on approval, so if he gets caught with the van out today he'll just say he's researching, getting some stock shots of the outside of the building for a future story. He's got himself covered. He's shooting another story in the area anyway."

The Common Good parking lot was manicured and Emmett quickly assessed their landscaping. Nothing outrageous. Nothing like his dreams. No commercial monolith. An unassuming building. Corporate identity took forefront, branded elements at all entrances and a looming presence in the cold glass lobby, with furniture meant to move along rather than comfort.

"Where's Mike?" Emmett asked as they walked toward the giant rounded front desk.

"Don't worry. He's coming," Larry said.

Larry told the receptionist why they were there. She directed the men to have a seat and she would call someone to escort them up. They walked to the windows out of earshot. Larry made a phone call. He said, "Hey. Okay. Great." And snapped his phone shut.

"I'm nervous," Emmett said.

"Shake it off. Don't say a word unless you're asked a direct question. Then defer to me. I'll let you know if it's okay to answer."

The elevator swished open and a young secretary, dressed more severely than her youth could carry, came toward them in sensible heels.

The men followed her up to a boardroom with a long shiny conference table and paneled walls hung with more corporate logos and official-looking documents.

"Please wait here. Someone will be with you shortly," the young woman said pertly.

When she had closed the door, Emmett said, "Wow. What a welcoming party."

Larry walked to the window and checked the parking lot below. He made another call.

"Back lot," he said and flipped his phone shut.

"You're devious," Emmett said.

"That's why they pay me the big bucks."

"I owe you."

"Don't owe me yet. We could just piss them off and make things worse."

"So what? They haven't done anything for me but give me grief. How much worse can it get?"

The door opened and four men in dark suits entered. They formally shook hands and took up positions on the opposite side of the table from Emmett and Larry. Oddly, each casually introduced himself, almost warmly, as if they were old friends, perhaps as a way of catching them off guard. Emmett felt a flare of anger. So these were the gatekeepers to his daughter's life. Their smug self-assurance rankled his nerves. He felt the sudden urge to jump across the table and pummel the smirks from their faces. He clutched his fists in his lap.

"Where's Tacket?" Larry asked, snapping his ink pen impatiently on his legal pad. Tacket was the lawyer Larry had agreed to let run the mediation. He was someone Larry only vaguely knew, but felt okay about.

"I understand he's in the building," one of the suits said.

The door opened and Tacket entered. He shook hands all around, then took up his position at the head of the table. After a quick review of the case, the mediator asked Larry to state his position.

Larry wasted no time in laying out his demands that Common Good pay the full amount required under the contract, which was valid at the time of the original diagnosis. There was hemming and hawing on the other side as they began, but Larry cut them off.

"A child is dying. We're tired of your delay tactics. I'd like to invite you gentlemen over to the window. There's something you need to see."

They moved to the window without a word. A freshly logoed CNN van gleamed in the parking lot below.

Shock flickered across their faces, but quickly an impassive, almost disinterested look returned.

Larry flipped open his phone. The van door slid to the side and a couple of guys spilled out. One held a camera. The other grabbed a phone from his back pocket.

"Up here. Third floor," Larry said. "Say hey."

The khaki-clad man with the CNN cap and sunglasses looked up and waved in their direction.

"That's my friend, Mike," Larry said to the suits. "We went to college together. Would you like to go down and have a little talk?"

"That won't be necessary," the one with the darkest suit said. "We get your point."

"So," Larry said, "here's the deal."

Larry told them they were going to pay everything contractually covered by the insurance policy and for a full checkup at Duke and would provide coverage for any medical expenses and drugs for any subsequent diagnosis from that visit. Larry relayed the moving story of how their small community had raised more than $13,000 to help keep the family afloat.

"Of course," Larry continued, "we would have no problems generating a good-sized letter-writing campaign, not only to your board members, but on the Internet and to newspapers, about how this child needs help because Common Good won't pay."

Larry held up a photo of Ainslie.

"She's a cute kid," he said. "And pretty articulate, too. People will just love her."

He held up a second photo. Ainslie was scrawny, her hair scraggly and sparse. There were tubes running out of her chest and she was even paler than the hospital bed sheets.

"Then of course, there's this image and the question

of how much damage was done because of delayed treatment while waiting for approval."

"You can't prove that," one of the shirts barked.

"I don't have to prove anything. This isn't a criminal trial. What we can do is make it a court of public opinion. Human interest stories are always an easy sell."

The Common Good representatives requested that Larry and Emmett wait in the hall. The mediator stayed in the room. Ten minutes later, the door opened and the suits strode away as if their minds were already on other, more important matters. They never turned their way nor raised a hand in acknowledgment. Back in the boardroom, the mediator told them Common Good had agreed to their demands and that papers to that effect would be drawn up immediately.

"You rattled their cage," he said with a wink that showed he was anything but impartial. "I'll see you get the appropriate papers on Monday."

CHAPTER 30

Baby Steps

Sloan rubbed sleep from her eyes as she waited for her computer's next response. She'd typed Verulo Moreno into a search engine. The computer screen flickered and a list came up. She scrolled down, but found nothing pertinent. She Googled Verulo. Still, nothing of any consequence. An hour later she had checked student listings at the University of Miami going back five years and there was no sign of him. She'd done every free online people search she could find, but still she came up empty—no Miami address, no telephone number. It was as if he didn't exist.

And why would he leave an information trail? Verulo was probably not his name. Criminals never give their real names. Maybe the University of Miami was a euphemism, a coy reference to where he got his real education. His UM shirts and board shorts were probably just his college kid cover. He could be thirty years old for all they knew.

The soft breezes of spring curled in the open window of her room. Her parents had informed the girls they wouldn't be turning on the air conditioner until mid-summer. Her father had repaired a few ragged screens but had finally given up. Screens were unnecessary anyway. Mosquitoes never crossed the creek, one of the reasons people had always flocked to the windy barrier islands in the heat of summer.

Sloan typed in "Mexican drug gangs" and a list of articles popped up. She found an article on express kidnapping. Apparently Mexican gangsters held people for a few days or a week while they maxed out the victims' credit cards and emptied bank accounts. Sloan thought of how they had innocently followed Verulo into the jungle to zip-line that day, and a little tingle of dread crawled her arms. She shook it off and continued to read. Hijacking and freight theft were also apparently major problems on Mexico's vast and sparsely patrolled network of roads.

Sloan remembered the rumors when they were in Cancún about heads washing up on beaches, so she added a plus sign to her search bar and typed in "severed heads."

The first article she opened was about Mexican drug wars, where organized crime rings fought each other for dominance and territory. The article was a B-movie account of rival drug gangs colliding at a disco where men dressed in black stormed into a crowded discotheque and rolled five heads onto the dance floor. A note attached to one read that they didn't kill women or children or innocents, only those who deserved to die.

Sloan went to the history bar of her computer and deleted her searches on Mexico. She had made her decision. She wanted absolutely nothing to do with Cal's big plan. In fact, if this was the type of thing Cal intended to do, she'd need to extricate herself from him as well. That would be hard. Cal was persuasive. Cal was

attractive. Sloan didn't want to break up with him. She
only wanted him to stop this crazy scheme. She'd heard
the characteristics that attracted you to somebody could
end up being the very things that caused you to eventually break up. Cal was so exciting, but this was too
much excitement. This was dangerous.

In her closet, Sloan found the shoebox of remaining
money she had earned from their Miami trip, just over
$900. She stuck a few bills in her pocket and the rest in
a manila envelope. She wrote *For the Sullivan Family* on
the outside. She would have to decide the perfect way to
leave it for her mother to find. She crammed it into her
backpack alongside pencils, oil pastels, and sketchpad.

"Ains, you ready?" she yelled to her sister in the next
room.

It was June and the day grew warm quickly. The entry
drive at Brookgreen was lush, flowers already thick,
birds crazed with desire swooping through the trees.
Sloan parked in a handicap space, clipped the handicap
pass on her rearview, and got out to wrestle her sister's
wheelchair from the back.

"I don't need that stupid thing," Ainslie complained.

"Just get in," Sloan said. "It was hard enough to get
Mom to let me bring you. She made me promise, so just
get in."

Sloan was glad to hear her sister complain. Since the
day of the storm Ainslie had lost her spark. She'd
stopped fighting. She would lie for hours in the same
position in bed, the television on her favorite channel,
but Ainslie wasn't watching. She no longer insisted
everybody in the family share her programs. She didn't
play video games or want to talk on the phone anymore.
One by one her school friends had dropped away. Now

Ainslie spent hours staring at the television, out her window, at the new fish tank in her room.

Ainslie took a few cautious steps and lowered herself into the rolling contraption. A recent checkup had pronounced her to be in remission, but their mother didn't take that as a good sign like most people would. Sloan had heard her mother worry that the doctors were simply writing Ainslie off because of mounting bills. Their father said to have more faith than that. Their mother said her faith was all used up. She said she wanted to send Ainslie to Duke University for a second opinion before she would believe everything was truly okay.

"Here we go," Sloan said. "Where's the ramp?"

Sloan found the concrete incline and rolled her sister up.

"Hey, want to go in the gift shop?" Sloan said.

"I don't have any money."

"It's your birthday. I've got money. My treat."

Ainslie shrugged. Usually she would have jumped at the chance to buy a beaded necklace or a book on animals. Inside the store Ainslie showed little enthusiasm.

"Here, try these on," Sloan said and held a pair of dragonfly earrings next to Ainslie's face. "These are cool. You like?"

"They're okay, I guess."

"Oh, come on Ainslie. We're out having fun. Buck up."

"I don't want any earrings until all my hair grows back."

"Okay. What about a hat then?" Ainslie's hair was growing back in unruly patches around the incision site. Pale scalp showed through a fuzz of dark hair. Sloan had drawn another animal on the other side of her sister's head, but it was fading.

"I have a hat. Let's just go," Ainslie said.

"Did you put on sunscreen like Mom said? You know you'll burn easy."

"YesIputonsuncreenlikeMomsaid."

"Okay. Okay."

At least Ainslie's thoughts and speech seemed to have returned to normal. But Sloan was still waiting for that curious little nature lover to appear again.

She pushed her sister through the gardens, past the frog fountain, where they stopped to watch water bugs slice across the surface. Through the allée of live oaks and back to their private corner. Lizards ducked for cover at their approach. Sloan pushed her sister's chair against a plant growing from one side of the black fountain. Ainslie eyed a couple of gray-green lizards too groggy from sunning to be alarmed. Usually Ainslie would have grabbed a couple of the slower ones, but not today.

"I'm going to go over there and sketch," Sloan said, pointing to the millstone.

Ainslie didn't reply.

Sloan settled in and pulled out her pad, intent on polishing a piece she hadn't completed on her last visit. But when she started, her fingers wouldn't make a decision about what to do. Often she became removed from herself while creating, and without thinking she would draw for an hour and suddenly wake up to a finished drawing or sculpture. But today, her hand was stalled. She turned the page to a clean sheet. Suddenly her hand was moving rapidly over the paper, her pencil scratching lightly. Sloan was barely aware of what she was drawing, and when she finished she was shaken by what she'd done. Staring at her from the page was the wide face of Verulo. This likeness had flaws, but she had captured his essence, his high cheekbones and close-cropped hair. She could see him perfectly in her mind, as if he were a photograph in a book. The only thing she couldn't remember about him was his eyes, so she had covered them with his aviators. She considered his image. *Who are you? Where are you right now?*

Blondie sang from her bag. As she was digging for her phone she glanced at Ainslie, and her sister wrinkled her nose in disapproval. Ainslie was the only one in her family who wasn't sold on Cal. Sloan hadn't asked her why, but she assumed it was because she had been spending so much time with him, time Ainslie saw as her time. Cal brought Ainslie gifts that she promptly gave away or threw in the trash.

Sloan couldn't find her phone and, frustrated, she emptied her bag onto the ground and picked the singing machine from the pile.

"Hey," she said into her phone. Ainslie was still looking at her as she crammed everything back into her bag.

"Hey yourself," he said. "Where are you?"

"By the black fountain."

"In the back corner?"

"Yes."

"I'm pulling into the parking lot."

"See you in a minute." Sloan snapped her phone shut.

"I can't believe you invited him."

"Get over it."

"Why did he have to come?"

"Why don't you like him?"

"He's bossy. He always tells you what to do."

"No, he doesn't."

Ainslie turned away and reached to rake a sunning lizard onto her lap.

Within minutes Cal rounded the hedge into their world.

"Hey, Ainslie," Cal sang. "What's up, dog?"

"I'm not a dog."

"Yes, you are. You're just a little shih tzu." Cal didn't

seem to notice Ainslie's glare. He sauntered over to Sloan and she closed her sketchpad on her drawing of Verulo before he leaned in for a kiss.

"Not in front of her," Sloan said.

"That's cool. Let's talk." Cal gently pulled her to her feet. "Let's take a little walk. She's okay here by herself for a while, right?"

"Ainslie, we're going for a walk, okay? We'll be right back."

Ainslie didn't answer, although Sloan knew she had heard her.

"I can't go far," she said to Cal.

When they were out of Ainslie's line of vision, Sloan said, "Hey, I heard your mom had to take a little trip. Is everything okay?"

Cal grinned. "Oh, you mean has my mom gone to rehab? That would be a yes."

"So she's okay?"

"Sure. Every couple of years she goes out west to dry out. Stays until the insurance runs out. Comes back and is fine for another couple of years. How'd you find out?"

"Doesn't matter. I just wanted to make sure you were okay."

Cal shrugged. "I'm used to it." He changed the subject quickly as if his mother didn't matter. "Anyway, everything's on. We're doing the drop tomorrow night."

"What? No. Why the rush?"

"I don't know. Apparently there was already a shipment on the way and their drop location got compromised."

"Cal, I did some research on the Web. There's no Verulo Moreno in Miami, or anywhere else for that matter. He gave you a bogus name."

"So?"

"So he knows us, but we don't know who he is. And he didn't want to have his photo taken that day when we were going on the zip-line. Remember? He practically ripped Ethan's cell phone out of his hand so he could take our photo and stay out of the shot himself."

"I repeat. *So?*"

Sloan paused, wondering if he was being intentionally dense. "Think about it," she said. "There's all kinds of drug-related murders going on down in Mexico. You don't know this guy. What if he's part of those drug-ring people?"

"You have a vivid imagination. And you worry too much. People do this shit all the time. Don't you know how much cocaine there is around this town?"

"No, I don't. I mean, I didn't until I met you."

"I've got this under control. Don't go all crazy on me. Besides, you need the money. You've got to get your shit together for school."

"Dad's working things out with the insurance company. Everything's going to be okay."

"And you believe that?"

"If Dad says they're going to pay us, then I believe him. I have to believe him."

"Whatever."

"Cal, don't say whatever. Look, you and Ronald go do your thing, but I'm out."

He reached up to run a hand through her hair. "Baby, we're a team. It's just one little boat ride and then we split the cash and voilà, we're rich."

"I said no. I'm not doing it."

He spread his fingers over her scalp and pulled her toward him. She thought he was going to kiss her and she was confused. He wound his fingers through her hair, massaging hard until she tried to push away. Her struggle made him grab a handful of hair and pull her head back.

His breath suffocated her. "Sloan, you're my girl. I need to know you're with me. You can't go against me."

"I'm not against you," she whimpered. "Stop. Please."

"You're not going to tell anybody, are you? If I thought you were going to fuck this thing up for me I'd be really upset."

His heartbeat vibrated into her scalp through his fingertips. Then suddenly, as if he had come to his senses, he released her.

She stumbled backward, stunned. She had to get away from him. She ran to where her satchel lay and started stuffing her art supplies in. She fumbled, and the bag spilled to the ground and he was there in an instant helping her.

"Stop it. I don't need your help."

He handed her a wallet, sketchpad, and manila envelope. She snatched them, shoved them in her bag and walked off toward Ainslie.

"Sloan, I'm sorry . . . it's just. Hey, don't walk away from me!" He followed her. She tried to suppress tears, but they crawled up and out of her fast.

He was there in an instant, leaning close to her, his voice softer, lower so Ainslie couldn't hear. "Baby, forgive me. You don't know the pressure I'm under. I need this money. My dad won't give me money anymore. He says my grades aren't up to par."

"Then you do it, Cal. I don't need money." Tears fell freely onto her sketchpad.

"I want to go to Europe this summer. I wanted to surprise you and take you with me. You'd like that, wouldn't you? You want to go to Europe, don't you?"

She faced him, still crying. "I can't believe it. You're doing this so you can go on vacation with your spoiled friends?"

"Don't judge me and don't judge my friends. You're lucky we include you."

"Lucky? I'm lucky you include me? Well, sorry to make you slum it. No shirtsleeves for you, huh?"

"Where'd you hear that?"

"It's your grandfather's platitude. Is that how you feel? That you're lowering yourself to be with me? Well, here's a fix for your problem, Cal. We're finished. I don't want to see you or your snotty friends ever again." Ainslie was already headed out of the fountain area. Sloan caught up and began to push her fast, but he was there in an instant.

"You can't break up with me. I won't let you."

He grabbed her arm and pulled her away from Ainslie.

"Hey, you let her go!" Ainslie cried.

"You don't know what you're saying, Sloan. You love me, don't you?"

"Let go."

"Because I love you."

His grip was beginning to hurt.

"Don't pull away from me," he hissed.

"What's wrong with you? You're hurting me."

"I'm hurting you? Sloan, do you know how much you're hurting me? You can't break up with me. I love you. Didn't you hear me say that? I love you."

She was crying then; she stopped trying to yank her arm free and simply stood there swiping at her face with her free hand.

"Cal, let me go," she said, but she put up no resistance when he led her away from her sister.

"I'm sorry," Cal pleaded, near her in a whisper. "Sloan, I said I'm sorry. Baby, I'm sorry. Please forgive me. I didn't mean it. I'm just really fucked up. You understand, don't you? I know you do. Nobody understands me like you do."

"I can't talk to you about this right now," she said.

"Can I call you later?"

Ainslie was twisted around in her wheelchair.

"Tell him no," Ainslie said. "Tell him no."

Sloan was crying openly. "Shut up, Ainslie. You don't understand," she said.

Sloan knew she should say no, never to call her again. But he said he loved her. He acted in love or what she thought in love should look like. But he was controlling. That was so not cool. He wasn't thinking clearly. Maybe he was coked out and he'd come down and reconsider. He'd be sorry for how he'd treated her. He was sorry now.

She said, "Okay. Call me later."

"That's more like it." He caressed her hair, but she ducked away and pushed her sister's wheelchair toward the exit.

He stood where he was.

"I'll phone you later tonight," he called after her. "I love you, Sloan. You remember that."

CHAPTER 31

Jezebel

Lauren couldn't remember the last time she'd been to church. Maybe it had been Easter. She stayed so exhausted she wasn't able to drag herself out of bed on Sundays anymore. Neither of the girls would attend with her. Even Ainslie refused now, pleading she couldn't stand the attention. Lauren felt ashamed to arrive by herself. Judged was probably the word, sitting there alone while other families packed whole pews. And to be honest, she had grown tired of fielding questions about Ainslie's health. And to be even more honest, she'd been avoiding church out of fear people had learned Emmett had moved out.

She'd never told a soul Emmett was gone and so far, not one person had had the guts to ask her what was going on, but she figured the topic might come up at lunch today. Some of the women from church had called her. She thought at first that they were checking up since she hadn't been to worship for so long, but instead they had invited her to The Rice Mill Restaurant in the Hammock Shops to organize a book club. Lauren thought it was about time she did something for herself. She realized she was becoming terrible company with no interests other than Ainslie. Something that, according to the therapist, was not good for her or Ainslie.

So here she sat in the same lot where only a week before she'd had her "Emmett's cheating on me" breakdown. She contemplated how she should respond to questions about her family. This attempt to shake things up and do something positive could backfire. Honestly, she wasn't sure she wanted to be in this book club, particularly if they were going to read books on theology or some other topic that would cause them to discuss God. She was in crisis about her own faith and she certainly didn't need other people imposing their own take on her situation. But if they wanted to read something like an escapist beach book or even one of those more literary novels she was always telling herself she needed to read, Lauren might actually enjoy it.

None of these people were anyone Lauren had ever called a real friend, only what she considered polite social acquaintances. She'd tried to be a part of the social fabric of the coast, had dragged poor Emmett to those fundraisers so she could pretend, if only for a while, that she was welcome. It wasn't that she wanted to be around these people all the time. She just needed to know she could belong if she wanted to.

Her husband played the community golf courses and that was fine with her. She'd never been the type to want to belong to a country club. That had been her intention when she'd joined a sorority in college, to belong. But something about that life hadn't really suited her either. It had been so much work and somehow seemed forced. While she still had a couple of friends she kept up with from college, overall, the sorority thing hadn't yielded the lifelong bonds she had hoped it would.

Now it was Sloan, who had always showed open disdain for Lauren's attempts to socialize, who suddenly had entrée into the moneyed world she'd always criticized. It was interesting to watch her try to rationalize her new place in life. Suddenly, her little girl was opening up and taking chances. Doing things she'd never done before, with that Wannamaker boy. Love and money made an intoxicating mixture.

Lauren wanted to tell her daughter that all the money in the world wouldn't make you happy. But then that wasn't exactly true, was it? It was one of those things people paid lip service to so willingly. People without money.

Lauren checked her lipstick in the rearview mirror and fluffed her hair. The Rice Mill wasn't too pricey, but if they wanted to meet at places like this, then Lauren would have to watch her money. Still, it shouldn't be too hard. It wasn't as if she ever ate much anymore. She shook off her negative thoughts and refocused on the meeting. She could be pleasant and social for an hour.

Inside the restaurant, Lauren found the loud gathering of women on the sun-drenched enclosed patio. They were festive in floral dresses and animal-print blouses. Lauren knew at least half of the fifteen women. They ordered white wine or sweet tea, then shrimp and grits, mustard barbecue sandwiches or chopped salads. While they waited for their drinks to arrive, the conversation was about their families. Lauren sat quietly, prepared to answer questions about Ainslie. She fiddled with the salt shaker, turning it slowly, exposing a few golden grains of rice there to capture moisture.

Somebody at their end of the long table said, "Where's Bitsy? Isn't she supposed to be here?"

"Didn't I hear Bitsy was sick?" somebody said.

"No," someone else said. "Heard she'd gone to a . . ." and here the woman made quotation marks in the air, "spa."

"Oh, bless her heart. She's drinking again." It wasn't a question.

"I'd drink, too, if my husband was treating me like that. I mean, everybody knows."

The women nodded as if they all knew something Lauren didn't know.

She wanted to shout, *What? Now you've got to tell me.* Instead, she kept her mouth shut. Her patience paid off.

"It's just depression."

"Well, I'd be depressed if my husband was cheating on me with the likes of that Caroline Crawford."

"Maybe she just needed to get away. Maybe it's not, you know, rehab."

"Well, if she turns back up in twenty-eight days, then you'll know what's what."

Lauren's shrimp and grits turned sour in her mouth. Was this true? Was Bitsy's husband the one having the affair? So Emmett had been telling her the truth. Caroline Crawford was in bed with Trip Wannamaker, probably in business, too, just like Emmett said. And she had kicked him out. She had accused him of being unfaithful. And he had taken it. And he had left.

She wanted to leave—to fly out the door and drive to Emmett's office and fling herself on his mercy. She wanted to tell him she was sorry. That she had been wrong. That she was crazy to have doubted him. But she didn't. She sat there, her meal growing cold in front of her. A tight smile pulled at the corners of her mouth as someone at the head of the table called out, "Now, let's talk about books."

Discussion began, but Lauren wasn't thinking about

books. She was thinking about the churchy gossiping busybodies seated around the table and how they should learn to keep a bridled tongue, because conniving Caroline Crawford, with her alluring Jezebel spirit, might just set her sights on one of their husbands next.

When books and meeting places had been selected, Lauren made her courteous good-byes and walked slowly to her car. She hadn't volunteered her home for a meeting as some other women had. No one expected her to host a meeting while her child was ill. It was all she could do to pull together a small party for Ainslie's birthday.

Lauren forced her thoughts to the small cookout she was planning to celebrate her daughter's tenth birthday this evening. With everything so crazy, Lauren had let Ainslie's birthday slip up on her. Ten was supposed to be a big birthday, but Ainslie was still so weak she couldn't take the excitement of a large party. So Lauren had called her parents and invited them up from Summerville for dinner. A party of five would have to do. Ainslie could have a big blow-out tenth birthday party when she felt better.

But in order to have a big party there would have to be more children, and since Ainslie had gotten sick her roster of friends had dwindled to nothing. All her friends from school had been overly attentive when Ainslie first became ill, calling, visiting the hospital, stopping by to drop off a stuffed animal. The mothers all brought food and stayed for a while to have a glass of tea. But people's patience had grown thin with her daughter's recovery. While other children were developing and changing, Ainslie remained a stark reminder that things could go very wrong. After her relapse, even the most hardcore friends had lost interest. It was as if they had decided to cut their emotional losses.

Lauren drove toward where Abraham Washington

usually parked his truck on Saturdays. He always had the freshest shrimp and he never underweighed. Lauren needed three pounds of shrimp to complete her frogmore stew for the cookout. This Lowcountry boil was one of Ainslie's favorite meals, although when she was smaller Ainslie had made her mother promise that there were no frogs in the stew. Lauren reminded herself that she needed to stop at the ice cream shop and pick up the cake she'd ordered. Her parents were coming at four. The plan was to have the yard decorated and everything ready when Sloan brought Ainslie back from Brookgreen at five.

Lauren hoped Ainslie wouldn't be disappointed by her small party. She knew how important parties and friends were to girls Ainslie's age, and it hurt to think of her child as lonely. Friendships at Ainslie's age were mercurial. Two girls who were best friends one day could be estranged the next. It was only natural for friendships to shift and dissolve and re-form, and it wasn't the fault of the children. And apparently some kids, like Sloan, didn't feel the need for lots of friends. Still, the real problem was that Ainslie was isolated in her illness. There were simply no new children for her to befriend. Lauren was incensed when old playmates slowly stopped calling and extending invitations. It wasn't as if Ainslie was incapable of going to a birthday party or coming over to watch a movie.

Lauren realized she was being a hypocrite, since the one person she should have invited to Ainslie's birthday party was Emmett. Ainslie would be hurt when her father wasn't there, but Lauren didn't have the guts to call him now. What would she say? That she was sorry she'd unjustly accused him, but she wasn't sure she wanted him to come home? That it was easier to be the one completely responsible and not expect anything of him?

That life had been less hassle without him there to disappoint her?

Lauren thought back on the book party and how the women had talked about Bitsy. That was another complicated situation to consider. While Lauren was sorry Bitsy's husband was having an affair, she was incensed that someone with Bitsy's overindulgent lifestyle could get insurance coverage to go dry out in Arizona while Ainslie couldn't even get the medical coverage she needed to stay alive.

The irony was enough to make a person laugh—or cry. Lauren drove into the lot where Abraham Washington's truck was parked. Before she got out, she found her cell phone in her purse. Her finger hovered over the speed-dial button for her husband, but she didn't push it. Hadn't Emmett said last week that he and Larry were supposed to go Raleigh-Durham? He hadn't called to tell her the results of their trip. Had they failed and he was too ashamed to call? Or had he succeeded and he was not calling to punish her? And wasn't she doing the same to him by not inviting him to Ainslie's birthday party? So this was what they were reduced to.

The sun was out in full force, flashing off windshields of passing vehicles. Lauren plucked a forgotten pair of Sloan's sunglasses from the seat next to her and shoved them on her face. She wouldn't call Emmett. He had to be the one to call her. She needed more time to figure out just how she felt about their situation. Maybe he needed time too.

CHAPTER 32

Winds of Fortune

Shrimp trawlers were not like other boats. They were a part of the family, working every bit as hard as the fishermen and shrimpers who toiled on their sun-kissed decks. Abraham Washington's boat, Jumbo, had been named by LaShonda when she was just a child. The Jumbo was like heavy construction equipment when in action, chains and levers and gears clanking, but she was also a graceful dancer, moving smoothly through the water, swaying and rocking in turbid ocean.

The morning was overcast, but LaShonda's father said it would burn off. In the pilot house, he took the wheel, steering a straight, slow course. LaShonda was trussed in the cumbersome orange life preserver, although none of the crew was required to wear one. Dolphins surfed their bow wave. Solemn pelicans perched on rigging, wearing expectant looks. All sound was muffled by the comforting grumble of engines.

LaShonda loved the vessel's outriggers, spread wide like the wings of a giant flying insect, black nets swagged down, then lowered into the water and dragged behind.

The nets fanned out in the boat's wake, opening a hundred feet wide before sinking in the hazy water. The first two hours of the morning were spent eating bacon and eggs in the galley then sipping coffee on deck until the sun made an appearance, a blinding reflection on the surface of the sea.

When the time arrived, the crew jumped to action. Suddenly, everything came alive and the deckhands focused on pulling in the catch. The men shouted to each other as they activated winches to haul in lines. Pulleys and hardware clattered as winches ground and lifted the old black nets heavy with water and life.

Nets were cranked in one at a time on rollers the size of tractor tires. A bulging teardrop of net was muscled over a counter-height boxed platform near the stern. They jerked a ripcord on the bottom of the net and the catch fell, sliding in a slick wave to the sides of the sorting box.

With rapid, practiced movements, the crew plucked shrimp from the writhing mass of sea creatures. The men whistled while they worked, their caps ringed with salty sweat, their rubber boots squeaking. In only minutes, plastic laundry baskets were filled with twitching shrimp. Pelicans and seagulls became aggressive and impatient, screeching and diving onto the deck, trailing the boat ready to snatch the random ray or crab flung back to sea. After the shrimp were collected, by-catch was scraped through a hatch at the stern with a flat deck shovel. Sea birds went wild over the dead starfish, flounder, jellyfish, and silver eels.

Her father ran a tight ship, so LaShonda jumped in to help, hosing down the deck. A prehistoric-looking pelican perched near her and she squirted him with the water hose. Her father laughed. The bird fell backward and glided away.

"You never did like them birds," he said.

"I hate how they stare at me," she replied. The crew laughed.

Her father inspected the catch stored in iced holding tanks. It was roe season and the white shrimp were large and plump and plentiful. Everyone would be well paid today. By afternoon they were chugging back to the dock, where her father would sell part of his catch to the purveyors at the fish house.

Her father saved some of the roe shrimp for himself, they headed out on his rounds, stopping at the back doors of a couple of restaurants where chefs came out and lifted the lids of the foam coolers. A smile jumped to their faces when they peeked inside. After the restaurants, her father drove to their favorite spot by the highway. It was Saturday and it would take them no time to sell the last of their catch to the locals. Her father proudly displayed his hand-painted signs with curled pink cartoon shrimp and waited for customers to arrive. Road prices were always better than at the fish house, so her father held back more and more shrimp to hand-sell. Commercial prices had held steady for years, but demand was down overall. With gas prices double what they were a few years ago everybody was struggling. Her father complained that the Americans now shopped at big-box stores for cheap, frozen, ammonia-laced shrimp farmed in crowded, man-made ponds in India, China, and Mexico.

The white shrimp of spring would soon be replaced by summer's smaller shrimp locals called brownies. With brownies bringing as little as a dollar a pound commercially, many shrimpers were talking of taking the summer off for the first time. Local folks would still buy brownies at a reasonable price since they had the good sense to appreciate the sweet white meat of wild shrimp.

Her father stretched a tarp over the bed of his truck to block the sun. He'd parked next to a massive live oak, and LaShonda took up residence underneath in a woven lounge chair and set to reading a novel, one of Oprah's picks. Her father sat on the tailgate and weighed shrimp out in pound bags. Every so often the musky smell of the sea would reach her nose.

They were there only a few minutes when Ronald arrived. He was riding with a friend, who didn't get out of his car but sat and smoked, the heavy base of rap rattling the dilapidated vehicle. Ronald sauntered toward them with an affected lope her father referred to as a shuck and jive. LaShonda watched her father stiffen at his approach. The two men talked, but LaShonda couldn't hear what they said. Ronald walked back to the car, a hitch in his step timed with a head turn. The music was cut and highway sounds hummed again.

"Now," her father said when Ronald returned. "Now that I can hear you, what is it you wanted to talk to me about?"

Ronald turned his back to LaShonda to block her out. To spite him, she got up and took a cold drink from the cooler. She walked over to them and challenged Ronald with a look. The can made a sucking pop when she opened it. She drank, beads of water running down the can. She could see Ronald's attention shift to her cold drink.

"Anyway," Ronald was saying. "I need to get me a new compass."

"What do you need it for? You're not going out in the ocean."

"Mine's busted is all. It's full of water. My boat's ragged out and I'm trying to restore it. Don't you got a compass around you can let me have?"

"Maybe."

"Maybe. Why you got to give me a hard time?"

LaShonda's father sighed and she could see him wondering why Ronald was suddenly so industrious.

"You're not going to sell your boat, are you?"

"No."

" 'Cause if you do, you won't be able to get back and forth from the island anymore."

"I know that. I might just be getting me a new boat."

"With what money?"

"Shit. Don't worry about it. Why you always got to give me a hard time? You got a boat compass I can have or don't you?"

Abraham Washington sighed. "Okay," he said. "There's a good one in my shed back of the house. Up on the second shelf above the tool chest. Don't you touch none of my tools now. You can have that compass. It's got brackets and all. Should still be in good shape. You'll have to attach it of course, but like I said, find your own tools. You can't take none of mine."

"Thanks, Uncle Abe." He only called her father that when he really wanted something.

Ronald reached into the cooler and snatched a soda before LaShonda could slam the top down on his hand.

He giggled and resumed his pimping swagger on his way back to the car that rumbled to life. They peeled out of the parking lot, cutting in front of oncoming traffic. Horns blared.

"You got any idea what he's up to?" her father asked.

"Nope."

"See can you find out."

"Yes, sir."

LaShonda recognized the next car to arrive. It was Sloan's mother. She got out, large sunglasses covering half her face. She wore a flowing pale dress. She looked like a movie star.

"Good afternoon, Mrs. Sullivan," her father said.

"Good afternoon, Mr. Washington. What's your shrimp look like today?" she asked.

He opened the cooler and pulled out a bag of gray-pink shrimp.

"Oh, they're just lovely," she said.

"Best I've seen in a while," he replied.

"How much?"

"For you, eight dollars a pound."

"Okay," she said. "Give me three pounds. I'm making stew."

"Fine shrimp for stew. What the occasion?"

"Oh, just a little party for Ainslie. She's turning ten. I can hardly believe it."

"Kids got a way of growing up on you, don't they? How's she doing?"

"Much better. Thank you for asking." A strange look came over her. She seemed harried when she got out of the car, but now her body language was droopy, almost relaxed.

"Honey," she said to LaShonda, "would you and your father like to come to our house for the cookout tonight? It's nothing fancy. Just our family. I know you and Sloan are friends, but you never come around. Say you'll both come."

LaShonda could tell her father was unsure how to answer her. "Well . . . I thank you, ma'am, but Mrs. Sullivan . . ."

"Lauren. Please call me Lauren. Our daughters are friends and yet we hardly know each other. I insist. I won't take no for an answer. Why don't you come around about six? Don't bring a thing. I've got everything taken care of. Say you'll come."

It was hard to tell what she was thinking behind those big sunglasses. LaShonda saw her father hesitate. Normally, LaShonda would have minded her manners and not put her father on the spot, but she wanted to go to the party.

"Oh, Daddy, can we please go?" she said.

She saw the furrows at the corners of his eyes grow deeper.

"Say you will, Mr. Washington."

"Well," he said. "I really appreciate the invitation. But the only way I'm coming is if you call me Abraham."

"Wonderful, Abraham. I'll see you both at six. Do you know where we live?"

"Yes, ma'am."

"Wonderful. We'll see you then. Sloan will be so pleased. How much do I owe you? Is that eighteen?"

"No, ma'am. It would please me if you took these free of charge," her father said.

"Oh, I couldn't possibly."

"Wouldn't feel right. Me eating my own shrimp you done paid for. You got to let me contribute."

"Well, all right then." She grasped the three pound bags of shrimp. "Thank you. I appreciate it. I'll see you then."

They watched her faded Volvo blend smoothly into oncoming traffic.

"That was strange," LaShonda said. "Thank you, Daddy. I know you don't want to go."

"Um," he said. "That woman's got a lot on her mind."

CHAPTER 33

Lowcountry Boil

Her mother had started the day setting up the gas burner on its stand in the backyard and filling the massive aluminum cook pot from the water hose. She shucked corn, sliced sausage, and peeled little potatoes for the Lowcountry boil. Sloan had to make sure Ainslie stayed in her room so she wouldn't notice her mother's preparations, an easy task with her sister engrossed in television. Sloan had spent the morning doing research on drug cartels, then bundled her grumpy sister into the Jeep and headed for Brookgreen. It was the first time she had taken her sister to the gardens in months.

Now, as they arrived at their house, Sloan was hoping her sister would keep her mouth shut about the unexpected turn of events with Cal.

"Ainslie, don't you tell Mom or anybody about my fight with Cal."

"I don't like him."

"I know you don't. You never have. Why?"

" 'Cause he's a jerk."

"He's not always a jerk. Look. I like him. I really do.

It's just things are a little complicated between us right now. I need you to promise you won't say anything about us to anybody. Okay?"

"He's a jerk, but I won't tell."

"Promise?"

"I said I wouldn't. I know all kinds of things I don't tell."

"I'm trusting you."

Their grandparents' car was in their drive.

"Hey, Grammy and Grandpa are here," Ainslie said as she crawled out of the Jeep and headed around the house, her wheelchair forgotten.

When Sloan made it to the backyard, Ainslie was folded into her grandmother's arms and soon squished in between her grandparents on the glider. The backyard was draped in strands of dangling lights shaped like starfish and a big banner that read "Happy 10th Birthday!" Sloan stopped short when she saw LaShonda and her father.

"Hey," Sloan said. "Wow. LaShonda. What are y'all doing here?"

"Your mom invited us." She leaned in to her friend and said low, "I know it's a little weird."

"It's cool," Sloan said low, then, "Hi, Mr. Washington. Nice to see you."

"Same here," he said and shook her hand. "Your mother was kind enough to invite us over."

Suddenly there were flashes and Sloan knew her grandparents had started their photography assault. Ainslie complained that people took photos of her as if she were going to die any minute. This past Christmas had been especially hard on Ainslie. At one point she'd even cried, "Stop it! You're burning my retinas!" Sloan wondered why adults wanted photos of a pale, skinny, sick child, a child nothing like she used to be. It was all

part of the strange way illness affected people. Her grandparents were uncomfortable around them now, always
trying to mask their anxiety with smiles and fake non-
chalance. Sloan understood when Ainslie said nobody
was real anymore.

The giant aluminum cook pot's top rattled with steam
and their mother raised the lid to check the progress of
the stew. The distinct tang of shrimp boil spices wafted
out. Her mother removed the foil from a large platter
and slid onions, corn on the cob, red baby potatoes, and
sliced sausage into the bubbling water.

"Sloan, honey," her mother said. "I'm about ready
for the shrimp. Would you run up to the kitchen and
get them for me?"

Always added last, shrimp cooked in a matter of minutes. Her mother used a slotted ladle to strain the stew
before she piled plates high. Conversation lagged while
everybody dug in. Mounds of translucent pink shrimp
shells and mangled corn cobs accumulated on plates.

Sloan popped her thumbnail into her shrimp, sever-
ing shell from meat. Southerners loved to have their
fingers scalded when they peeled their shrimp. That
shelled, deveined, and chilled on the side of a fancy
bowl was for Northerners. No, Southerners liked everything fried or boiled, from vegetables to peanuts to
seafood.

Sloan loved oysters the most, but there would be no
oysters today because it was May and every person in
South Carolina knew the R rule—only eat oysters in
months that contain the letter R. You could eat oysters
in other months, but the slimy little creatures didn't
have the same sweet, wonderful taste that cooler waters
brought.

Blondie called from Sloan's pocket and she checked
the number even though she knew who it was. Ainslie

wrinkled her nose and LaShonda raised her eyebrows in a knowing look. Sloan shrugged and went back to peeling shrimp.

Cleanup was easy, since everyone simply tossed out their soggy plates. Sloan was dispatched to get the ice cream cake that had been removed from the freezer twenty minutes before. LaShonda came along to help.

When they hit the kitchen, Sloan said, "What are you really doing here?"

"I already told you. Your mother invited us. Sloan, I'm sorry for what I said about Cal's mom."

"Look, LaShonda. I've got a lot on my mind right now." Her phone sang out again and this time she pushed the OFF button.

"What's the matter? Trouble in paradise?"

"Grab the candles and let's light this puppy," Sloan said, ignoring LaShonda's sideways inquiry.

The party broke into the birthday song as they descended with the flaming cake. Her mother had ordered an ocean theme. Fish jumped waves of frosting. Shells and sea stars were strewn on a brown sugar beach.

Ainslie clapped her hands as Sloan set the cake in front of her.

"Make a wish," Sloan said.

Her sister squeezed her eyes tight and blew out the candles. Their mother began to serve the cake as Ainslie turned her attention to the meager pile of presents at the other end of the table. Ainslie selected a large red and white polka-dotted package with a giant red bow.

"Who's that from?" Sloan asked.

Ainslie opened the card. "It's from Daddy."

"That's right," their mother said. "He dropped it off earlier this week. He said he was sorry he couldn't make it today, but that he loves you."

"Oh, okay," Ainslie said. She ripped open the package and squealed. It was a Wii.

Sloan locked eyes with her mother and knew it was all a lie. Had her father truly forgotten? It was more likely that her mother hadn't invited him. That she had made him stay away.

Dark was closing in and cicadas began their scratchy trill. Suddenly, headlights raked the dock and crawled across the lawn. Everyone turned to the front of the house.

"What's *he* doing here?" Ainslie snarled.

"I don't know," Sloan said.

"You didn't invite him?" LaShonda asked.

"No. We broke up."

"Do I need to go talk to him?" her mother asked with trepidation.

"No. I'll take care of this." The walk out to Cal seemed like the longest of her life. Sloan knew everyone at the party was watching. Cal sat behind the wheel waiting for her. She walked up to the driver's side. At least he had enough sense not to come barging into the party.

"What are you doing here?" Sloan stood away from him, her arms crossed over her chest.

"You won't answer my calls."

"That's because I don't want to talk to you."

"You said I could call you tonight."

"Is this important, because we're right in the middle of my sister's birthday party."

He sighed. "I didn't want to bother you. I'm sorry for what I did today. It was wrong to treat you like that." He seemed contrite.

"Okay. Is that all?"

"No. I've got some news you won't like."

"What?"

"I told Verulo you were out and he said no way. He said we have to keep the circle tight. He said you know too much."

"I don't know too much. I don't know anything at all."

"Well, he thinks you do."

Sloan could feel her family staring at her and she moved out of their line of vision around the side of the house.

"Whatever gave him that impression, Cal? It wasn't you, was it?"

"Look. Don't go all crazy on me again. It's just that we need assurance you're not going to go to the cops or something." He had that fidgety way about him that let her know he'd been snorting.

"We?" So he didn't trust her either.

"I say we because if you did something like that, well, I don't know what Verulo might do. He might hurt us or, you know, our families or something."

She caught her breath.

"Did he actually say that? Did he actually say to you he'd hurt my family?"

Cal stepped out of the SUV. "He knows where we live."

"Did he threaten us?"

Mr. Washington approached with a garbage bag in his hand.

"Cal, you've got to go," she said.

"Tomorrow night. We're doing it tomorrow night."

"We'll talk later."

"Say you'll do it."

"Tomorrow night's too soon."

"Sloan, this isn't about your schedule."

"You've got to go."

"Say you love me," he whispered as Abraham Washington drew near.

"Not now, Cal."

Mr. Washington opened the garbage can and dropped the bag inside.

"Say it," Cal said and grabbed her arm.

Mr. Washington stepped from the dark into the glow of moonlight.

"What's going on out here?" he said. "Let go of her, son. That's no way to treat a woman."

Suddenly Cal's silky smoothness came back. He said, "Oh, this is nothing, sir. Just a little personal thing between Sloan and me."

"I'd like to hear that from Sloan."

Sloan crossed her arms in defiance and stared at the ground.

"Say everything's okay, Sloan," Cal urged, but she remained mute.

"Okay, son. It's time for you to go," Mr. Washington said as he stepped forward to move Cal back into his vehicle.

Cal threw his arm up and blocked the other man's attempt to touch him. "Go away, old man. This is no business of yours." Sloan had never seen him lose his cool around adults.

"I've seen you before. I've seen you with my Ronald down at the boat dock."

Cal ignored him and got back into the SUV.

"Be ready, Sloan," he said. "Answer the phone when I call you."

Cal spun gravel on his way out of the drive.

"Are you okay?" Mr. Washington asked her.

"I'm fine. Thank you."

"What was that all about?"

"It's nothing. I broke up with him."

"Then maybe your daddy needs to have a talk with that boy. Calm him down some. Help him see the light."

"My dad's not around right now. He and my mom are split up."

"Well, that's a sorry state of things."

Sloan agreed. "But thank you for your help. I'm sure Cal won't bother me again."

"Let's hope not. Now come on. Let's join the others for some more of that good cake."

"You go ahead, Mr. Washington. I don't feel like cake."

Sloan took the steps two at a time until she arrived at her room. She locked her door and threw herself onto the bed. Cal's words swirled in her head. She kept playing their fight over and over looking for a clue to how to get out of her predicament. If she didn't go, would Verulo actually track her or her family down just because she didn't show up? Sloan doubted it, but still, how could she know what he was capable of?

And what about Cal? Cal had gotten them into this awful situation and now he didn't trust *her*. He was pissed that for once she wasn't following along like a little puppy. She didn't want any part of his big deal, but she also didn't seem to have an out. She could not show up, not answer her phone and just see what happened. The best-case scenario was that Cal would break up with her for good. The worst-case scenario . . . well, that was something she didn't even want to think about.

She had that feeling again. That empty, sad sensation that called her to the beach when the last light had leaked from the sky. That pull that beckoned her to stand at the edge of the world and feel the earth draw breath. She pushed that feeling down.

There was a timid knock on her door.

"Go away," she said.

"Sloan? It's LaShonda. Are you okay?"

Sloan hesitated. She didn't want to talk, not to anybody, especially not to LaShonda.

Reluctantly, Sloan opened her door. "Did they send you up here to check on me?"

"Yeah."

"So, have I ruined the party for everybody?"

"No. Not really. What's up?"

"Nothing."

"You know, somehow I don't believe you."

"I can't tell you anything so don't ask."

"You know you can't keep a secret for shit. Besides, I've got some idea what's up."

"No, you don't."

"Why don't I tell you what I think is going on and you tell me if I'm hot or cold?"

"That's a child's game."

"Maybe. But I'm old enough to keep a secret."

CHAPTER 34

Limited Options

On Sunday, Sloan sat through her mother's abusive-boy speech, but when her mobile vibrated soundlessly in her pocket she answered Cal's call. She texted him back and then waited until her mother got into the shower to slip away that night. Before she left, she checked on Ainslie, who was sleeping the sleep of the fevered. She'd exhausted herself and spiked. Sloan ran her hand over her sister's sweaty forehead and felt guilty that she couldn't alert her mother, but she had to go.

Cal's vehicle sat dark a few houses down. She hesitated with her hand on the door. His windows were open and he said, "What are you waiting for? Get in."

She climbed in and he started the vehicle.

"Turn your phone off," he said.

She glared at him, but it was dark and she knew he couldn't see her reaction.

"It's off."

He reached over to kiss her and she flinched.

"Don't be mad," he said. "You know this would have

been easier if you'd just told your mom we were going to a senior party."

"On a Sunday night?"

"Tell her tomorrow's senior skip day."

"Cal, all I've done since I've been with you is lie to my parents."

Once off the island, he drove toward Georgetown, not toward the school-boat landing as she had thought he would. They passed dark business fronts and mom and pop restaurants where only a few cars sprinkled gravel lots. The South shuts down on Sundays, church being where the energy is placed at week's end, with fishing and crabbing running a close second.

"Where are we going? I thought we were going to the school-boat dock."

"I don't want to leave my ride there. Ronald's picking us up at another landing. Minimum exposure."

Sloan snorted. "So none of you white boys with Daddies' fancy boats know how to get up the Waccamaw to the school-boat landing? It's like, what? Two miles?"

"It's like a damn maze."

"Why do we have to do this so fast? Why not plan a little?"

"You saw how they were in Miami. They're like, *move and do it now.* I guess less time for something to go wrong."

"But we're delivering to the school-boat landing?"

"Why are you so interested all of a sudden?"

"I'm scared."

"Just chill. Don't ask questions. Don't do anything. Okay?"

"Okay."

Trees hung low and crowded the sides of the dirt road. Dust swirled behind them like a funnel cloud in their taillights. When they arrived at the isolated dock,

Cal pulled into a gray fishing shed and fastened the door behind them. Sloan was always fascinated by Cal's attention to detail.

Ronald was waiting at the dock in his old center console boat. They stepped down into the dilapidated vessel and found seats on the cracked bench. The seat's fissures pinched her legs and she readjusted her position numerous times before finally sitting on her hands.

"Drive on, brother," Cal said.

"All right, then," Ronald said. "Let's do this thang."

Cal pulled an impressive GPS system from his pocket and gray light pressed against their faces.

"Here." He held it out for Ronald to take. "Take us to those coordinates."

"No problem." Ronald cranked the boat to life and Sloan's heart rushed her ears.

Sloan scanned the boat for a life preserver but found only a moldy old orange thing a size too small. She shoved her hands down into her jacket pockets. The moist night air eased its way into her bones.

They clipped along in twilight, Ronald navigating by a three-quarter moon. He had lowered the sunscreen canopy, but even at rest its ragged edges snapped in the wind. He guided the boat expertly along the river overhung with branches. The watery road eventually became a wide labyrinth of marsh grass that they maneuvered through until it opened to ocean.

Sloan sat shivering from fear as much as from the cool ocean air. She knew if something should go awry, Cal's important father would get him out of trouble. If something bad went down, Sloan was sure she and Ronald would be the ones to pay and pay big. Even Ronald had less to lose than she did. She was the one who wouldn't get to go to college. Her family didn't even have enough money or time to defend her. She'd end up with one of those substandard public defenders you saw all the time on those crime shows.

The boat cut cleanly through the ocean's heartbeat. No rough water.

Sloan had expected they would go out a ways, but in a matter of minutes they pulled aside a sleek cigarette boat that dwarfed their vessel. While they traded ropes Verulo stepped on deck. The boats docked and Verulo's man jumped to action.

"Hello, chica," Verulo said. "I have a present for you."

When he reached down to help her climb aboard, a long pinky nail on his right hand made her pause. Sloan willed Cal to turn and see what was happening, but he was offloading cargo and paid her no mind.

"Time is swift," Verulo said.

Sloan couldn't say exactly why she reached to take his hand, but she did. In only a second, she was down into the galley of his boat, all shiny wood and brass and pale blue leather seats. He handed her a black pouch.

"Go ahead. Take a look," Verulo said. "Then take it to your man."

"I don't want to look. And he's not my man."

He smiled, showing plentiful teeth. "Interesting."

"I don't want to be any part of this. Look, I don't know you. I've never met you. I have no idea about any of this."

"A little late for this regret, don't you think?"

"Please don't hurt my family." It came out in a pleading, breathless stream of words.

Uncertainty flashed Verulo's eyes, then was gone. He reached up and snapped the clasp loose from her hair and her curls fell forward. He touched the end of a lock, then raised her hair and inhaled. He walked her back against the small sink and leaned close.

"Chica," he said. "You are confused. You need to talk to your man about why you are here."

She was a column of fear.

He kissed her lightly below her ear. Chills oozed down her arm.

"If you were mine I would take better care with you."

"That will never happen."

"What if we took a ride?"

Panic caught her. In a softer voice, she said, "Verulo, you're scaring me."

He backed away, snapped open a shiny lighter, and flamed a cigarette.

"Your man and I will do business, but you stay away. Never talk. If you talk, we will know. Then, as you Americans say, all bets are off."

She stared at him, struck dumb for a second. "Really?"

"Yes."

"Thank you." She started to leave and then hesitated. She had something she needed to ask.

She walked back to him and stood strong. "Did you ever threaten my family to Cal?"

"No. If he said so he lies."

Verulo smirked as realization came to her. She ascended the galley, the bag clutched to her chest. She climbed down onto Ronald's boat. The two watercrafts were disengaged and the cigarette boat zoomed away, immediately engulfed by the dark. Things were moving too fast.

Ronald cranked the engine and started toward land.

Cal reached for the pouch Sloan clutched.

"You lied!" Sloan yelled over the engine. "You lied to me!"

"Give me the money."

"No!" She twisted away from him. "You asshole!"

"Give me the fucking money, Sloan."

"What if I throw it over? Huh? How about I throw it overboard, Cal?" She held the pouch over the side.

He lunged for her.

She struck at him, only a small blow, easily deflected.

He grabbed her forearm and she cried out when he forced her down onto the windshield. Ronald cut the engine and they both fell forward onto the bow decking, where they thrashed around. Ronald moved to break them apart. Cal hit him with an errant swing. Ronald tumbled backward out of the boat.

"Ronald!" Sloan screamed and jumped to help, but she couldn't reach him. She searched frantically for the life preserver to throw. The boat was still drifting forward at a good clip and Ronald, quickly distant, was beyond Sloan's ability to throw the light life preserver she'd found. She dropped it and watched as Ronald went under, then clawed his way above the water line again.

The sound of his choking quickly dissolved in saltwater.

Cal jumped to the captain's chair.

"Get him!" Sloan screamed. Cal fumbled with the starter. She didn't think before she leaped. She hit hard and submerged. She forced herself to hold her breath even though she felt her chest was going to burst. When she finally came up, she saw Ronald in the distance, barely above the water line. He sank and then clawed his way to air again. Sloan knew if she approached, he would drag her down with him. There was no way she could save him. Cal had to get him back in. He had to. The boat idled up to her, blocking her view of Ronald.

"Get in," Cal commanded as he flipped the ladder down.

"Go get Ronald," she yelled.

"Come on. We're going to miss the drop. Get in," he yelled. "Then I'll get him."

"No! Get him first!"

Cal scanned the ocean in Ronald's direction. "I don't see him. He's not there!" he shouted. "We'll miss the drop. These people won't wait. Get in the goddamn boat!"

Sloan calculated the distance to shore and started in. She'd have to conserve energy, but she could make it.

"You're crazy!" Cal called. "Don't do this. Get in the boat."

She continued to plow through the water, the tide coming in and pushing her gently forward. She heard Cal calling, but his words were lost to her. The boat sped away. Sloan swam steadily. Her jeans dragged her down and she stopped and shed them as she had learned to do one year in camp. She kept swimming. Was it a mile to shore? Her arms began to ache long before she expected and land seemed to move away from her at times. Sloan flipped onto her back and kicked, Ronald was at the edges of her mind, but in the forefront she was just willing herself to put one aching arm in front of the other. To continue, simply continue was her goal.

Fatigue grabbed her and she had to rest. She floated on her back and her muscles twitched and screamed inside her. Would she make it? She was cold. Her muscles could refuse her. If she cramped, she'd drown. She had to stay loose. She started again, but the waves picked up and while they carried her inland she found it harder and harder to stay above water. Every stroke hurt. She gulped water. Cough. Pain. Another wave. Water in her lungs. Cough. More water. Stabbing pain. She was drowning. Drowning. And she would never be found. Never.

She was lifted. There were stars. Her lungs purged onto the scarred hide of a dolphin. She screamed, fell away from the animal and went under again. She came up choking. The animal was there, close, but still. Sloan grabbed at him. He was slick and her cold hands failed.

He nudged under her and she grabbed on as best she could.

"Don't leave me," she sputtered. "Please, don't leave me."

The animal, one giant muscle, was easing her toward home. She tried to swim, but quickly failed and he bumped her up as if she weighed nothing.

They moved toward the beach. Another dolphin appeared in the distance. And then a third.

They left her in two feet of water. She crawled to sand and rested her head in the sea foam line. She turned to find her rescuers, but they were gone. Apparitions now.

"Thank you," she whispered.

Ocean still roared in her ears. She threw up then; salty bile boiled out of her onto the sand, quickly taken by the surf. When she caught her breath the beach was peaceful, the architecture familiar. She had washed ashore at the far end of her island. She could make it home.

CHAPTER 35

A Call for Help

LaShonda loved the metal taste of the shed, gasoline and oil and smooth silver tools she sensed in the air like a spoon in her mouth. Her father sipped a can of beer and stared out the window over his workbench at nothing LaShonda could see in the dark. Ronald had taken the compass.

"What you reckon that Ronald's up to?" he asked LaShonda.

"I don't know. He's always up to something," she replied as if uninterested.

"Maybe so, but I get the feeling something's going on with that white boy. They're not hanging around with each other because they're friends. Something's going on."

He raised an eyebrow at her. "I don't know, but I'm betting it's illegal. And what's illegal mean? That means drugs. Well, there you go."

LaShonda was always shocked by his perception. She watched his big hands delicately mending a shrimp net draped from the ceiling of the shed. His gray mustache twitched as he moved his fingers. He wrinkled his brow and the lines on his face grew deeper.

"What?" her father said. "You don't think I'm right on this? I know something's going on."

"I didn't say a thing."

"But you're thinking it. What are you thinking? Do you know something?"

"No."

The phone rang in the house and LaShonda ran to answer it. This late, their phone rang only at times of trouble. LaShonda knew before she scooped it up that things were going to get interesting.

The voice on the other end surprised her for the second time in as many days. It was Sloan's mother.

"Hi. Is this LaShonda?" Mrs. Sullivan asked.

"Yes, ma'am."

"LaShonda, do you know where Sloan is?"

"No, ma'am."

"Would you tell me if you did know?"

"I don't exactly know. You want to talk to my father?"

"Yes, please."

When her father came to the phone, she lingered nearby, pretending to watch an *ER* rerun with that good-looking black doctor.

"Mrs. Sullivan, good evening. No, I haven't seen her. What's the matter? For how long?

I see, well, we haven't seen her but if we do I'll be sure to give you a call. You take care now. Okay. Good-night."

He carefully placed the receiver back.

"Sloan Sullivan's gone missing."

It was after midnight.

"Her curfew's eleven. Anybody could be an hour late," LaShonda said offhandedly. "Her mother just freaks when she does the least little thing. I wouldn't worry about it."

He scanned her up and down, LaShonda thought looking for a crack in her façade. He considered her silently as if he could force the truth from her mouth by a single stare, but LaShonda wasn't moved. Her father folded his arms across his chest.

"What do you know?" he asked. "Is Sloan out with her boyfriend?"

"I don't know."

"You mean to tell me you spent an hour up in that girl's bedroom last night, all that going on with her boyfriend, and she didn't tell you nothing? Hard to believe."

"She broke up with him. That's all I know."

Sloan had been quite the soap opera the last few months. LaShonda had been more intrigued by her friend's exploits than she should have been. And she was sure that if asked, her father could come up with a passage from the Bible to address such things. Something about guilt by association or something. So she just never mentioned anything. She was proud of herself for keeping a secret.

"What's that boy cooking up with Ronald?"

"I don't know. Ronald doesn't tell me nothing."

Heat bugs scratched outside their door and LaShonda knew her father was going to push her to admit what she knew. But what did she know really? Not everything, just bits and pieces. Ronald hadn't told her much, just insinuated that he was going to be in the money soon, nothing unusual for him. Sloan hadn't really told her anything exciting or juicy. Sloan was guarded and defensive when it came to that rich boyfriend of hers. But there were clues enough. Enough for LaShonda to figure out what was going on.

And she felt smart for figuring things out before her father did. He was always the one who could read people, who knew what you were thinking before you did, what you were going to do before you did it. LaShonda could never resist her father once he started asking questions, but everything in her being told her to keep her mouth shut this time.

CHAPTER 36

Home Calling

Emmett stared at the glass that had been attached to his hand the last few weeks. It was way after midnight, but he couldn't nod off. Since moving in with Larry, he'd picked up his friend's habit and become a night owl, too. Insomnia wasn't his only new trick; he'd started to drink more during the day. Emmett knew it was a problem and he fully intended to do something about it. Soon. Emmett slowly swirled bourbon in a crystal highball, the tawny liquid refracting lamplight in a beautiful dance.

"Here's to you," he said and raised his glass to Larry. "You slew the dragon."

"Don't throw a party just yet," Larry advised. "They could still hold out on us."

"So we're supposed to hear from them, what, on Monday?"

"Right. Tomorrow. That's what they said."

"I know Lauren's probably wondering what happened, but if you're not absolutely positive that things are settled then I'm not going to call her yet."

"Probably wise."

"Ten months. That's how long those assholes dragged this thing out. Think they were just hoping Ainslie would die so they wouldn't have to pay?"

"It happens. It's not a bad strategy on their part."

"Fuckers."

"You can say that again."

"I think I just did." Emmett threw back the last of his drink and rose to get a refill. Larry's bar was a thing of beauty, fully stocked, fancy cocktail shaker and monogrammed napkins. Clients frequently gave him alcohol and bar accessories as a thank-you.

Unlike Larry's personal disheveled demeanor, his boathouse was a well-maintained jewel on a tidal creek. He kept it clean by owning few things. He lived a Spartan existence that Emmett now found appealing. Owning less, meant less to keep up, less to own you. Larry was a solitary person. Emmett spent his life in constant flux living in a household of females with raw emotions and unpredictable reactions. Larry ate what he wanted when he wanted, scratched when necessary, and watched ballgames on the tube until he fell asleep.

But Emmett's life was full of women, and try as he might to figure them out, he was forever one step behind, one decision late, one compliment shy.

Larry got up to make another drink. Outside a bird flew in and perched on the deck railing. It was an egret, stark against the shadowy background—a rare treat from a bird that usually shied from humans. The bird didn't leave but scrunched down searching the water, patient.

They'd spent many evenings fishing off Larry's deck into the flat, glossy water that mirrored the forest walls.

"I wonder if Lauren'll take me back."

"She'll take you back. Y'all have too much history."

"I don't know. She doesn't act like she misses me

much. Total noncontact except when it comes to the kids."

"You don't look like you're freaking out about it."

"Honestly, and I'm a total bastard for saying this, but it's been a relief to be away from all that for a while."

"You are a shit."

"Well, she kicked me out. I didn't leave. And let's not forget I'm unjustly accused."

"Point taken."

"Don't get me wrong. I'm embarrassed about it, our being separated, I mean. But we needed a break."

"Be careful. A lot of people who take breaks end up taking them for good."

There was a familiar ring tone from Emmett's phone.

"Well, speak of the devil," Emmett said. "I wonder what's wrong this late."

"Maybe she misses you."

"Yeah. Right." He flipped open his phone.

"Hey, Lauren. What's up?" he said.

Lauren was not hysterical, but Emmett could tell she was worried.

"Emmett, you haven't seen Sloan, have you?"

"Not in a couple of days."

"So she's not with you now? You wouldn't *not* tell me, would you? I mean if she was with you."

This hurt his feelings some, but he said, "No. I wouldn't lie to you. Why? What's wrong?"

"She's missing."

"For how long?"

"I guess a couple of hours now. I thought she was asleep in her bed. I went to check on Ainslie and just thought I'd look in on her. She's been so strange lately."

"Stranger than usual?"

"Yes, stranger than usual. Please don't make light of this, Emmett."

"I'm not. I swear."

"She had a fight with her boyfriend yesterday. I . . . well . . . I had a little party for Ainslie's birthday yesterday and my parents came and it wasn't a big deal or anything."

Emmett felt a stab in his stomach, but he said, "Okay."

"So anyway, Sloan didn't invite Cal, but he showed up. They had a pretty heated exchange out in the driveway."

"Did she say what it was about?"

"She's tight-lipped about it. I mean, you know how she is, but she did say she'd broken up with him and he wasn't very happy about it. He grabbed her arm and hurt her, I think."

"That little shit."

"I told her she couldn't see him anymore for a while. I explained to her about abusive situations, but she just rolled her eyes at me."

"So she's okay?"

"I thought she was. I can't believe she isn't here. I have no idea when she left. She won't answer her cell phone. The weirdest thing is her Jeep is still here."

"Maybe she went for a walk on the beach."

"This late at night?"

"Maybe, I mean if she was upset. You know how she likes to run off on her own."

"I guess it's possible she's out celebrating the end of school with some other seniors, but she could have told me. I would have let her go."

"Have you called any of her friends?"

"That's just it, Emmett. I just realized that I don't really know her friends anymore. I mean, other than Cal Wannamaker, who does she run around with? I don't know."

"I surely don't know either."

"I need you to come home."

Emmett held his breath.

There was silence on the other end of the phone.

Then she said, "I mean, would you please come home and help me find her?"

"I'll be right there."

Emmett drove faster than he should have, considering he'd been drinking. He wasn't panicked about Sloan. She was just being a teenager, breaking away, making her own decisions. She'd been on that trip to Mexico, so she surely could handle being out a couple of hours on her own. But Lauren saw this as something more than just her being out past curfew. She was truly worried, and if this did indeed have something to do with that boy Sloan was seeing, well, Emmett would just deal with him in a swift fashion, man to man.

He took the front steps two at a time and stood on the porch wondering if he was required to ring his own doorbell. What an odd sensation. He was unsure if he was welcome in the house he had lived in his entire life. He let himself in.

"Hey," he said to Lauren, who was seated at the kitchen table, phone at the ready. She took one look at him, put her hands over her eyes, and burst into tears. Unsure of what to do, he approached her slowly and reached to touch her shoulder. She kept crying and he kept moving closer until his hands rested on her shoulders and she was hanging on to his waist, sobbing into his chest. He caressed her hair. Tears flowed freely, and when she finally regained control of herself, she had a blotchy face and eyes like roadmaps.

"Should we call the Wannamakers?" she asked between shudders.

"That would embarrass her. Let's don't just yet. She's not that late. Look. This is probably just the first time of many more times of her being late. You're overreacting just a bit at this point. Let's be patient."

She considered this, then said, "I need a glass of wine."

"I'll get it," Emmett said and moved to the wine cellar, but it was empty.

"There isn't any. There isn't much of anything around here anymore."

"Rum and Coke, maybe?" he asked.

She was frustrated and let out an angry cry. "God!" she said. "I can't believe we're having this conversation."

"Look, there's nothing we can do right now. Just chill."

Larry called then and Emmett answered and blurted out, "Hey, how long do we have to wait before we can file a missing-persons report?"

"Twenty-four hours, but shut up a second," Larry said. "I was listening to the scanner. There's some drug bust down at the school-boat dock. Cal Wannamaker's name came up. Are you sure Sloan isn't with him? If she is, she may be headed to jail."

"Shit," Emmett said. "What do we do?"

"Don't do anything. I'll be there in twenty minutes."

"What is it?" Lauren asked after he hung up.

"Cal Wannamaker's just been busted for some sort of drug deal. If Sloan's with him, we're going to be bailing her out of jail."

"Are you kidding me?"

"Do I look like I'm kidding?"

"What are we going to do?"

"Larry said sit tight. He'll be here in a few minutes."

"What are we going to do until then?"

"I don't know. Look, you said her car is still downstairs. I'm going to go walk the beach and look for her. Call my cell if anything changes. I'm going up to scan around before I leave."

Emmett let himself into Ainslie's bedroom. Her lizard tanks were empty but she would be filling them with critters again soon. For a second he saw her as she had always been. Her head was buried in a pillow and only her face showed. She seemed so calm and even happy, Emmett thought. He touched the linen at her chin and bent to kiss her forehead. She was hot and sweaty and he checked her for fever but decided she was fine. He had become aware of so many of those caregiver things Lauren had always done.

Emmett grabbed a pair of binoculars from Ainslie's shelf and climbed up to the widow's walk. The alcohol had burned away and his mind was razor sharp, his vision very clear in the cool air. The ocean rumbled in like thunder, and like thunder it rolled off down the beach. When he was a child, he believed thunder was arriving waves on the flip side of the sky.

He glassed the beach with Ainslie's binoculars. Flashes of white surf tumbled in, illuminated by the light of neighbors' windows, lights that Ainslie would have scolded them for allowing to shine out to the beach. He stood this way for some time, rigid and thorough in his scanning of the beach and the creek behind him. She wasn't down on their dock, she wasn't at the neighbor's pool. Back on the beach, something caught his attention. He trained his glasses on the small figure. The person stopped and teetered a second before crumbling to the sand. A moment later the figure stood again and started up the sandy trail toward their house. Emmett recognized her pale legs.

Down the ladder, the stairs inside, then outside and to the path he ran. She was looking to the house, longing written across her face. Her gaze slowly shifted, and when she recognized him, she crumbled down. He ran to her, soft sand pulling at his every step. He fell to his own knees, ignoring the sting of sand burrs.

He gathered his daughter to him and held her tightly. She was cold, so bone-achingly cold he knew she must be in pain. He stripped his jacket off and pulled it around her. He carried her then, through what seemed like quicksand, back toward the light of home.

CHAPTER 37

Treading Water

"They're going to question her," Larry said. "She's the girlfriend."

For the last two hours Sloan had slept in Emmett's leather chair near the fireplace, a blanket wrapped around her. She was shivering when he brought her inside, and Lauren had quickly plied her with hot cocoa. Within ten minutes she was asleep. It was nearing dawn, with none of the adults having slept.

Emmett, Lauren, and Larry were sipping coffee and taking turns pacing the kitchen. Lauren wanted to let her sleep. The men wanted answers.

"She's back here safe. That's all I care about right now," Lauren said.

"Aren't you just a little curious as to where she's been?"

"It looks as if she went swimming. That's all I know."

"Help me here, Larry."

Larry shrugged as if to say he couldn't convince her.

"She'll tell us. Don't push her," Lauren said.

* * *

As the morning wore on and the phone didn't ring, Emmett began to feel relief. Sloan slumbered, occasionally jerking from a fitful dream. Lauren had finally taken a nap, too, and Larry was snoring on the sofa. It was nearing lunchtime and Emmett's stomach was growling. As he searched the refrigerator, Ainslie came into the kitchen. He'd almost forgotten about his other child.

"Daddy," she said. She hugged his waist and buried her face against his chest.

"Hey, baby. You slept a long time," Emmett said and held her tightly.

"Did Sloan come back yet?"

"Yeah, she's back. Did you know she was gone?"

"I'm hungry."

"Okay. I'll make you some scrambled eggs."

Ainslie rubbed sleep from her eyes and said, "With cheese."

"With cheese."

Emmett was stirring the eggs in the nonstick skillet with the soft spatula when Sloan stepped into the kitchen. He'd been meaning to ask Ainslie what she knew. It would have to wait.

"Eggs?" Emmett asked.

"Yes. I'm starving," she said.

Emmett added more eggs to the skillet, and when they were still slightly wet, he sprinkled in a handful of grated cheese, folded it in, and divided the eggs three ways onto plates. Ainslie made toast and buttered each side. Emmett poured orange juice, and they sat silently eating. The girls had their heads down, concentrating on food as hungry children can. At this moment, here with his daughters, life was perfect again.

Emmett was startled from his thoughts by the doorbell. He heard Lauren move toward the door. He sat still, dreading what could be next. It was probably the cops come to question Sloan, and they had accomplished nothing. Sloan had yet to say one word about where she had been early this morning.

Lauren's tone was full of venom. "What are *you* doing here?"

An indiscernible, female voice drew Emmett and Larry to the front door.

To Emmett's astonishment, Caroline Crawford stood on his porch.

"Please," she said to Emmett when she saw him. "I'd like to speak with your daughter. Is she here?"

Lauren stood her ground. "What could you possibly want with Sloan?"

"I'm sorry. That's confidential."

"What confidential business could you possibly have with my daughter?"

"I'm sorry. I simply can't say. Is she here?" This last question was directed at Emmett.

Lauren turned on him, daggers flying from her eyes. "What is *she* doing here?" she hissed.

"I don't know. I'll take care of this," Emmett said. He stepped outside and pulled the front door closed behind him.

"Caroline, what in the world *are* you doing here?"

"I need to talk to your daughter. She *is* here, isn't she?"

"Why wouldn't she be?"

"Look, Emmett. I don't have time to play games and neither do you. I need to talk to her. She might be in a lot of trouble and I have to talk to her before the police get here. You can rest assured they're not too far behind me."

"What do you know?" he asked.

"What do *you* know?" she replied.

"Caroline, this is my child we're talking about."

"I know. That's why you have to send her out to talk to me. I can protect her. I can make this whole thing go away from your family."

"What thing are you talking about? We still don't know what's going on and I'm very confused as to why you're here."

"You haven't talked to anybody yet, have you?" she asked.

"Not a person."

"Great. Then there's still time. Send her out, Emmett. This affects a lot more people than just Sloan."

He hesitated. "Wait here," he said finally.

"Fine."

Back inside, Emmett brushed past his wife and leaned down to whisper into Sloan's ear, "There's a woman outside to speak with you. Her name's Caroline Crawford. I'm not exactly sure what she wants, but I think you should talk to her. She's not with the police."

Sloan sat rigid, her hands spread on the table.

"Go on," he urged. "It'll be okay."

He followed Sloan outside and watched as she shook hands with Caroline. The woman motioned for her to follow her and they walked down the stairs and headed toward the beach. He thought briefly of Caroline's shoes and saw that she wore sensible ones today. This was when he realized his daughter was barefoot. He hadn't thought to have her put on shoes.

CHAPTER 38

In Over Her Head

There was no way anyone could hear their conversation on the beach. Nature had a way of swallowing words uttered near the ocean. Sloan knew her father was trailing behind them, keeping an eye on her. Her mother had probably sent him out to stand guard, to make sure she didn't collapse or maybe even run away again.

Somehow Sloan knew this woman. She was pretty in an uptight kind of way. But it was apparent her mother didn't like her and Sloan had some suspicion why.

They walked for a while and then the woman said, "Sloan, I know you were with Cal and Ronald last night."

She stopped short.

"Don't be afraid. I'm here to help you. I'm friends with the Wannamakers."

Sloan knew her now. This was the woman everybody said was having an affair with Cal's father.

"We were afraid something had happened to you," she said. "We were very relieved to learn you made it home okay."

Sloan detected a note of insincerity in her words.

"What do you want?"

"Sloan, what happened in the boat? Cal said Ronald fell out and drowned. He said you jumped out to save Ronald and when you couldn't you swam away from him and refused to get back into the boat. Is that what happened?"

"Sort of."

"So Cal tried to help you two?"

"What?"

"I'm saying, Ronald drowned, but Cal was trying to help him. You remember that, right?"

"Cal knocked him into the water. Then he wouldn't save him."

"Sloan, I don't think you know what you're saying."

"I know what I'm saying."

"I want you to listen to me very carefully. Nobody knows about you. Nobody has to ever know about you or Ronald. We don't want you involved in any way."

"We who?"

"The Wannamakers. Cal. Cal wants to protect you. You want to help Cal, don't you?"

"Not really."

"But he's your boyfriend."

"He's not my boyfriend."

The woman sighed then. She said, "Okay, let's cut to the chase. The police are going to interview you just because you are Cal's girlfriend. At this time, there is no evidence you were involved. You weren't at the school-boat landing when Cal was busted. He never said a word about you. They know about Ronald. He apparently tried to cut a deal through his parole officer to turn you two in."

"Both of us?"

"Yes. But you weren't there, so it's misinformation at this point."

"How do you know these things?"

"Honey, I work with the city. I know things."

It was Sloan's turn to stare out to sea.

"Ronald's dead. The police won't investigate that?" she asked.

"Ronald could be anywhere. He skips town all the time. He's frequently unaccounted for. There's no body. Everything is circumstantial. Ronald's information is unreliable. Keep your mouth shut and everything will work out fine."

"How's Cal explaining away having Ronald's boat?"

"Cal says he borrowed the boat."

Sloan nodded. "Guess a drug rap's a lot easier to beat than murder."

"Sloan, nobody said anything about murder. Besides, even if this whole thing blew apart it would still only be manslaughter. He tried to help Ronald. But then, we're trying to make sure things don't get to that point."

"Where's Cal now?"

"His parents bailed him out this morning. They're shipping him off to rehab today. Out in Arizona I believe."

"I know the place. I guess that'll help his case, to say he's been through rehab."

"Don't worry about Cal. His parents will take care of him."

Sloan snorted at that.

"You need to worry about you and your family. You don't want everybody around here to know you were a part of this. Right? So, here's the deal. You don't know anything."

"I don't know anything."

"You were home playing cards with your family all night or some such shit. Make up a story and stick to it. Can you get them on board or will they be a problem?"

"Don't worry about it. I can handle it."

"As long as you don't talk, you're safe. If you talk, well then, we can't protect you."

"What does that mean?"

"It means Cal might start naming names."

A dagger of panic shot through Sloan's heart. "He can't. Nobody can. Doesn't he understand? It's dangerous."

She held up a hand to stop her. "Sloan, Cal told us everything. We know about your Mexican connection."

"Not *my* Mexican connection."

"No. Let me rephrase. Cal's contact information and names he had wouldn't be useful. It's all a bunch of lies, dead ends. DEA would never find them."

"I figured as much."

"So authorities are going to press hard to get who they can locally. Let's just make sure they don't get you."

"Why do you care if they get me? What's it to you?"

"It's nothing to me personally, you understand. Let's just say that it is in nobody's best interest for you to be involved. Can we just keep it at that?"

"Won't the cops ask where Cal got the drugs?"

"I said don't worry about it. That's what lawyers are for. You just keep a low profile, don't add to the problem, and we're going to make this all go away."

She nodded. "Okay."

"Then we have an understanding. What have you told your parents?"

"Nothing."

"Nothing."

"No. I haven't talked to them at all."

"I'm the only person you've talked to?"

She nodded yes.

"Excellent. That way you won't have to involve anybody else." She opened her purse and showed Sloan an envelope.

"What's that?"

"Something to help you remember to forget."

"Money?"

"Smart girl."

"What if I don't take it?"

"You'd be a fool not to. Take it and keep your mouth shut. It's easy."

"How much?"

"Twenty thousand."

Sloan had the feeling if she didn't take the money that it would disappear and the Wannamakers would still think she had it.

Besides, she would never talk. She had every reason in the world to keep her mouth shut. She'd promised Verulo her silence and she would stand by her word. She'd protect her family no matter what happened to her. She'd go to jail before she'd give up any information. But she didn't tell this woman that. She would never reveal what happened, not to anyone, not ever.

Up the beach, Sloan saw her father sitting on the steps at the end of a neighbor's boardwalk. She turned her back to him, reached for the envelope and slid it into her sweatshirt. She zipped it up and said, "Don't you talk to my family about this. Not one word. I'll take care of everything."

The woman's lips made a knowing, disturbing smile. "I think I can trust you."

"I can do it."

"So we have a deal?"

"Yes."

"Good. You need to understand, Sloan. This is bigger than just what was going on with you and Cal. There's much more at stake here than you know about. You're in over your head, so don't fuck up."

* * *

The detectives arrived in a sleek black unmarked sedan. It was dusk when Larry answered the door. He was around as the family representative, although he said very little. The cops already had some information, such as the fact that Sloan had gone to Mexico with Cal's friends. They told her not to be afraid, that they were talking to everybody who had gone on the trip.

One officer, an attractive young fellow who they probably thought Sloan would relate to, asked questions first. When this softer approach yielded no results, an older cop got more pointed with questions.

"Did anyone approach you while you were in Mexico?"

"What do you mean?" Sloan asked.

"Anybody you were unfamiliar with? Did you notice Cal talking at length with anybody you didn't know?"

"Cal's outgoing. He talks to all kinds of people all the time."

"You ever see anybody doing cocaine?"

"No."

"It's okay. You can tell me. Even if you participated, you won't get in trouble."

"I'm not very good friends with the rest of them. I'm not really a part of their little rich clique. I just dated Cal. He wasn't my boyfriend or anything."

"Really? Because when we were asking around, your name came up a lot in connection with Cal Wannamaker."

"I don't know why. I think he had a couple of other girls he dated down at the College of Charleston."

"Got names?"

She shook her head. "Why would I know the other girls he dated?"

"Good point. Look, the reason I ask is, clean-cut college kids go down to Cancún to have a good time, and before you know it, they're hooked up with some sleazy characters. Spring-breakers are attractive targets since they don't fit the profile of the typical drug runner. Living on the South Carolina coast would make your group particularly attractive."

"Why?" Emmett asked.

The younger cop answered her father. "DEA's shut down a lot of Florida drop points. Smugglers are looking for new inroads and South Carolina's got a lot of unmonitored coastline, thousands of estuaries and rivers and creeks. All along the coast there are points of entry to the Intercoastal Waterway. Prime real estate for illegal activities. We're seeing an increase in illegal drug activity every year. Even in our ports."

The older cop focused back on Sloan. "Where were you last night?"

"Here," she said.

"All night?"

"Yes." She held her breath, hoping her father wouldn't correct her.

"You didn't leave the house?"

She decided not to omit turning up on the beach wet and exhausted. "I did for a while. I went swimming."

"When?"

"Around midnight."

The cops paused at the unlikely story and gave a questioning glance to her father.

"First I've heard of this," Emmett said and shrugged as if it didn't matter.

So he would have backed up her lie.

"That's a little dangerous, don't you think?" the cop said.

"I do it all the time," Sloan replied.

"Okay," he said. Doubt tinged his voice. "Why don't

you tell me what you know about the Wannamakers? You dated their son for how long?"

"About three or four months."

"Which is it, three or four?"

"Well, um, we met in February but didn't go out for a while after that."

"Have you been over to their house for supper or parties?"

She nodded. "A couple of times."

"Did you ever see anything when you were over there? Anything like strange people or them acting secretive or just anything you would consider out of character for them?"

"Why are you asking her this?" Emmett said.

"Just let her answer the question."

"No. They're just normal. You know, like everybody else."

"Did you ever see anybody there from Mexico or South America?"

"Other than Al from the restaurant, no."

"So Mr. Wannamaker is friends with Al?"

"Everybody knows they are."

"How frequently did you see Al Aldrete?"

"I don't know. I was only there a few times."

She wanted to ask why they were so interested in the Wannamaker family. She flashed on what that Crawford woman said. *"There's much more at stake here than you know."* She focused on moving the cops out of her house as quickly as possible.

"What about gangbangers? Ever see Cal hang around with any of those guys? Anybody unusual for him?"

"My daughter doesn't hang out with thugs," her father said.

"Mr. Sullivan, gangs are one of the main distribution channels for drugs."

"It's okay, Daddy," Sloan said. "No gangsters. Really. Nothing like that."

"What about bikers? Did Cal know any bikers?"

"Like motorcycle riders?"

"Yes. Three members of a bike gang were arrested at the school-boat dock along with your boyfriend," the young officer said.

"It's Bike Week in Myrtle Beach," her father surmised. "They come from all over the United States."

"Yes, sir," the officer continued. "They were the next leg of the transportation chain. It's good they were caught before disbursal began because it would be like a spider web from that point."

Now Sloan understood the rush to make things happen this weekend. So Verulo's connection had fallen through and he had pressured Cal to make a quick drop in order to meet the bikers this week. She wondered how much money Verulo had paid Cal. It must have been a sweet deal, and Cal had been afraid she would mess it up for him. He'd wanted to keep her involved so he could control her. Now it all made sense.

Suddenly Lauren pushed Ainslie into the room in a wheelchair that hadn't been used for weeks. Ainslie slumped over and at first Sloan was alarmed, but when her mother spoke, Sloan understood.

"Excuse me," Lauren said sweetly as she made a show of setting the brakes on each side of the chair. "I hate to interrupt, but how long do you think y'all are going to be? Ainslie's not feeling well and all this excitement is making it hard for her to sleep."

Recognition washed the faces of the detectives. Sloan could see they were mentally debating how much longer they should push the suspect. She wasn't giving them anything. She was playing the innocent so well.

The officers rose and made polite comments. They

apologized to Ainslie for bothering her on their way out.

The family stood rigid in the foyer as they watched the lights of the unmarked car scrape the night.

"Smooth," Emmett said.

"You're welcome," her mother said, then, "Ainslie, go to bed."

As Ainslie climbed the stairs, Sloan thought to follow her, but then she heard Larry talking. The cops had wanted to know why they had a lawyer there, but her father had assured them he was only a family friend. As their family friend cracked the seal on a fresh bottle he'd brought with him, he said, "I heard they've been watching the Wannamakers."

"Why?" Emmett asked.

"All that coke at their parties. They think they're local royalty, above the law."

"Guess they're getting ready to find out different," Emmett said.

Larry turned to Sloan then, a glass of bourbon clinking softly in hand. "Now young lady, are you sure there's nothing you want to tell us?"

The three suspicious adults waited for her reply.

"No," Sloan said as she thought of the envelope of money tucked away in her closet. She'd have to find a way to get it out of the house along with a few other things that could be considered evidence in this ordeal. "I swear there's absolutely nothing to tell. I'm really, really tired. Can I go to bed now?"

CHAPTER 39

The Drug Dealers Next Door

The water was warm and inviting. The ocean was calm, Sloan's buoyancy effortless. She moved her arms gracefully away from her body, slow angel wings in the deep, dark sea. Now, when she swam at night, she was always searching for her friends, waiting for their fins to emerge, for a gentle nudge from below. She called to them in her mind.

"Come back to me," she would plead. "I want Ainslie to know."

But she could never tell her sister how the dolphins had saved her. She would never be able to divulge their kindness, at least not until they arrived again under different circumstances.

She floated on her back, her hair tugged gently away by the water's movement. She felt a swirl of action beneath her and she bolted upright in the water. Her heart rushed into her ears.

"Show yourself," Sloan whispered. "Please. Come back to me."

And then a smooth, gray body sliced the water to her

side and she reached toward him, but her fingers didn't touch. The animal surfaced again and she waited, hoping he would come closer.

She felt happy, comforted by his presence, and when she felt the rush of water beneath her she waited for his contact, braced for his muscular push. Water swirled between her fingers and she reached for him, and up from the depths came a face, bloated and torn, eaten away, frantic crabs crawling from the maw of Ronald's mouth. He moved into her outstretched hand and she tried but couldn't pull away. When she touched him, Ronald opened his eyes and eels spilled out. He coughed and spewed vile mud into her face and she screamed and screamed and screamed.

"Sloan, honey, wake up." She heard her mother's firm voice commanding her back to consciousness. "Sloan, I said wake up. You're having a bad dream."

Sloan jerked upright in bed.

"Honey, you're having another nightmare. Are you okay?"

Sloan was disoriented. She wasn't sure where she was, and then, slowly, she realized it had all been a dream. She hadn't been in the ocean since the ill-fated night Ronald drowned. At least not physically.

But every night since the incident, as she had come to think of it, she had gone swimming in her dreams. Her mind was always on Ronald and how he was still out there, bits of him floating around, food for the sea. Nobody was looking for him, nobody was asking questions, so he came to her, night after night. He never spoke. He only spilled his guts onto her and smothered her with his suffocating stench.

"What is up with you?" her mother said. "Maybe you need to go see somebody about these nightmares."

"No, Mom," Sloan said. "I'll be fine." Sloan wouldn't be sharing her stresses with anybody, ever.

Her mother pushed Sloan's hair back from her face. She placed a hand against her forehead to check for fever. "You're clammy."

"I'm hot. That's all. It's hot in here. Can't we turn on the air conditioner?"

"It'll cool off soon. Look, it's almost nine. Why don't you get up and help me? I've got to go to the grocery store. Can you come with me? We can stop and get some waffles on the way if you like."

"Sure, okay. Just give me a minute to get ready."

"I'll wait downstairs. Hurry up. We have to pick up Ainslie from your father at noon."

In her bathroom, Sloan stared into the mirror at her pale, sweaty self. When would this stop? It seemed she spent every waking moment anxious. She couldn't shake it. Couldn't put it out of her mind. But she had no alternative. She didn't have the freedom to unburden herself. Everything seemed to be going better for her family right now and if she opened up about Cal and Ronald and Verulo, things would spiral right back into the dark abyss they were only now beginning to escape.

She watched her mother's mind wander as they meandered through the inland grocery store Sloan had come to loathe. Her mother insisted they continue to shop here, since their money situation was still dire. Even though she had planned their meals for the coming week, it took her forever to make selections. Her mother seemed particularly overwhelmed by the cereal, so Sloan had made those decisions. As they rounded the end of an aisle next to the checkout counters, her mother stopped at a stack of Sunday newspapers from Charleston and suddenly became engrossed.

The Post and Courier headline above the fold read, "Millionaire Real Estate Developer's Financial Fall Leads to Drug Charge." The story featured a photograph of Cal's father exiting a yellow courthouse, wearing a crisp tie under his tailored jacket, the air slightly lifting his smooth hair.

Her mother read down. "Says here Trip Wannamaker is going belly-up on a couple of his larger developments. Apparently his McMansions aren't selling and he was looking for some quick money to keep his real estate company afloat." Her mother paused in her reading and then said, "They're getting it on conspiracy and money laundering too."

"They who?"

"The article says, 'local restaurant-owner and wine expert Alejandro Aldrete was also indicted. From Mexico City, Aldrete has been living in South Carolina's coastal community for a dozen years, allegedly plying his neighbors with more than fresh gazpacho and thick steaks.'"

Her mother scanned the rest of the article. "Apparently, the Wannamakers have been of interest for a while. Seems authorities suspected the restaurant was a money laundering scheme and that cocaine was fueling Wannamaker's commercial development company. Even Joseph Wannamaker's container business in the Port of Charleston is being investigated."

"Can I read it?" Sloan asked.

Her mother handed her the paper and then checked the grocery list. Sloan read quickly and flipped the paper open to an inside page where the story continued. She found Cal's arrest referred to in one paragraph as "the incident that triggered local and state authorities to move in earlier than planned on their investigation into Wannamaker and Aldrete." The raid on the restaurant had been the talk of the town. So, what started as party favors ended up as charges of conspiracy to possess and distribute.

Cal was lucky to be hiding out in rehab and missing

all the excitement. Sloan would always wonder if he had known Verulo before the Mexico trip, if it had all been planned, their meeting like that, becoming involved so quickly. There were so many things about Cal and his family that she would never know.

Sloan finished the article and breathed a sigh of relief. Once again she had escaped mention. Every day she expected a call from an investigator. But one day slipped into the next without incident and after a while she allowed herself the smallest hope that she would survive. She didn't fear Verulo as much as she once had. She'd overheard Larry say Cal's cargo had been so light that it must have been a trial run. Larry said the line of distribution was cut in this area so smugglers would simply move on to other opportunities. The entire coast was like a sieve of rivers and estuaries. Sloan felt assured that Verulo would just wait in Cancún for his next set of college kids to approach so he could start the whole process again.

She'd never told anyone about Verulo. Even LaShonda, who had tried so hard to get Sloan to unburden herself, had ended up empty-handed. LaShonda had phoned her shortly after the bust, but Sloan had quickly asked her to never call again and then, as an added measure, she had blocked her number. LaShonda wasn't really her friend. She was only interested in Sloan for the same reason Sloan had been attracted to Cal—the rush of being included, a glimpse into another life. It had been a minor friendship and one Sloan could no longer afford to keep. She made an effort to avoid any place LaShonda might be, including the gardens.

Her parents hadn't pressured her, but they had fished for information, always examining what Sloan said, asking questions when opportunities arose, probing where they shouldn't have. Larry had lurked around their house for a long time like some sort of lie detector, but he'd eventually given up and gone home. Sloan wasn't giving out information. Not to anybody.

"Honey, we need juice and milk. Would you mind running over to the dairy case?"

"No. I'll be right back." As she walked away her phone vibrated in her pocket and she checked. It was Cal calling from rehab. She never answered, but afterward she listened to the messages he left. They were nice messages, nothing that would implicate her. He was careful. Just short bursts of emotion, how lonely he was, how much he missed her. She'd never called him back. If there was one thing she'd learned from Cal, it was to be careful about mobile phone records.

She'd thought about him so much over the past few weeks. Tried to dissect him and figure him out. Was Cal a good person who did bad things or was he a bad person who struggled to be good? Maybe that was something he could find out while he was in rehab . . . or prison. It was certain she wouldn't be in his life to find out for herself. Still, she missed him every day.

Sloan hated the sour funky smell of the milk case. Cold kissed her arms as she reached for a white carton. She had forgotten to wear her sweatshirt and she was freezing in her flip-flops and shorts. Grocery stores were like meat lockers compared to the searing heat of a South Carolina summer. She was thinking about Cal, wondering if he was sweating his upcoming hearing, what the weather was like in Arizona, if he was lounging around by a pool or sitting through a counseling session. She was ripped from her thoughts when she heard her name.

Abraham Washington sauntered up the aisle toward her. He wore faded blue coveralls and had a grocery basket looped over one arm. His coveralls made a soft brushing sound.

"Hello, Mr. Washington," Sloan said. She prepared for questions.

"Miss Sullivan, nice to see you."

"Yes, sir. Nice to see you."

"Miss Sullivan, I'd like to ask you something."

"Yes, sir."

"My nephew, Ronald, do you know where he is?"

"No, sir."

"Is he dead?"

Sloan's heart thumped over in her chest, but she kept the calm expression she had perfected over the past few weeks. She paused before she spoke, selected her words carefully.

"I'm sorry?" she said.

"Just tell me if he's dead or alive so I can stop thinking about him. I worry about him, I do."

"I don't know anything."

Abraham Washington was standing there as if he had all the time in the world to listen to her. As if she could take a week to think about her answer and it wouldn't make any difference to him.

"Honey, please tell me what happened to Ronald," the old man said softly.

She felt the burn of tears threatening, so she cast her eyes down. *Suck it up*, she told herself. *Don't fall apart now.* She raised her head and stared him directly in the eyes.

"I don't know anything about him," she said as she pulled a thin smile across her face. "I really don't, Mr. Washington."

She had been expecting to flip through the paper one day and there would be Ronald staring back at her. It would be a small story, a sidebar, below a photo of him. His body would have been recovered by an angler or the article would state how long Ronald Jones had been missing. There would be a number.

"Nobody has to get in trouble. I just need to know, for my own self," the old man said. "I'd never tell a soul. I just want to lay my worries down."

Verulo's rhythmic words were tattooed on her mind. *"If you talk, we will know."*

A sincere threat.

"Mr. Washington," she said, "again, I'm so sorry, but I can't help you."

CHAPTER 40

Sea Change

L auren pushed the file cabinet drawer shut with a solid thud and handed the new volunteer an information sheet to fill out.

"Just take your time," she said to the bright-eyed, hopeful young woman. "Bring it back to me when you're finished."

Lauren watched the prospective volunteer move into a waiting area to fill out her form. She scanned the room for anyone else needing help, anyone looking for directions to the cafeteria or maternity. Seeing no person in need, she refocused on her computer screen where she was completing her volunteer list.

In August, Ainslie had returned to school and Lauren had had a reality check about their financial situation. Even after paying off every bill, there was substantial debt.

Larry had come through in a big way. Instead of allowing Common Good to pay the outstanding bills, which would have meant more months of delay while they negotiated with healthcare providers over what they called reasonable and customary charges, Larry had forced the insurance company to cut a lump sum check. He'd also taken some money out to pay his expenses.

It arrived in Larry's office the second week of June.

"I'm holding the check in my grubby little hands," Larry said when he called. "It's all going to be okay. We'll get your bills paid and get ya'll back on track ASAP."

Lauren had wept with relief. Larry had been as good as his word. He'd totaled Ainslie's bills and paid the healthcare providers each bottom line without question since they had waited so long. The medical savings specialist had found only a few small discrepancies, and overall, the billing statements were accurate, if not user-friendly.

Larry had tacked on a "dicking around fee" which paid off his costs and those of the medical savings specialist. But even with that cushion, the money was quickly dispersed and there was very little left to pay other non-medical outstanding bills.

Lauren spent weeks making sure their credit rating was repaired. It was during one of these financial marathons that she realized she had to get a job, at least a part-time job. Emmett hadn't made any move to come back. If they got divorced, she would need a source of income. He didn't make enough money to keep two households. Lauren had been looking at For Sale signs in yards of smaller homes. She'd even been wondering if she should move to Summerville and live with her parents for a while. Ainslie would be closer to MUSC, and surely the job market would be better there.

While she waited for things to pan out or go ahead and fall apart with her husband, Lauren had started scanning the want ads. One Sunday she found an in-column ad in the jobs section for a hospital volunteer coordinator. Lauren recalled what Emmett had said about her organizational skills. She surely knew more about hospitals than the average person. She could direct people to the right place, help them find information. She certainly had the understanding and compassion the job would require.

Lauren searched the Internet until she found a site with a quick reference for creating a résumé. She printed the guide, then set about enumerating her qualifications. Her résumé was nothing to be proud of, or so she thought at first. But once she started listing all the committees she had served on, all the fundraisers she had chaired, all her volunteer work, Lauren had had to cut information to contain her experiences on one page, as suggested by the guide.

She'd asked Sloan for help, and her daughter had quickly created a polished document. She selected a font Lauren had never seen before and staggered the information in a way she said implied Lauren was dependable, yet flexible. Lauren's résumé was an unexpected thing of beauty.

Sloan then suggested she wear the navy blue dress to her interview.

"Nothing flowery or pastel," she'd said. "This is a professional place. You need to project confidence." Lauren had worn her grandmother's pearls and pulled her hair into a chignon. Sloan had insisted on more severe lipstick.

"You're a big girl now, Mom. Rock some red."

Lauren had been so nervous the morning of the interview she could hardly eat, but as soon as the double doors swished open she'd felt a surge of desire to prove herself in this carefully constructed atmosphere. She'd adjusted her posture and found an unexpected determination to get the job.

Now she was the Director of Volunteer Services for Waccamaw Hospital. A few months ago, Lauren thought the best life in the world would be never to set foot in a hospital again. But oddly, some days she couldn't wait to get to work. Emmett had been right when he said she was good at organizing people and arranging things. She ran a staff of two dozen volunteers who delivered flowers and gave directions and helped people who needed wheelchairs.

She knew the main reason she was hired for the job was her understanding of local nonprofit organizations—everything from AA to cancer support, from emotional-health groups to assistance with the financial stress of illness. She was able to recommend churches and synagogues where people could find help, as well as government programs that provided assistance. She knew the ropes.

Sloan didn't go to college in August as she had hoped, so she was home until January. This meant she could pick Ainslie up after school and drive her to physical therapy, allowing more time for Lauren to concentrate on her new job. The girls had both been very supportive of her new ambition, and Lauren often worked more than the thirty hours per week for which she had been hired. She hoped to make the job full time after the first of the year. A full-time position would mean health benefits if she and Emmett divorced. Health insurance would forever be a focal point of her life.

Ainslie's health insurance situation would always be dire. Would insurance companies continue to consider her a risk? Would they exclude any type of cancer from future policies for her? She'd certainly have to stay employed by a major company with a large risk pool before she would be able to afford health insurance for a number of healthy adult years.

But when Lauren was helping other people she was able to forget about her own problems and the problems of her family. She felt satisfaction when she was able to give people even the smallest amount of advice, point them in a new direction of hope. And while a heavy hand pressed against her heart each day as she passed the turnoff to Emmett's office, she'd learned to shake it off and focus on her job, on her girls, on her future. She no longer had to force herself out of bed each day. She was moving on.

CHAPTER 41

Sister Secrets

The shaggy-haired teenager pulled into a reserved parking spot and got out. Ainslie watched her sister to see what she would do.

"Dude," Sloan called from her driver's window. "Don't park in a handicap space. Please."

"I'll only be a second," the boy said defiantly and walked toward the front door of the Y.

"Just move. You can walk a few more feet," she yelled, but he ignored her and kept moving. "Jerk!" Sloan parked her Jeep around the side of the building and cut the engine.

"Mommy would've gone off on that guy," Ainslie said.

"I know. Geez, what's wrong with people? Can't they read a dumb sign?"

"I don't know. Maybe he's mentally handicapped."

"Haaa. Funny."

The smell of chlorine assaulted the girls as they walked into the YMCA. Ainslie checked for the parking offender, knowing Sloan would probably continue her assault on the guy, but he was nowhere in sight. The building echoed with the shrill voices of happy children, the sounds of divers plunging into water, a whistle for roughhousing.

The girls' dressing room filled with the sound of wet feet slapping tile. Ainslie began to change from her school clothes into her bathing suit.

"Do I really have to wear this stupid swim cap?" she whined.

"Pool rules."

"So what? I don't care about rules. This thing pulls my hair out when I take it off."

"Just wear it."

Ainslie tried to yank the ugly piece of rubber down over her head, but her right hand failed her. She attempted to stretch the cap, but it kept popping out of her grasp.

"Let me help," Sloan said.

Ainslie's head stung as Sloan shoved little bits of baby fine hair into the clinging material. Happy swimmers pushed their way out to the pool and the girls were suddenly left alone with the drip, drip of the showers.

"There," Sloan said. "I've almost got it."

"I know you left with Cal that night." Sloan stopped torturing her sister's hair. Their eyes met in the full-length mirror.

"What?"

"I saw you. I got up to go to the bathroom and I heard the door close downstairs. I looked out my window and I saw you go down the road. Then a car started and lights came on and you pulled away. It was Cal, wasn't it?"

Sloan bent close and said, "Did you tell anybody?"

Ainslie let the question stand. Then she said, "No."

"Nobody."

"No. You know I don't tell your secrets."

"Do you know anything else?"

"I know you swim at night sometimes."

"You do?"

"Sure. I used to watch you go out. It kind of scared me."

"Why didn't you ever say anything?"

"Geez, Sloan. I said I don't tell your secrets."

"Well."

"Why do you do it?"

"I don't know. I guess to scare myself."

"Why do you want to scare yourself?"

"It's a thrill, you know, like a roller coaster ride."

"You really should stop."

"Don't worry. I've had enough swimming for a while."

Ainslie looked at her beautiful sister in the mirror. There were so many questions she wanted to ask her, so many things she wanted to say to her. Everybody was talking about Sloan in those quiet adult voices and Ainslie was afraid that Sloan would end up in jail like that mean boyfriend she'd had. It seemed like everybody knew she was involved in something bad, they just couldn't figure out what. And Sloan never said anything to anybody.

Ainslie blurted out, "I know you gave that envelope of money to Mommy and Daddy."

"What money?"

"That money you had after you went on that trip and you came back all sunburned. I saw that envelope fall out of your backpack at the gardens that day you had a fight with Cal."

"You're delusional."

"Yeah. Right."

"I'm not admitting anything to you."

"But will you tell me some day?"

"Sure. When you're, like, an adult." Sloan got up from the bench and started gathering swimming gear. She handed Ainslie her fins and towel. "This conversation i over," she said. Sloan checked her cell phone before shoving it into her backpack.

"Has he quit calling?" Ainslie asked.

"Yeah. Finally."

"Promise me you won't ever call him back."

"I promise," she said.

"Promise?"

"I said I promise." Sloan bent forward and looked Ainslie directly in her eyes. "How come you never tel on me?"

Ainslie shrugged. "A sister's supposed to help, no get you into more trouble."

Sloan nodded. "Thanks." She motioned toward the exit. "Now come on, your therapist awaits."

Ainslie pushed through the thick door and poo sounds vibrated against her. Her physical therapist was already in the pool, a sleek, tanned young man fresh out of college.

"Oh, he is so cute," Sloan said. "Try to swim on thi end a lot."

Ainslie rolled her eyes and walked to the pool.

"Hey, Ainslie. Get on in here," Kevin said. "How' your right hand doing?"

"I think it's getting better."

"Motor skills improving?"

"I think so."

"Hey, how's that new dog of yours?"

"He's so cute. I just love him."

"What kind is he?"

"Just a mutt. Mixed breed, but he's cute."

"Let's throw this ball back and forth and work on

your motor skills and you can tell me all about him, maybe bring me a picture sometime."

Working out with the physical therapist was a drag when all Ainslie wanted to do was swim and splash and have a good time like all the other screaming kids in the pool. He'd make her use the kickboard until she was exhausted, to build back her strength. She was getting strong, but her weak right hand made her writing hard to read. Her teacher cut her slack, but she hated special treatment and she hated having to sit out kickball and dodgeball games because of her head surgery.

After physical therapy, Sloan said she could play in the pool, probably because she wanted to flirt with the physical therapist, but Ainslie was too exhausted and hungry to stay. On the way home, they stopped at Pirate Dogs, their favorite hot dog stand. Before Ainslie got sick, their mother hated for them to eat chili dogs and fries and soda. She always tried to make them drink soy milk and eat fruit. But she'd let up on the food rules because she wanted Ainslie to gain weight and the girls had taken full advantage of the opportunity.

They carried their paper-wrapped food to a red and green splotched picnic table plagued by flies under a stand of palmetto trees.

Sloan swirled a French fry in a puddle of ketchup as she said, "Yum. Salt and preservatives and fat."

Ainslie stared at the hot dog-eating pirate on the roadside sign. She said, "We're studying pirates in school. South Carolina used to have a bunch of pirates. Blackbeard and Calico Jack and a woman who dressed up like a man and killed a bunch of other pirate dudes."

"I remember studying that stuff."

"They used to come ashore and pillage the locals," Ainslie said around a big bite of chili dog.

Her sister laughed and swatted at a fly.

Ainslie swallowed and sucked on her soda straw. "You know," she said. "I bet there are still pirates out there somewhere."

"Absolutely," Sloan said. "I'm sure of it."

CHAPTER 42

Testing the Waters

They waited on their dock. It had been a crystal clear day, and even though the sun dropped toward the tree line on the mainland, the light was still white and pure, making colors pop, delineating each strand of graying marsh grass, every cloud in the indigo sky.

Her mother leaned against the railing, jacket pulled tightly against the November chill off the water. She held a book, but didn't read the moisture-warped pages. Sloan's hand moved across her sketchpad capturing the scarlet of her mother's scarf and hat against pale skin, dark sunglasses, the weathered wood of the dock.

She drew her mother's image over the faint impression of another portrait, a ghostly outline of Verulo from the previous page. Sloan had ripped that portrait from her book of drawings and stashed it in a secret place along with the metal cuff bracelet Cal had bought her in Mexico. She also kept some money there, just in case. Sloan planned her life more carefully now. She kept a contingency plan, a just in case scenario.

As she drew Sloan tried not to look at the great swaths of cordgrass that had been carved away behind her house. The machine that cut back the vegetation of their choked creek had started on their end and would work its way south. Every day, Sloan stood on her back porch and watched the machine gnashing away. She waited for the workers to suddenly stop and shout and scramble down to stand in shock over Ronald's gnawed remains.

"He's late," Ainslie said. She poked at barnacles collected on the wooden steps that disappeared down into the creek. She already had mud on her shoes.

"He'll be here in a minute," their mother assured her.

Her own hands were cold, but Sloan continued to draw, smudging uneven color with a finger.

"Let me see," her mother said.

Sloan held up her artwork.

"You're very talented," her mother said. "Just like your father."

"When's he coming?" Ainslie asked again.

"Patience, child."

"Mom?" Sloan said.

"Yes?"

Sloan had wanted to ask this question for a long time but had been too afraid of what the answer might be. "When will Dad move back into our house?"

She took so long to speak that Sloan wondered if she was going to answer at all. Sloan could feel her sister tense, listening for their mother's reply.

"I don't know," she finally said. "We're talking about it."

Sloan had wondered all summer why their father had not moved back in now that their financial situation was better. She knew her mother had accused him of messing around with the city manager woman, when the truth was it had been Cal's father who was having the affair. So why hadn't their father come home?

Sloan whispered, "You know he didn't do anything. Why can't you just let him come back?"

"Sloan." Her mother leaned forward and took off her glasses. She got close enough that Ainslie couldn't hear. "Did it ever occur to you maybe your father hasn't yet decided what he wants to do?"

"But you told him you forgive him, right?"

"Yes. But maybe he needs time to forgive me."

"What did you do?"

She sat back on the bench, pulled her jacket tighter. "Oh, I don't know. It's complicated. I guess you could say I lost faith in him. He's a good man. I know that. But he isn't perfect. Nobody's perfect. I'm not saying I didn't have good reason to be suspicious and angry and hurt."

"You were scared."

"Sure. But so was he. We were all scared. That's when it's supposed to mean something to be a family. Family is supposed to stick together, support each other, and I, well . . ."

"Did you tell him you were sorry?"

"I did. I apologized . . . for being so hard on him . . . and for other things."

"For kicking him out?"

"Yes. For embarrassing him."

"Didn't he forgive you?"

"Honey, it's not that simple. He needs time to think."

"It's been, like, six months."

"Not quite."

Her mother paused and Sloan could tell she was considering if she should say what she said next. She checked on Ainslie, but the girl was once again busy with something at the waterline.

"Sloan," she said in a low voice. "Don't be surprised if he decides not to come back."

Now it was Sloan's turn to lower her voice.

"Are you going to get divorced?"

Her mother sighed then, but it was no longer the same way she used to sigh from exhaustion or frustration when Ainslie was so sick. It was a sigh of resignation.

"Your father and I have a long history of being disappointed in each other. We need to get past that and decide what we want our future to be. Things change. People change."

Sloan thought about this. And about how much she missed Cal and how he had made her feel good about herself when they were first together. He'd told her she was special and she had wanted to believe him, to fit in his group, to live his life, to be his girlfriend. Still, his increasing drug use, his abrupt meltdown, his crazy changes that frightened and disappointed her only made her miss the old Cal more. She missed him every day, longed for his crooked smile, his slash of shiny hair, his hands on her body. But she had never contacted him, never returned a phone call, never written a note or sent a text. He had finally stopped calling after his indictment. He had kept their secret.

"Don't you miss him?" Sloan asked.

Her mother sighed again, and Sloan knew she was unaware of this, her new habit, that made melancholy cling to her like a haze. "I miss something, but I'm not sure what. I'm not sure if I miss the familiarity of having him around or if I miss him."

"Mom!"

"Well, you're asking adult questions, I'm giving you adult answers. I love your father and he loves me. We just have to decide, after everything we've been through, if we're still *in love*. There's a big difference between loving somebody and in being *in love*."

And there it was. Sloan had been *in love*, but she hadn't

loved Cal. She had been swept up in the heat, crazed with passion, in love with the idea of love, but she had never actually loved him. For all their adventure and sex and fun, he could have been anyone, any guy who could distract her and entertain her and make her forget her problems.

Her situation was the opposite of what her parents were going through.

"So you're not in love with Dad anymore?"

"Oh, sweetheart, I didn't say that. I shouldn't even talk to you about these things. It's just that I guess you have the right to know. Life has a way of beating up on people, of wearing them down. It's hard to stay married and . . . well . . . you know that marriage counselor we went to that one time when Ainslie was sick? She said we had to be careful, that the strain of illness points out all the strengths and weaknesses in people. It exposes all the cracks in a relationship. It accentuates the negatives. Honey, it's hard to hold a marriage together under normal circumstances." She shrugged then as if to say she had resigned herself to the fact that she had no control. "It's really up to your father now." She turned away then as if the matter were closed.

Sloan focused back on her artwork, but her mind lingered around her parents. So her father had chosen to stay away. He had been there for her and Ainslie in so many ways over the past few months, taking on responsibilities formerly left to their mother. He had helped Ainslie with her summer homework. He'd been diligent in helping her study so she could start fourth grade with the rest of her class. And Ainslie had slid back into her school routine without a hitch.

Since their parents weren't officially separated, their father had no custody. He came around on occasion to visit, to fix something broken—to test the waters, was how Sloan viewed it. Their father stayed for dinner on many occasions, but he always went back to Larry's afterward. The first few times he arrived, the girls had hoped he was trying to mend more than a leaky faucet, but that hadn't been the case. It was confusing.

Their mother tried to make things normal, to do some of their things their father had done. One job that seemed to be beyond her was grilling steaks. Her steaks were always tough or undercooked or not seasoned properly. Ainslie had complained once and their mother had taken her glass of wine to the end of the dock where she sat for hours until it turned dark. Sloan had finally cleared the plates and told Ainslie to just eat her stupid steak and say it was good the next time.

Sloan could tell her parents missed each other. One evening their father had arrived and swept the platter of steaks from the counter. He'd opened the spice cabinet, shaken his secrets over the meat, and gone out to the grill as he had a hundred times before. After a while, their mother brought him a glass of red wine and they stood there, sipping, bathed in the barbecue smoke as if nothing unusual had transpired between them.

The girls watched from the kitchen window.

"Are they making up?" Ainslie asked in a hopeful voice.

"I don't know," Sloan replied. "I can never tell what's going on with them anymore."

He had left that night, as he had all the other nights, and Sloan had decided then to stop speculating about her parents. The steaks were tough and that was life.

"Hey! There's Daddy!" Ainslie said and pointed to the mouth of the creek. Their father drove the gleaming boat around the bend. It shone with polished brass and wood, all new hardware and seats.

"Ahoy, there!" He waved and smiled as he floated toward the dock. Ainslie jumped to grab the rope and tie her expert nautical knots around the dock's cleats as her father had taught her. She was always his helper. Sloan had no idea how to tie a knot.

"Emmett, she's beautiful," their mother said. "Just spectacular!"

"And I've got a surprise. The best part."

"What? What?" Ainslie asked.

"Check the name."

All three women moved to the back of the boat and there they saw in script, "Arion."

"It's a Greek god dolphin name," Sloan said. "Dad let me pick it."

Her father said, "It means lofty native. I thought Sloan made a nice choice."

"But I thought it was bad luck to rename a boat," their mother said.

"I don't believe in luck," he said. "Besides, it's time for a change. All aboard."

They purred along in their sleek boat, seabirds embracing the sky at their approach, wide white wings soundlessly lifting into flight. He navigated the creek to the public boat landing where they tied off and disembarked. Beach music drifted toward them and Sloan recognized, "Under the Boardwalk." Lights twinkled into action on their approach. Dusk was falling as they made their way down the boardwalk out to the party at the new pavilion. The whole island had pitched in to raise money to finally rebuild the pavilion Hugo had crushed.

Autumn always came late to South Carolina and was heralded by the smell of propane and boiling seafood. At the party, bowls of cocktail sauce and anemic sleeves of saltines were strewn along eight-foot rectangular tables draped in newspaper. Men hovered over cook pots, poking inside with slotted ladles, discussing the contents with serious expressions. Beer flowed freely. People laughed. Couples of all ages shagged outside, holding hands, dancing smoothly in six-count patterns, most of their movement below the waist.

Someone handed Sloan a blunt oyster knife and a thick glove and she stepped up to the table across from her parents. Two men overturned a giant cook pot onto the table and steaming oysters rolled out, smelling metallic and muddy. With gloved hands, neighbors distributed them down the table. There were familiar pops as shells cracked. Sloan found a weak point in a shell, inserted her stubby knife, and twisted. The shell broke open, and inside she found a fat, steamed oyster. She expertly scraped the animal from its shell, eased it off onto a saltine, topped it with cocktail sauce and popped it in her mouth. Heaven. At another table, others ate oysters raw, preferring the sweet taste of the sea unsullied on their tongues.

Her mother struggled with a shell and her father reached for it and shucked it with one try.

"Grab a cracker," he said, as he scooped the oyster out. Then, "Hold on. Let's make the first one of the season perfect." Her mother held the cracker as he squeezed lemon juice and added a dollop of cocktail sauce.

"Now," he said. "See what you think."

The cracker crunched in her mother's mouth and she rolled her eyes in pleasure.

"Perfect," she said. "Absolutely perfect."

The DJ put on "Carolina Girl" and shaggers rushed the dance floor.

"May I have this dance?" her father asked.

Her mother nodded and stripped off her glove. They held hands as they moved toward the dancers and joined the flow, their arms sliding smoothly together and apart. Sloan wondered if her sister saw this, but when she finally found her, Ainslie was engrossed in a moth stuck to a wooden pylon.

Next the DJ spun Van Morrison's "Brown-eyed Girl,"

and her father grabbed Ainslie and pulled her onto the dance floor. He twirled her, his hand skimming her waist. He acted silly, pointing at Ainslie and mouthing the lyrics, "You're my brown-eyed girl." Ainslie laughed and clapped. Her mother jumped in and they all held hands, a dancing triangle.

The pavilion vibrated and Sloan sensed the steps of her family and friends in her own feet. A rumble like distant thunder meant another pot of oysters had been dumped. The shadowy creek below reflected faint purple and orange, lingering at the edges of the evening sky. The creek was rising. The ocean was on its way in.

**Please turn the page for a very special
Q&A with Janna McMahan!**

The Ocean Inside is a deeply layered family story much like your first novel. Do you see this as your hallmark?

I like to think my novels are about communities and how the social mores, politics, and economics of a place affect my characters. In *The Ocean Inside*, I see the community as a complicated mix of altruism and greed, of concern and deceitfulness. The Sullivans are ultimately able to overcome their financial woes with the help of friends like Larry. Then there are the random acts of kindness, like the church collecting money and people bringing food and gifts that is an important means of support for the family emotionally, as well as financially.

The Ocean Inside is set in contemporary times, unlike the 1970s era of your first novel, Calling Home. *What are the differences in writing something set in present day versus a period piece?*

The Ocean Inside required something entirely different. Instead of relying on my own memories of what it was like to grow up in the late 1970s, I needed to know what it's like to be a teenager now. Technology, music, and language presented a challenge. Kids today communicate nonstop, they have information at their fingertips, they're latchkey kids early and have cars given to them at sixteen. There's a freedom and a maturity to children that didn't exist thirty years ago. Family dynamics are very different. Parents don't shelter kids as much and they allow them decision-making power, both socially and financially. While the daughter in *Calling Home* feels responsible only for herself, Sloan recognizes all the pain and struggles of her family. She tries to help where she can, but she's unable to affect her sister's situation or her parents' imploding marriage. Sloan's maturity allows her sympathy for others, but it also leads her to believe she can handle situations she really can't handle.

Sloan does get in over her head and she never really gets out of trouble.

Sloan's situation has no immediate ending. I've left a lot up to reader interpretation. Sure, she made some lousy choices. What teenager wouldn't when faced with young love and a chance to escape unhappiness at home? So she ran off to Mexico with a guy she barely knew. She agreed to a shady road trip. When things got scary, she tried to pull away only to find she couldn't escape Cal's control. In the end, she protects the people she loves. She could have unburdened herself and drawn her family into a larger drama, perhaps even endangering them, but she chose to live with guilt and dread. That emotional sacrifice took a lot of maturity and strength of will. We know from the beginning that she's a fragile person, but when things get dire she reaches down inside for the strength to do what she thinks is right. Her power is in keeping secrets.

So is that how the title came about? Does The Ocean Inside *refer to Sloan's secret?*

I think it reflects something inside us all. Everybody has a secret, a fear, a regret, a longing, an emotional burden of some sort. The ocean inside is what lies behind the cultivated façade we show the world. I think midlife crises are built on suppressed desires and questions that visit us more as we age. The ocean inside is a universal feeling. I loved the title for all the possibilities it embraced.

Much like your first novel, there is a strong connection between siblings in The Ocean Inside.

Characters need alliances just like real people. The strong bond between siblings, people who will never betray each other, who will always be allies, is a relationship worth writing about. The connection between the sisters is integral to the story line. Sloan kept Ainslie going. She was the only one who actually let the child be herself and helped her without question.

What a complicated relationship Lauren and Emmett have.

They are a mess. Before any of the big drama of the story begins they are already at odds. Emmett, with his feelings of inadequacy, rejects Lauren in a physical way. Lauren, missing physical intimacy, questions his love and commitment to the family. They fight about money. They fight about sex. They fight about social obligations. They have differing philosophies about religion and parenting and it seems just about everything. They've reached the point in their marriage where they're simply polite to each other for the children's sake. So when a huge family crisis comes along they aren't much of a team. It's a widely held belief that most marriages that experience a major illness or death of a child end in divorce. If this is true, how can Lauren and Emmett make it?

Are you veering into the realm of magical realism in the part where Sloan has an encounter with the dolphin pod?

Not at all. Dolphins frequently act in altruistic ways toward humans. I found a newspaper article about recreational fishermen whose boat capsized off the coast of Georgetown, South Carolina, the same waters in *The Ocean Inside*. According to these guys, they were in the water for more than a day surrounded by hammerhead and tiger sharks. They said a dolphin pod stayed with them, repelling the sharks. After many hours the men floated into the Gulf Stream and were rescued.

I suppose you could find how Ainslie attracts butterflies and lizards to be a little magical, but I firmly believe that some people have an animal vibe. A lot of Ainslie's animal interaction is based on my daughter. There's something about Madison that animals love. She's definitely the one who attracts butterflies. It was a month of mourning in our house when Steve Irwin died. I had to mention him as a sort of memorial. He had such an amazingly positive influence on children.

The Ocean Inside *addresses the issues of coastal development of natural habitat. Would you say that you are a conservationist?*

I'm a realist. I know some about the economics and politics involved in land development because I'm married to a landscape architect. While the story portrayed here is totally of my own creation, it does have basis in reality. There is no stopping what some people call progress, but I get angry when a development company comes into a natural area, denudes it, then names the neighborhood for the natural amenities they destroyed— Whistling Pines and High Dunes Estates and such. We need stricter, more sensible regulations on development, but we also need incentives for developers to do the right things. Local governments find it difficult to balance the needs of an ever-increasing population with the divergent demands of developers and conservationists. The point is to find a way that benefits the community while respecting natural resources. That's a tall order.

Is Sandy Island a real place?

Sandy Island is real. I was intrigued by the concept of an isolated community, so I finagled an assignment to write about the school boat so I could visit. I loved the school boat kids and I hope that comes through. Sandy Island has an interesting history typical of how land has changed hands in South Carolina. Of course, that land was originally occupied by tribes of Native Americans, thus the name the Waccamaw River. Then came the white man with his plantations. After the Civil War, slaves were allowed to settle on barrier islands because the sandy, windblown land wasn't desirable for crops. Black families lived there for generations until the islands became attractive to developers, and once again, those with less money and power were pushed off their land. So far, Sandy Island has deflected attempts to "log" their island. All this background came from research. My story is a fictionalized account of what could have happened.

Today even middle-class families are finding it hard to continue to live along the coast because of rising property taxes and upkeep and insurance and such. The coastal ring of superrich that Emmett predicts is a creeping certainty.

Do you base your stories on actual events or people?

All writers do. Sometimes real life is so much more interesting than anything you can think up on your own. Then sometimes life and fiction collide. When I finished my original outline for *The Ocean Inside* one very important reader told me that she didn't find it credible that people in their forties would be doing cocaine at parties. The next week our state's treasurer was indicted on cocaine charges. While sad for him, it was a gift to my story. He's a young fellow, upper crust, and he just considered his habit a "social problem." I've had people say they didn't like it that Emmett participated at the party, but casual drug use is rampant and I think that particular weakness made him a more believable character.

There are always the small liberties a writer takes. I know the bumper stickers for Pawleys Island read "Arrogantly Shabby" rather than "Shabby Chic." It just wouldn't have worked as well to refer to Charleston as the most arrogant of shabby places. Just isn't the same as "chicest of shabby places." Sometimes you make choices based on how true the language will ring.

You tend to set a lot of your stories around bodies of water.

I grew up water skiing and swimming in Green River Lake in Central Kentucky. Now that I live in South Carolina I have the opportunity to be at the beach quite often. Any time spent around water is a luxury to me. It makes me contemplative and sets my imagination free. I always wondered what's under the water. When I was a kid my parents forbade me to go to the movie *Jaws*, but I sneaked to see it anyway. That entire summer I couldn't bring myself to swim in the lake. I'd barely have my skis on before I was yelling at my father to gun the boat and yank me up out of the water. A vivid imagination can be a curse at times.

So you were an imaginative child?

Let's just put it this way, my Barbies weren't of the milquetoast variety. Jacques Cousteau was big when I was a kid, so my dolls were deep-sea divers and marine biologists and sometimes astronauts. They also had babies before they were married and fought over Ken like soap opera queens. My Barbie beauty pageants always ended in a big cat fight. I may have frightened some of the other little girls with my story lines. I've always had very vivid and elaborate dreams. I would dominate breakfast conversations relaying these involved dream sequences from the night before. I'm sure my parents are grateful that my imagination finally manifested itself in a positive way.

Did you start writing early?

I've written stories for as long as I can remember, even in elementary school. I once wrote a poem for a friend in high school, a class assignment that she didn't want to do. It was a sad poem about a depressed girl. The day after we turned in our poems my friend stopped me in the hall and said, "Thanks a lot for that stupid poem. I got called into the guidance counselor's office because of it." Apparently they thought she was in danger of harming herself. That was the first time I realized how writing can impact other people.

The Ocean Inside *is about a family dealing with the turmoil of cancer. You're a cancer survivor yourself.*

I was diagnosed with breast cancer at twenty-eight. At first, I didn't want to admit weakness and I continued to work. I completed and defended my thesis while doing chemo. I just looked at it as something that happened to me and moved on.

A couple of years later I stopped trying to prove how damn strong I was. Acting like nothing had changed was exhausting. I was constantly frightened that every day would be relapse day. I asked myself what I really wanted to do with my life, however long or short it might be. The answer was write a novel. I'd always wanted to see if I could do it. My husband encouraged me to quit my job and give it a try. He just wanted me to be happy again. So, you could say that having cancer made me pursue this lifelong desire of being a writer earlier than I would have otherwise.

But you didn't want anybody to know you were a cancer survivor?

I didn't want that label. The Big C takes center stage when you bring it up. While being interviewed for my first novel I once let it slip that I had been spurred to write because of illness. That immediately became the dramatic headline. The article became about cancer and not about my writing. I decided then that I would never mention cancer again in an interview.

But I think things are different with *The Ocean Inside*. My diagnosis and treatment lends me credibility to speak about the emotions and financial tensions involved. I understand the guilt of being the one putting strain on the family. I understand the fear and the pain. Major illness sorts out your true friends. It emphasizes strengths and weakness. It's an eye-opening experience in so many ways.

You proved that you could write a novel—two, in fact.

I now feel as if I've contributed, that if I died tomorrow I would leave something of significance behind. I love the fact that my novels are in libraries across the country. It's now documented that I existed, and I think that's what matters to me on some basic level. I want my daughter to be able to pick up one of my books when she's an adult and say, "My mother wrote that." It may sound strange, but now I feel as if I'll live forever.

From an extraordinary new voice in fiction comes a haunting, powerful novel about mothers and daughters, choice and regret, the mistakes we make and the ones we hope we can correct before it's too late.

Nothing much ever happens in Falling Rock, Kentucky. Nothing good, anyway. So when Virginia Lemmon's husband takes off in his Trans Am to take up with a beautician, there's not much to do but what people in rural Kentucky have always done—get on with it. Now, overwhelmed and unsure, Virginia's got her hands full trying to keep it together, body and soul, while raising her two teenage kids—eighteen-year-old son, Will, and her spirited fourteen-year-old daughter, Shannon.

But Shannon has her own ideas for breaking free of Falling Rock, and in her reckless, wild-child daughter, Viriginia sees echoes of herself and her own painful past. She'll do whatever it takes to keep her daughter from making the same tragic mistakes, and saving what's left of her fragile family just may be the biggest fight of Virginia's life.

In this compelling, heartbreaking first novel, Janna McMahan brings to authentic life the dreams, passions, and troubles of one southern town, where choice isn't always easy to come by, and living the hand you're dealt with is a grace all is own.

Please turn the page for an exciting sneak peek of Janna McMahan's CALLING HOME, now on sale at bookstores everywhere!

The window gave a couple of inches. Virginia, poised on a cinder block, put her hand against the bottom of the sash and shoved again. Paint fractured and fluttered down as the frame broke loose and slid up. The reek of nicotine tinged with perfume seeped over her, a sour contrast to the clean air outside.

It was a vivid day. The sky seemed close as Kentucky skies can, as if you could just reach out and touch the pale smear of clouds. Virginia squinted into the dark interior. She could see it was a bedroom, as she had anticipated. Not hard to figure out where things were in these rectangular brick boxes. People had started trading tall breezy farmhouses for the central air of squat ranches with hardly enough room to make up a bed and no kitchen big enough to have a family meal.

She hoisted herself up onto the ledge. Her pants snagged on rough brick and ripped. She stopped, balanced on her stomach, half in, half out of the window, to inspect the dirty, thin streaks of blood where her forearms had scraped the window ledge.

She hadn't expected to have to go to so much trouble. Most people around Falling Rock never locked their doors. But this woman was from Louisville. She had paranoid city habits.

Virginia dropped down onto the floor, her heart beating in her ears as if she were underwater. She felt submerged, her movements measured, her legs heavy. What was she looking for? What did she hope to find, to not find, in this woman's house?

The louvered closet door screeched as she pushed it aside and there she saw what she came for. His frayed jeans with the torn pocket. Scarred hunting boots. Proof.

A metal tang came to her mouth—an angry taste she recognized. Her fingers itched to rake everything in the room into a shattered pile. She imagined the perfume bottles on the woman's vanity, the hand mirror and brushes and combs in a grotesque dance on the hardwood. The cut-glass lamps and crystal ashtrays—one with Roger's cigarette stubs, the other with her long skinny ones all crinkled down—she could sweep from the bedside tables with one swipe. She could find scissors and cut blouses and skinny little jeans to shreds. Bleach would ruin every carpet and drape and bed linen in the house.

She felt a stinging on her leg and turned in the vanity mirror to check where she had caught her pants. A right angle was neatly cut from the thin material and her skin underneath was abraded. She saw herself fully then—ruddy cheeks and dark hair in riotous curls around her shoulders. She didn't like what she saw, this woman with a set jaw and hollow eyes.

She jerked suddenly, her attention focused down the narrow hall. Was that a car door thudding shut? Virginia reactively laid her hand to her heart. Its staccato throb under her fingertips threatened to burst through her bones. She crept to the kitchen, where she scanned outside through the kitchen sheers. Nothing in the carport. She peeked through dust-filmed windows in the front room. No truck on the gravel road beyond. She moved from window to window, checking every possible angle before she was satisfied that nobody had arrived. It was her imagination. She'd checked to be sure they were in town before she came.

She gave a little laugh then. *Silly,* she whispered. Why was she so jumpy? She'd thought this through. She knew what she was doing. Her car was hidden on the other side of the woods behind the house. There was a farm road that cut through fields to the next road over. She'd have to open and close a few cattle gates, but she could slip away and never have to drive back down the road in front of this house.

But even if she got caught breaking and entering, nobody would blame her. She'd never spend one night in jail, not with the way Roger was doing her. Did he think she was stupid? Didn't he know how the town talked? How people were always primed for gossip?

At first, Virginia hadn't realized anything was amiss. Then her sisters had come to her with what they'd heard at church, at the factory. Virginia chalked it all up to how much she and Roger fought. They didn't make a big secret out of their intense marriage. But when she really paid attention, Virginia recognized that Roger's absences had grown longer and more frequent. One night at supper, she'd watched his mind wander. He'd turned preoccupied, even when he was physically there.

Virginia hated to admit she missed Roger's touch, but she did. She missed his hand on the small of her back when he kissed her in the morning. He'd grown to treat their infrequent contact as an obligation and then finally stopped altogether. The past few months, he'd grown more distant from her and the kids. Her children didn't seem to notice, but once Virginia realized something was wrong, she saw it in his mannerisms and inflections and even his appetite. What had been a sort of foreplay in their high-tension marriage now held no interest for him. He had changed. It was as if, after all these years, their roles were reversing.

Now her whole body ached for his weight against her. She regretted the times she'd pushed him away, imagined she was somewhere else when he reached for her. Now that his interest had shifted, it might be too late. He was getting his fantasies fulfilled elsewhere, from this whore nobody around here knew. So she was all painted up and teased and bleached. So she owned a beauty shop. Roger probably thought that was exotic. Maybe he was tired of a good woman who cooked his meals and took care of his home and children.

Maybe this woman reminded him of those whores in that movie *Shampoo.* Roger had insisted they make a special trip up to Louisville to see it. Three women were practically clawing the hair off Warren Beatty's chest to have sex with him. If that was Roger's fantasy, he could just dream on. In real life, things were definitely the other way around. Even after they'd been married a number of years, it was a constant source of tension between them. This movie was apparently another of Roger's attempts to "spice things up." He talked about that awful movie for days, pointing out things he found enticing, but it made Virginia feel dirty. Roger knew she couldn't handle strange sex, and he knew why.

She turned her attention back to the woman's house, to the kitchen, where she opened the refrigerator. There wasn't much. Beer. A bottle of wine. Butter. Pickles. Old bread. There was a fast-food bag stuffed in the garbage under the sink. This woman didn't cook. Virginia opened drawers and picked through mail on the counter. She didn't think Roger had enough sense to forward his mail.

She opened and slammed cabinets. There were no *Sports Afield* among the *Hair Styles* and *Beauty Salon* magazines on the coffee table. She went through the bathroom cabinets and saw medicine for yeast infections and birth control pills and an old-fashioned silver razor. She went through the dresser and found leopard print and red lace. She slammed those drawers. She even looked under the bed, but she didn't find the second thing she had come for.

A sign. Any sign that her husband intended to stay.

Virginia checked her watch. She'd been inside twenty minutes. She lowered the bedroom window and shut the closet door. In the kitchen, she locked the door handle and was ready to pull it closed behind her when she saw the photo. It was pinned to the side of the refrigerator with a magnet, nearly hidden by a newspaper clipping. She slid it out.

The shot was grainy and dark, probably taken at dusk. They were seated at the picnic table in the backyard. She was on his lap, kissing him on the cheek. He was laughing. His hands nearly encircled her tiny waist.

So this was it. They looked like a couple. They took photos. It wasn't just sex. Somebody had snapped the photo, so at least one other person knew. Maybe that person had been talking. Spreading lies was what Virginia had thought. But it wasn't a lie. She had known. Inside she had known or she wouldn't be here.

She considered taking the photo as evidence; had actually put it in her pocket. But at the last moment, she balked. What good would it do? She would obsess over it, make herself sick with it. Plus, they might wonder where it went. Women know where things like a favorite photo live. She pinned the glossy paper back under the torn newsprint, checked that the handle locked, and pulled the kitchen door closed behind her.

Her vision was liquid. The cool of shadows brushed

her shoulders as she moved beneath the heavy canopy of oaks and tulip poplars toward her car. Although vines tripped her up and logs blocked her way, she walked with purpose. She knew now. At least she had that much. She was no longer a fool. Now she knew.